# JACKAL IN THE MIRROR

## BOOK THREE
### of The Perils of a Reluctant Psychic

# JACKAL IN THE MIRROR

## A NOVEL

## V. & D. POVALL

Publisher: Dragonfly Media
ISBN-13: 978-0692136737 (Custom Universal)
ISBN-10: 0692136738
Library of Congress Control Number (LCCN): 2018948992

Dragonfly Media, Oceanside, CA

Writing never happens in a vacuum.
Many are those who help in different ways.


Thanks

To
The guides and residents of Old Town Eureka and
Clear Lake for their input and assistance while conducting our research.

And To
The ghosts we encountered, who made us feel right at home.


A Special Thank-You

To Jennifer Silva Redmond, our exceptional editor,
for her invaluable advice and her unique ability to elevate our prose
while honoring our voice.

# CONTENTS

# 1

# THE BOOK

The moment Sarah entered the timeworn bookstore her heartbeat intensified. The hairs on the back of her neck prickled, and her hands tightened into fists.

Made wary by her body's reaction, she took in her surroundings. The quaint Booklegger bookstore appeared harmless. New and used books of every size and shape crowded worn-out wooden shelves that lined the narrow aisles, and welcomed the curious to peruse and browse, enveloped in the scent of thousands of new and experienced tomes.

When selecting a spot for their first all-women four-day escape, her friends had suggested the Victorian seaport of Eureka, California, south of the Oregon border. The location made it easy for all of them to reach. It also had the added thrill of plopping their psychic friend Sarah into the heart of a town famous for its paranormal stories.

The decision had been made before they called Sarah. Not that she opposed the idea—after all, she hadn't spent any time with her California friends for over a year. And, truth be told, the minute they mentioned Eureka, something had stirred deep within her.

At first, she attributed the feeling to a natural interest in the eerie tales that made up Eureka's distinctive history. But she soon realized that tourist allure wasn't the whole reason. A presentiment about the town created an internal vibration, as if an electrical current was passing through her body.

Curiosity aroused, she decided to arrive a day early to get a feel for the place, just in case. In point of fact, she had no idea why, except for a strong urge to get ahead of any surprises.

Aside from the constant vibration that still coursed through her, the trip had been an uneventful one. After kissing her husband Conrad goodbye and appeasing his many concerns, she'd driven south across Washington State from their home near Winthrop, and stopped for the night in Bend, Oregon. She'd driven on early the next day and arrived in Eureka's historic Old Town by mid-afternoon.

After a quick bite, she made her way down 2nd Street and discovered the Booklegger bookstore, surrounded by refurbished and updated buildings erected more than a century earlier. One window sign said *Used Books,* the other proclaimed *Rare and Antique Books.* Sarah had no reason to go into the bookstore, but the front door beckoned like a long-forgotten friend. The instant her feet crossed the threshold, she froze, overwhelmed by the sensation that her arrival had somehow been preordained. She spotted an arch to her left that led deeper into the store.

*I'm expected. Okay, then... let's get on with it.* She headed resolutely through the arch and toward the back of the bookstore.

A couple of years earlier, these kinds of feelings and impressions would have caused her to turn away or even flee in haste. But after years of painful denial, she had finally come to terms with her unique ability to discern a reality beyond the four-dimensional plane that most people inhabited. She no longer dreaded its effect. The sensations her body experienced when entering the bookstore were no longer to be feared. She viewed them as harbingers of things to come, her internal alert system.

Stopping in front of a shelf like many others in the bookstore, she selected a hardcover book from the far end and opened it.

A piercing scream escaped from its pages.

After the scream, came a rush of air, as if a door had been opened allowing the encased energy to escape. A mist seemed to emanate from the ground and engulf the corner where she stood, leaving behind a whisper that echoed through the aisles.

*Sarah, please help me.*

Sarah spun around, searching for the origin of the voice, but found no one.

She stared down at the book and turned to the first page. A terrible pressure built inside her chest—the deep pain of profound disillusionment. Instinctively, she brought her hand to her heart to ease the agony.

She stared at the book and realized the words had patiently waited for her to find them. She obliged, and read the first chapter.

# CONSEQUENCE

A heavy mist hung above the lake, causing the moonlight to cast a shadow-less glow across the water. An abrupt embankment that shot up to the surrounding forest bordered the mirror-like surface. In a clearing a few hundred feet from the lake, sat a two-story house engulfed in darkness, except for a pale yellow glow that spread from a window.

Inside, the home appeared silent, cold, except for the flickering shadows cast by a few votive candles set in a circle on the living room floor. A woman, clad only in a long white nightgown, her grey hair tousled, her anguished face bathed in tears, stepped over the candles. She reached a barely illuminated staircase and stared at a crack of light that seeped from under a door on the upper floor.

"Why?" she asked, as she made her way up the stairs.

"You know why," a man answered from somewhere in the shadows above her.

"No, I don't. I can't understand. Please, help me understand," she pleaded as she slowly ascended.

"It's what I do," he said, his voice cracking.

"No! It's not you. How could you do such unspeakable things?" When she reached the top of the stairs she stretched out her hand to touch him, but he recoiled.

"Don't!" he snarled and slapped her hand away.

The force of his blow propelled her backwards. She lost her balance and cried out, "Dear God!"

"No!" His cry emanated from the gloom as he reached for her, but she plunged helplessly down the stairs. A moment later she lay dead on the floor, eyes fixed on her killer.

Engulfed in darkness he froze, staring at her body sprawled on the floor below. He took the stairs, one step at a time, his left hand tightening around the banister. "No," he whispered with each step. "No." On the back of his hand a rose-shaped red birthmark seemed to darken with the pressure of his grasp.

When he reached the bottom, he sank to his knees. With great tenderness, he unbent her limbs, straightened her hair, and caressed her face. He picked her up gently, as if handling precious crystal, crossed to the living room, stepped over the candles, and gently set her down in the middle of the circle. He adjusted her nightgown, brushing away any wrinkles, cleared the loose strands of hair from her face, and kissed her forehead.

He lay on the floor next her, curled up against her body, and sobbed.

Sarah snapped the book shut and stared at the title, *Jackal in the Mirror.* She shoved the book back onto the shelf.

A piercing scream in her head made her clap her hands over her ears. "Stop."

The discordant scream gave way to a murmur.

*Help me Sarah. Please help me. Take the book.*

She stood in stunned silence, considering the scene she had just read, and the pleading request. After a few seconds her heartbeat and breathing returned to normal. She knew there was a reason she had felt compelled to visit Eureka, but the intensity of the past few minutes had come as a shock. After a few deep breaths, Sarah grabbed the book. "All right. What now?"

Silence.

"Read the book? Is that it?"

Silence.

Reluctantly, Sarah opened it and continued to read.

Mist floated above the serene water of the mountain lake. Crickets chirped in the distance. A rhythmic paddling joined the sounds of nature. A small rowboat, its cracked paint starting to peel, glided gently across the water. The woman's body lay across the stern; her white nightgown twisted, her hair snarled, one of her arms dangling in the water. The red birthmark was visible in the moonlight on one of the strong hands powering the oars.

The man ceased rowing and secured the oars. Ripples lapped against the boat, rocking it gently. He lifted the inert body, slid it into the water, and pushed it under.

The crickets stopped. Only the gurgle of water, as the lake slowly swallowed her, could be heard. As the body vanished beneath the surface, the scene regained its stillness. The crickets resumed their song.

With a shadow at the oars, the small boat disappeared into the mist.

Sarah shut the book and returned it to its spot on the shelf. "No," she said, "I don't wish to read this."

As she turned away, the sharp cry threw her off balance.

"Stop!" Sarah yelled, covering her ears and shutting her eyes.

A tall white-haired man approached Sarah and placed a hand on her shoulder. "Are you all right?"

Sarah shook her head as she struggled to focus.

"Would you like to sit down? Are you dizzy?"

Sarah steadied herself and regained her composure. "No, thank you. I'm all right. I was a bit startled."

"Poetry will do that."

Sarah turned to the shelf behind her noticing a sign that read: *Poetry*. "Yes, I guess so."

"One can become completely enraptured by a poem."

Sarah shrugged. She could tell he was humoring her and offering an elegant way out. She chose to take it. "The images were too vivid and I didn't...well I couldn't get all weepy here in the middle of the bookstore...so I called out to myself to stop that silly behavior...sorry. I didn't realize I was so loud."

"No need to apologize." The man smiled. "If you need anything I'm right over there." He indicated the desk at the front of the store.

"Thanks," Sarah said.

He nodded and walked away.

Alone again, Sarah turned back to the bookshelf. She recognized the cover, pulled it out, and stared at the title. "*Poems For My Love?*" she whispered. She examined the book. "This is the same book."

She scanned the bookshelf. "Where is *Jackal in the Mirror?*" She searched the shelves above and below, but found nothing. She stared at the book in her hand. "This *is* the book. I'm sure of it. What's with this title?" She opened it to the first page and read.

### *YOU*

> *You are my eyes*
> *My hands*
> *My voice*
> *The feeling of love that I need*
> *The slow tender moments that kisses prolong*
> *The only peace that I know*
>
> *I wish sometimes I were the wind*
> *To follow wherever you go*
> *To be part of your breath*

*To be every caress*
*To be with you all of the time*

Sarah closed the book and carefully inspected it. "It looks like the one I grabbed, but—" she scowled at it, "—where the heck is that awful chapter I read?" She looked past the book in her hands to the shelf in front of her and slid the poetry book back onto the shelf.

Instantly the scream pierced through her. Sarah yanked the book out and the shrieking stopped.

"All right, all right. I get it. This *is* the book and you need to come with me... whoever or whatever you are."

Having made a decision, she made her way through the bookstore and handed the book to the man behind the desk.

He raised his eyebrows at the sight of the book. "Ah, is this the book that moved you?"

"You could say that."

His eyes widened. "This is marvelous!" he said, admiring the book in his hands, before quickly handing it back to her.

"Is it?"

"Look at it. It's in such good shape."

"I couldn't find the price. How much is it?"

"What?"

"I'd like to buy it. How much is it?"

He looked shocked. "I didn't realize we had this book."

"Is it well known?"

"Its history is, within certain circles."

"Can you tell me about it?"

He took the book back. "Well, to begin with, look at the cover. There's no author listed." He flipped to the title page and pointed. "Or here."

Sarah glanced at it. "Why not?"

"That's the conundrum, isn't it?" He grinned. "The story is that only three copies were ever printed. The printing house refused to reveal the author's name or who received the three books. Needless to say, that created great speculation regarding the author, which in turn generated a huge interest in these books."

"Why?"

"The reputation of the publisher itself had a lot to do with it. They specialized in creating exclusive editions by elite authors with a limited number of books available."

"But why no author? Wouldn't that decrease the value of the book?"

"You would think so, yes, but the mystery of anonymity coupled with the publisher's status made the three books a rarity."

"Was it a stunt to create demand?"

"Some surmised as much, but that didn't turn out to be the case."

"If there were only three copies, how did you learn all this history?"

"One of the books ended up being auctioned off at an estate sale after the death of its owner. Not the original owner, mind you, but a man who had obtained the book—how he acquired it remains a mystery to this day. Anyway, he gave it as a gift to his wife. His good intentions backfired, apparently."

"Why? What happened?"

"No one knows for sure, but the story goes that the wife hated it. She couldn't stand it. Supposedly she kept it locked away in a trunk in her basement for years, and when her husband died, she was quick to get rid of it. And that story gained momentum among collectors of such rare and unusual books. Eventually, a publisher purchased that copy and tried to get the rights in order to distribute it. He issued a public appeal in an attempt to locate the author. That's when we, the public, first learned about the existence of the books. The media pushed and pushed. A few people stepped forward claiming to have written it. However, the original publisher denied their claims. They admitted to printing the three books, yet never divulged the name of the author. As you can imagine, endless speculation ensued, but to no avail."

"What happened?"

"The publisher never obtained the rights and eventually gave up on the idea altogether. After that, the buzz surrounding the book died. We all assumed that someone paid the publisher some good money for it."

"What about the other two copies?

"Their whereabouts are a mystery."

"How did you come to have it here?"

"Like I said, I'm clueless, truly baffled. I don't remember seeing the title on any of our inventory lists. It's strange, very strange. But if you wait a moment I'll check with the owner, she might have more information."

"You're not the owner?"

He laughed. "No, I'm a devoted volunteer. I love this old bookstore and I'm a good friend of the owner. She's a brilliant woman, and I enjoy her company." He winked and disappeared through a door at the back of the bookstore.

Sarah examined the book. She ran her fingers over the leather binding. It had a texture both soft and grainy to the touch. The spine only bore the title *Poems For My Love*. She opened the book to the first page, which showed the title. She turned to the next page and found no date, no identifying numbers, only the name of the publisher. The following page showed the first poem.

The man returned and took his place behind the desk. "I was right; we don't have any record of acquiring this book. Are you sure you found it here?"

"Yes, of course, in the back corner. On the poetry bookshelf."

"Well, we have no idea how it came to be there or how long we've had it."

"May I buy it?"

"The owner says it doesn't belong to the Booklegger so, technically, it's not ours to sell. Someone must've placed it on the bookshelf. Let me take a look." He took the book from Sarah and studied it. "The binding is unusual but typical of the press that issued it, and it has no real defects. It's been read, but with care. There are some handwritten notations in the back, but that hasn't damaged the book. I can't find any flaws. Here," he gingerly handed the book back to Sarah. "This book certainly doesn't like being handled by me."

"What do you mean?"

"Just that."

After a brief awkward silence, Sarah smiled nervously and shrugged. "This may sound strange, but I have the opposite feeling."

She hesitated. "The book—how should I say this—won't let me go. It *demands* to be with me. Odd, isn't it?" She felt her cheeks burn with embarrassment.

The man chuckled. "Darling, in this town that statement isn't strange at all. I've witnessed and experienced many unusual things in my lifetime." He stretched out his hand. "I'm James Horton." He shook Sarah's hand vigorously. "Born and bred in Eureka with a long line of peculiar ancestors and enough paranormal stories to bore you to death."

"Nice to meet you. I'm Sarah Thompson."

With her hand still in his, he raised his eyebrows and cocked his head. "A psychic?"

Surprised, Sarah mumbled, "Yes."

James squinted as he studied her. "And a medium too, I'd venture. Clairvoyant for sure."

"Wow. How can—"

"Been there, done that." He released her hand.

"Really?"

"You doubt me?"

"No, no. It's just that I've never been around someone who spoke so freely about it."

"Ah, you've only recently come to terms with it."

Sarah nodded.

"Yet I sense a very strong energy from you. You may have accepted your gift recently, but you must've been born with it. It's quite powerful."

"I hid it and denied it most of my life."

"Your parents?"

Sarah looked down. "They meant well."

"Yes, I can sense you loved them. Your nana as well."

Sarah was so stunned she stepped back from the counter. "My goodness, that's extraordinary. How on earth can you deduce all of that?"

"Same way you do. I sense it."

"I can't sense anything about you."

"Sure you can, only you're not focused on me right at this moment. This book gave you a heck of a jolt."

"You saw that?"

"No," he smiled. "I heard you."

"That's embarrassing." She shook her head. "I'm so sorry."

"I told you, there's no need to apologize. I can see that whatever the book showed you really shook you up."

"I'd say. The worst part is that I'm clueless as to why it showed me what it did. Any ideas?"

"That's not for me to understand – otherwise the book would've revealed itself to me. I've been coming to this bookstore since I was a kid, and that's about seventy years. No telling how long it's been here, but I never sensed its presence. Lots of other psychics and the like have been through here, too, and never found the book."

"How can that be?"

"Entities that are attached to earth-bound objects—in this case the book in your hands—are highly protective of those objects, and can create powerful energy barriers to shield them. That book may have been here for years, or days, or hours. Hard to tell, but it waited specifically for you."

Sarah furrowed her brow as she examined the book. "What should I do?"

"I can't help there, but I'm sure you'll figure it out. Take the book."

"Okay, but I must pay you something."

"No, you don't. Owner said we couldn't charge you for something we didn't buy. The fact is that however it got here, the book was meant for you, and only you. That means the book is yours."

"But you can't simply give it to me."

James shook his head. "I'm not the one giving it to you. Whoever placed it on that shelf is the one who gave it you. I'm sure you'll find out soon enough what that's all about."

Sarah stared at James, feeling she had known him forever. Kindness emanated from him, and his good looks no doubt contributed to the overall impression of affability. Deep blue eyes danced with joy, an effusive grin enhanced the wrinkles in his face, and loose, wavy gray hair perfectly framed his face, neck, and shoulders. He looked rugged, yet refined. His stylish white goatee, peppered with black, added a look of distinction.

She snapped herself back to reality and cleared her throat. "But, what if someone else—"

"C'mon Sarah, trust your instincts. Take it away from here, and give it time to acquaint itself with you. If anyone comes looking for it, I'll call you. But I guarantee they won't."

"James, you're something else," she said with a smile. "Don't take this the wrong way, but I'd like to visit with you while I'm here, if that's okay. I can learn a great deal from you."

He placed his hands on the desk and leaned toward her. "Darling Sarah, given what I'm sensing, I'm the one who can learn from *you*." He placed the book in a small bag and wrote his address and phone number on a piece of paper and handed it to her. "I'm here off and on most days, but you can reach me at home or leave a message in either place."

Sarah jotted down her cell number and handed it to him. "I'm here for the next four days."

He stepped around the desk and gave Sarah a warm embrace. "It's been a real pleasure to meet you, Sarah Thompson."

"Delighted to meet you, James Horton."

# 2

# THE STORY

"Extraordinary," said Conrad. "This James fellow sounds like someone I'd like to meet."

"Peculiar, for sure, but he knows what he's talking about." Sarah took a sip of wine and set the glass on the table near the fireplace. "I'll have loads to tell you tomorrow once I walk around this city. Hopefully I'll find out why it's so open to the paranormal."

Her room in the Carter House Hotel featured exquisite antique furnishings, a grand four-poster bed and a marble fireplace, the very one she now sat beside in her nightgown. The hotel, one of four beautifully renovated Queen Ann style properties that constituted the Carter House Inns, was perched above Humboldt Bay, a slice of which she could see out the window.

"I expect detailed reports. But what are you going to do about the book?"

"Follow James's advice and allow the book to become acquainted with me. I know that sounds like an odd thing to do, but…"

"Not for you."

"C'mon, I'm not exactly—"

"Wait. What have you done with my wife, the woman who talks to our attic?"

She snickered.

He laughed. "Well, it's true. Telling me that the book needs to become acquainted with you is not that far-fetched, for you. So, how are you going to do it?"

She sighed. "No clue. On the one hand, I'm reluctant to open the darn book and find the pages of that terrifying *Jackal in The Mirror* staring back at me. On the other hand, I'm curious. The first poem is beautiful and I imagine the rest might be as well, but the other stuff is simply…unsettling. Yet, I'm intrigued about what that story is all about. How could such a bizarre set of events and the death of that poor woman be part of a book of love poems?"

"No idea, but let's face it, stranger things have happened to you, so don't shut it out."

"Stranger? C'mon, that's not—"

"Strange in the sense that in the past you've attracted entities that—"

"Whoa! Entities? Since when did you start using words like that?"

"Um, since I started reading about psychics and mediums."

"You've been reading about psychics?"

"I'd planned to surprise you when you got back. The point is, if I'm going to be your sidekick, I should study what this whole phenomenon is about beyond simply accepting that it happens,."

"Sidekick?"

"Sure thing, Sherlock. I probably should've learned about it long ago, but I wasn't curious. When I was young and saw my grandmother and aunties do the kinds of things you do all the time, I took it all for granted. Never wondered why or how. But with you, so far it's been an unexpected rollercoaster of intrigue and plot twists. I need to be up to speed."

"So, tell me, my dear Dr. Watson, what have you learned?"

"You apparently attract entities that share their stories in bits and pieces. They have an agenda, a purpose. They take you on a journey of discovery. They need you to do things for them in a way that explains or forgives their actions. They need you to uncover a wrong and set it right for them."

"Wow! I'm impressed."

"Me, too."

"Don't let it go to your head, Watson."

"Not with me, I'm impressed with you. The more I read, the more I realize how incredibly special your talent is."

"Gosh, Watson, what a compliment. So, my darling sidekick, what do you recommend I do about this book?"

"Open it up, and let it guide you. Even though it's a book, whoever is using it to get to you has a plan."

Sarah heaved a deep sigh. "I wish you were here."

"I miss you, too. But you'll enjoy spending time with your friends. In fact, I demand it. In the meantime, I'll be diligently reading and preparing myself to be the best Watson ever. Stay grounded, and don't forget how much I love you."

"I love you too. Good night, darling."

"Good night, my love."

Sarah pressed the cell phone to her chest and sighed. She set the phone down, nibbled on a piece of cheese from the platter on the table next to her, took a sip of wine, and gazed at the flames in the fireplace. The book rested silently on the table next to the platter and wine. She turned to it, hoping for a hint of what she would find if she opened it. But it offered nothing.

She picked up her glass. "All right, Book, let's get acquainted. We'll start with a bit about me. I'm a psychic, but you've already detected that. Although I dislike that label because it comes with too much negative baggage, and hatred from folks who don't understand people like me." She stared at the book as she sipped her wine. "If I avoid the label, I can describe what I do and you can decide if I am indeed the one to help you. So here goes. I can perceive, at times witness, or even be present with individuals who have departed this world.

"These beings—or entities as Conrad calls them—reside in alternate realities, in their own time, which can be either past or present, or both. Like you, I assume, whoever you are." After another sip of wine, she went on. "What you must understand is that I cannot will these connections to happen. Quite the opposite, in fact. I'm the recipient, not the initiator. So it's up to *you* to communicate with me."

Not a sound from the book. She put down her glass, and leaned back with a sigh.

After a long silence, she continued. "When I was little, I could see the future. I haven't sensed the future in a long time, but it wouldn't surprise me if one day my ability to do that should pop up again." She leaned forward and grabbed the book. "I have no idea why I can do these things. It simply happens. For many years I stifled these abilities. I'm only now learning how to navigate in these realms, Book, so don't expect too much of me unless you're willing to help. After all, you picked me."

She shook the book. "C'mon, talk to me!" Frustrated, she set it down, nibbled on her cheese with crackers, then sipped her wine. "You could at least give me a sign."

She waited.

Nothing.

"When I started talking to my attic at least it cricked and creaked. It communicated with me—at least, I chose to interpret it as such. The attic opened the communications. It worked. And trust me, talking to an attic isn't any crazier than talking to a book, so you need to find a way to get to me."

Silence.

"Are you uneasy? After all, I took you away from your shelf in the bookstore. My attic was comfortable and at ease in its familiar environment. Is that it? Do I need to tell you where we are? Acquaint you with your new surroundings?" She stood and looked around the room. "Okay, so, we're in the Carter House Inn." She picked up the hotel's information packet and read. "It says here the house was originally built in 1884 in San Francisco and was called the Murphy House. The original structure was destroyed in the San Francisco earthquake and fire of 1906. In 1978, Mark Carter found the plans for the house in a Eureka antique store."

She returned to the table, gently stroked the book, and waited to see if it reacted.

When it didn't, she took her seat by the fireplace again and placed the book on her lap. She stared down at the cover, tan leather with rust tones forming a narrow frame around it, and at the center, in gold letters, *Poems For My Love.*

"Why were you waiting for me?"

She flipped the book over and examined the back. The surface mirrored the front cover. The spine was entirely tan with the title in gold.

"How did you predict I'd come to Eureka?" She placed the book back on her lap. "I've never been here before, and I know next to nothing about this part of California. My information is limited to a handful of facts I read before I came on this trip. Other than Old Town Eureka, the rest is unremarkable—a small town that happens to be on the famous U.S. Route 101, north of San Francisco, and south of the border with Oregon." She paused and sipped her wine. "The thing I find most interesting about this place is it's said to be open to paranormal activity."

She stared at the book and shook her head. "C'mon, Book. I'm running out of things to say here, and if I continue to sip this wine, I'll get tipsy and be of no use to you."

Silence.

She set her wine glass down and ate a few grapes. "What else can I tell you about this place?" She looked around the room searching for ideas, and noticed a painting depicting the original settlers and the indigenous peoples that lived in the area. "Could that be a connection with you? What's the tribe's name? I read it somewhere."

She opened her iPad, and clicked on her bookmarks. "Aha. Here it is. They were the Wiyot people and they called this place Jaroujiji, which means 'Where you Sit and Rest.' What a splendid name, isn't it?" She read on. "Says here that the gold rush miners renamed it Eureka, a Greek word meaning 'I Have Found It.'" She chuckled. "They most certainly found it, and they lined their pockets with the riches from mines and lumber."

*You must help me.*

The whisper traveled through Sarah's loose hair as it swirled around her shoulders.

"At last. You sure took your time. Are you ready to share?"

Silence.

Sarah closed her iPad. She picked up the book, set it on her lap, closed her eyes, inhaled deeply, and slowly breathed out. "Okay, here goes nothing." She opened the book and gasped.

# YOUNG LOVE

The girl dove into the lake, and swam effortlessly to a powerboat that drifted a few yards from the shore. A young man helped her climb in. Once she was safely on board, he shot her a disapproving look, then turned to the controls and sped away, leaving a trail of churning water in his wake.

They raced the length of the lake in silence until they reached a secluded cove. With a dexterity born from years of experience, he slowed down and steered the boat under some overhanging branches to hide it from sight. He dropped anchor while she dove into the water and swam ashore. As soon as the boat was secured he stripped down to his trunks and followed her.

They sat side by side in silence on the small beach, their feet mere inches from the water. After several tense seconds, the young man ventured to speak. "How did it happen?"

She looked into his pained eyes. "He asked my father."

"And he said yes without even asking you?"

She closed her eyes and lowered her head.

"I see."

She reached for his hand. "No one knows about us, so how could anyone guess? Why would my father even doubt that I'd be thrilled about the match?"

"You encouraged him?"

She yanked her hand away. "How could you ask me that?"

He reached toward her, but she rejected his touch.

"I'm sorry. Please understand...it hurts, it really hurts," he whispered.

She turned to find his eyes flooded with tears. She caressed them away. "If only you had asked before he did."

"I couldn't."

She shook her head. "You wouldn't."

They looked into each other's eyes, realizing that the distance between them was quickly becoming a chasm.

He looked down at the sand. "So, now what?"

"We go back and..." she turned her gaze away from him.

"And what?"

"We do what we have to do."

He gently turned her toward him searching for hope somewhere in her deep blue eyes, but found none. He stood abruptly and dove into the lake and made his way back to the boat. Moments later, she followed.

Sarah wiped away her tears. "I feel such pain...a hurt deep within me." She set the book down, sighed, and stared into the fireplace. "Who are these teenagers? Could they be the children of the woman who was killed? Obviously, you expect me to do something with this tiny glimpse of their situation." Her voice became laden with frustration. "What's the message, Book?"

Silence.

She picked the book up and read on.

# ARDOR

The cavernous art studio was cluttered with paintings, many hanging on the walls or leaning against easels or furniture, some lying on the floor. Alabaster sculptures sat on pedestals and tables, crammed among the paintings. A large easel stood at the center of the loft covered by a white sheet dappled and smeared with a kaleidoscope of colors. A table crowded with tubes of paint of every imaginable hue, surrounded by rags and brushes, stood beside it.

From behind an oversized screen that separated the studio from the makeshift bedroom, the moans of a man and woman involved in fervent lovemaking echoed through the room.

Bodies entwined, they writhed and moaned atop a king-size mattress that rested directly on the floor. Pillows and covers lay strewn where they'd fallen or been flung away.

A large painting hung precariously above the bed, dominating the room in a disturbing way. It was a stylized rendition of a jackal snarling at an unseen enemy, while a pale, delicate hand reached from the upper right corner of the canvas toward the beast.

After an exuberant climax, the couple's breathing slowed to a series of heavy sighs. The man attempted to withdraw, but the woman wrapped her arms and legs around his body. "No, wait, Andrew," she moaned.

He surrendered to her embrace, kissing and nibbling her neck. Something he did around her ears caused her to giggle. "Stop." She laughed and struggled in vain to escape, as he growled fiercely and tickled her without mercy. In the struggle, he rolled off the mattress and she snatched up the sheet, taking refuge beneath it.

He sat up on the floor and leered at her. A stunning man in his late thirties, with long black wavy hair, gray eyes, dark olive skin, and taut muscles, Andrew exuded an irresistible combination of razor-sharp intensity and animal presence.

He pushed back the sheet and caressed her buttocks. A rose-shaped red birthmark decorated the back of his left hand. He chuckled and slapped her behind, causing her to squeal with delight. His eyes wandered to a covered sculpture on a table across the room. He rose to his feet and padded across the studio toward it.

Bewildered, the woman emerged from under the sheet to see what had caused their game to come to such an abrupt and unexpected end. She spotted him next to the sculpture and eyed him with curiosity.

Andrew yanked the cloth away and tossed it aside, revealing a half-finished sculpture of a jackal cradled against a reclining nude woman. He studied it intently for several seconds, then reached toward the mass of clay on a small table nearby.

"Was it something I said?" the woman asked with a hint of sarcasm.

Andrew, clay in hand, didn't respond; his attention fully focused on the sculpture.

As she stood, the sheet fell to the floor, revealing her soft and attractive figure. Her wavy auburn hair fell loosely over her shoulders. She was an eye-catching woman in her late twenties. Picking up the sheet, she wrapped it around herself, and sauntered over to him.

Without looking at her, he acknowledged her presence with a smile. "Animals, like women, are exhilarating."

"Andrew, tell me—"

"No questions. You agreed. Let's deal with what you can observe and feel in this room."

"Okay, but first—"

"Hush..."

He dropped the clay, wiped his hands with a rag, turned, and pulled her to him.

"Karla, all you need to know is that you enthrall me." He caressed her cheek with the back of his right hand.

Karla sighed as she gave in to the sensation of his touch.

"Model for me," he said.

"Now? Just like that?"

"Just like that."

"I can't stay in one position for that long."

"You don't need to be motionless. I'm not after a duplicate of you. I seek who you are. I crave losing myself in the depths of those crazy hazel eyes of yours." He cupped her face in his hands. "The tones of gold around your iris that fade into pools of blue and gray pull me in. "

"Aren't we metaphysical today?"

He stared into her eyes. "You've bewitched me."

She smiled. "I could say the same thing about you."

"Say yes. Let me take you all in."

"How do you propose to do that?"

Andrew snaked his arms around her waist. The sheet dropped as he delicately ran his hands over her nude body. "Slowly. Very, very slowly."

With an impish grin, Karla broke away from his embrace, and ambled about the studio studying his work. "Is that how you've created all these…creatures?"

"Ask them."

There were sculptures of every size, all of women and animals. The paintings depicted the same subjects. She ran the tips of her fingers over the sculptures, feeling their vibrations, listening, expecting them to spring to life. A quiet intensity, buried anger or hidden pain, emanated from all of the figures.

"Can you hear them?"

Startled, Karla jumped. "Yes," she gasped. "In a way. They're so real."

"They are real. They're my most intimate friends. Without them, I couldn't survive."

He walked up to her and combed his fingers through her hair.

She tilted her head back to meet his sensual touch without taking her eyes off the painting of two jackals standing over a nude woman, whose lustful eyes stared back from the canvas.

"What do you mean, survive?"

His lips tickled the nape of her neck. "They take care of me. Look around. What can I tell you that they haven't already captured? My work speaks for me. I cannot. If I knew how to express myself in words I'd be a poet, or a writer like you."

"How will I—"

"You'll work it out. You're good at your craft. I like what you do. You grasp things other art journalists don't." He spun her around and touched her lips gently with his. "I long to read what you can do with me."

"Without talking?"

"We don't need to talk."

"You're a strange man, Andrew."

"Am I?" He pulled her toward him and kissed her.

The words dissolved.

Sarah blinked and stared at the page only to find the first poem staring back at her. She flipped to the next page and encountered a second poem.

"Where's the story?" She flipped through the pages, but saw nothing but poems. She scanned the book deliberately, but the poems didn't change. She slammed it shut.

"This tale appears and disappears at will. Who are these people? They don't look like the teenagers—well, maybe a little. Andrew has some resemblance. But the girl was a blue-eyed blond. Karla looks different." She stared down at the cover. "Why show me their lovemaking? What connection do any of these people have with the woman who fell down the stairs and died? I don't get what this story is about."

Silence.

She sighed and forced herself to rein in her frustration. "Why would you make the story disappear? Unless you need me to read the poem—is that it?" She shook her head. "I need to think about these scenes first. Give me a minute."

She rose from the chair and paced up and down the room. "There's a definite connection between these poems and the stories. There has to be. So, do the poems need to be read before the story goes on?" Sarah mulled that over for a moment and shook her head. "No, I saw the death of the woman first, the poem followed. Which means the story comes first and the poems appear to explain—what, the plot of the story? No, no, no. That doesn't add up. The woman's death happened, and then the first poem expressed the love and need of the writer for his lover… unless the poet is a woman. Either way, the poem was followed by the two chapters about love, one of deep disappointment, possibly betrayal, the other—" She stopped and stared at the book from across the room. "Jealousy! The story is about jealousy and the poems are..." She shrugged. "I'm not sure what they are. The man who sent the woman flying down the stairs, is he the jealous one? Is he the one I'm supposed to find? Is that what you need from me?"

The book refused to answer.

"Your silence is very annoying." She yawned, grabbed the book from the table and carried it back to her bed. "Fair warning, I'll read the next poem, but after that, I'm going to sleep, unless you give me something."

### WORDS

*I love you more*
*Than words can say*
*No language could express*
*The things I feel for you*

*My need for you is greater*
*Than fear or joy could ever be*

*The only anguish great enough*
*To make me lose my mind*
*Is knowing that for just a day*
*You won't be by my side*

*And if I were God*
*For just a single day*
*Some changes I would make*
*To be the only love for you*
*The only thing you had to do*
*Your only thought*
*Your only sight*
*To reach inside of you*
*And stay*

*Both night and day*
*Throughout the substance*
*Of your life*
*To repeat in every way*
*I love you more*
*Than words can say*

# SURPRISE

The morning sun glared down through the skylight onto the bed in Andrew's studio. Only Karla lay beneath the messy sheets, squirming sensuously into consciousness, moaning softly. She felt about the bed searching for her lover. Squinting against the bright sun, she sat up and glanced around the room.

"Andrew?" she called out. The only response was the echo of her voice.

She crawled out of the bed naked, spotted his T-shirt on a nearby chair, and slipped it on. She peeked around the screen, half-expecting Andrew to burst from some hiding place to surprise her, but found no one. She ambled over to the kitchen in the far corner of the room, filled a kettle with water, and placed it on the stove. After rummaging through the cupboards, she found a satisfactory type of tea, removed a bag, and dropped it next to a cup.

She wandered about the studio, peering at the paintings strewn about the room and stopping to examine a sculpture. The shrill whistle of the teakettle demanded her attention so she scurried back to the kitchen, filled the cup with hot water, and placed the tea bag inside. She found a bottle of honey on the shelf above her, poured a few drops in, and swirled it with a spoon. She removed the bag, sipped her tea, and turned back toward the studio.

This time the large easel at the center of the room caught her eye. A mischievous smirk crossed her lips as she headed over to the easel. She reached for the cloth that shrouded the painting.

Something on the table next to it caught her attention. A page from a local newspaper was pinned to the table by a large sharp knife that had been stabbed through the photograph of a woman labeled: Martha McKenzie. The headline above read: *McKENZIE MATRIARCH FEARED DROWNED, Lakeside Community Shaken by Inexplicable Death.*"

# 3

# THE FELLOW TRAVELER

Sarah bolted upright in shock. The four-poster bed in her hotel room squeaked and wobbled with the sudden jolt. She grabbed the book from the nightstand, opened it, and stared down at the page before her. A new chapter titled *Surprise,* silently waited for her reaction.

"The murdered woman is Martha McKenzie. Wait a minute, did I dream this chapter exactly as it's written?"

Her eyes frantically scanned the pages. "I'll be darned, the exact description, the same images. When did all this stuff happen?" She reread the chapter, but found no mention of a date anywhere in the narrative. "Did this just happen or did it take place a long time ago? I didn't notice a date on the newspaper. I don't get it."

The book offered no answers.

She looked at the clock by the bed. "Oh, my God. I slept for eleven hours straight. That's a first. Well, at least it's not too early to call James." She pulled James' contact information from her purse and dialed her cell phone.

James answered. "Hello, Sarah, how are you?"

"How did you guess it was me?"

He chuckled. "The Washington State area code on your phone number. What's up?"

"Good morning James, first of all. Sorry to bother you, but I'm enormously puzzled by this book. Is there any way we can get together for a chat this morning?"

"Sure. I'd love to have you to come to the house, but I'm afraid the book may shut down with all the stuff I have around here. Where are you staying?"

"The Carter House Inn Hotel."

"Tell you what, meet me at Café Waterfront. It's on the corner of 1st and F streets. The front desk can give you directions. How about we meet in one hour?"

"Great. I'll be there. Thanks, James."

An hour later, Sarah entered the small restaurant and scanned the tables.

James stood and waved her over.

She was grateful that he'd picked a corner table that offered a bit of privacy.

He welcomed her with a warm embrace. "Good morning, my dear."

"Good morning, James. Thanks for seeing me so soon."

He motioned for her to sit and followed suit. "Welcome to the Weaver Building, built in 1892. In my opinion, it's one of the most interesting in town, and quite a beauty. Back in its heyday, it boasted a saloon downstairs and a brothel upstairs. Some years later, it became the Blue Bird Cabaret where men paid a dime a dance. Imagine that."

"I noticed the sign in the front. It's a Eureka historical landmark."

He leaned toward her with his elbows on the table. "You haven't had any breakfast. It shows in your eyes."

"You're right."

He relaxed back in his chair and grinned. "Well, you're in for a treat."

"I'm not really hungry, I—"

"You must eat, at least a bit. Your body is going to need all the energy it can muster to deal with whatever is bothering you. I recommend their *huevos rancheros*. They're super good."

Sarah smiled. "*Huevos rancheros* it is."

After they placed their orders, James reached over and held Sarah's hand. "I can tell that you're uneasy. Tell me about it."

"Okay." She took the book from her purse and placed it on the table.

James yanked his hand away and frowned. "This book refuses to be shared with me."

She glanced back and forth between the book and James, puzzled. "What do you mean?"

His voice fell to a whisper. "I sense a strong force pushing me away. It won't allow me to interfere. Please put it away." Stunned, Sarah did as he asked. "If you'd like you can ask me general questions, that should be fine, but don't reveal any specific names or events. The book is adamant that its contents are meant *only* for you."

Sarah nodded. "This is a book of love poems. Beautiful poems, I may add. But—how can I put this? It also reveals a story. In bits and pieces, mind you, and...well, the text appears on the page and then...it disappears. Like magic."

"I understand."

"Doesn't that strike you as odd?"

"No, my dear, not at all, certainly not in these parts, and definitely not with someone like you. You *are* quite special."

"How can you say that? We only just met."

He shook his head and peered deep into her eyes. "We may have only met in person now, Sarah, but I feel a very strong connection to you—a sense of partnership—as if we've been friends a long while."

"Well, ditto, my friend. Any idea why we have that impression?"

"I suspect it's aided by our surroundings. Our subconscious minds and spirits are connecting. They're at ease. There's trust and comfort. Like a favorite blanket cuddling you."

"What's so special about our surroundings?"

"Ah, well..." He leaned closer. "For starters, there's the shape of the bay, and our local geography. It is said, and this goes back generations, that it forms a kind of tuning device that opens a gateway between our four-dimensional plane and other planes in other dimensions."

Sarah furrowed her brow, staring at him skeptically.

James smiled. "A bit outlandish, I know. Many have been hard pressed to explain the strange electromagnetic energies of the region and, let's not forget, the hauntings and visions in unusual spots. Yet, there it is. We're proof that some kind of inexplicable energy is enabling our communication at a deeper level, far beyond being right here chatting over breakfast."

Sarah gave a slow nod of agreement. "You've got a point there."

"Let me tell you a bit about Eureka's...hmm...let's call it a special attraction. According to the owner and operator of Old Town Ghost Tours, there are twenty-seven spots in Old Town Eureka that are haunted or have reported ghost sightings. This is a man who's a natural skeptic, who has researched the history of this area extensively, and examined all the reported paranormal events in depth. He claims Eureka is one of the most haunted places on the West Coast." Before she could speak, James held up a hand. "Sure, these claims are good for tourism, and provide him with some extra money. But he is not making it all up. One of the reasons Eureka has so many hauntings is most certainly because of its longitude and latitude, but also because of its past, going all the way back to the original inhabitants."

"You mean the Wiyot people?"

"You've done your homework. Yes, the spirits of the native peoples permeate our atmosphere. The Wiyot considered this bay sacred. History tells us this part of the world remained hidden from outsiders until the mid-nineteenth century when Europeans took over."

"A difficult transition for the Wiyot, I'd imagine."

"As you're well aware, the spirits of the dead, particularly those who are unhappy or in search of closure, have a propensity to stay behind. Most of the time their energy is interpreted as haunting places or objects. For folks like you and me, that energy manifests differently. Spirits entrust us with their desires and needs. They strive for a resolution, and use us as vehicles to accomplish that."

"Yes, I've had that experience."

"On the other hand, some spirits are not unhappy or desirous of anything, they simply don't wish to depart. They're not ready to leave this plane of existence, and their energy creates unexplained phenomena.

Eureka was a lively port town in the nineteenth century, crowded with saloons, brothels, and other sordid establishments. History tells us that a tremendous amount of violence occurred in those days, people died terrible deaths, and as a result, many a place is haunted. Not to mention the old Victorian buildings, which lend themselves to stories of haunted houses inhabited by ghosts or evil spirits. Don't get me wrong—I'm not saying that all the stories like the one of the woman who haunts the alley between H and I Streets are fabrications to entice tourists. Many of the stories are true, and the spirits do stay and visit us."

"You've seen them?"

He nodded. "And I speak with them when they wish me to." The waitress brought their orders and James took a sip of coffee. "I do like their coffee."

Sarah sipped hers. "It *is* good. These eggs look great."

"Wait till you taste them." He dug in.

She took a bite and savored it. "You're right, they're delicious."

James chewed and swallowed. "Anyway, some wandering, restless souls get attached to objects, places, or people. In your case, it appears that there's someone attached to that book of poems and is using its energy to connect with you."

"I suspected as much. But why use a book and not simply converse with me? And, why this business of vanishing poems replaced by equally ephemeral chapters?"

James laughed. "Raw talent, I might venture, in terms of your abilities. As much as you've been through, you're still learning to harness your gift."

Sarah blushed.

"No need for embarrassment. Quite the opposite, I'm paying you a compliment. I'll take your raw talent any day. The world is full of charlatans claiming to be special. Rubbish."

"I'd like to understand more about it, though. Learn how it works, how come I have it—*we* have it, and others don't."

"Understandable. Yet beware of too much dissection. It might interfere with the free flow of information if you anticipate or expect things to occur according to some other person's research. Our abilities—yours and mine—are embedded in our being, our senses, our entire makeup, our DNA, and rational scientific explanations tend to fall short. At least in my opinion."

"I'm sure you're right, but nevertheless—"

"Let me give you a taste of the research behind psychics, mediums, and the like. Einstein is quoted as saying that 'everything in life is a vibration' given that everything is made up of atoms, molecules, etc. Atoms are in a constant state of motion, and depending on the speed of these atoms, things in our four-dimensional plane appear as a solid, liquid, or gas. Well, sound vibrates, even though we can't see it or touch it. We simply hear it. For folks like us, we tune into the vibrations from another set of dimensions where the speed of the atoms or the energy, or whatever is there, travels at very different frequencies without the drag of time or location."

"Are you saying that's how I can observe the future at times?"

"Yes, obviously you can tune into other planes where the future becomes visible to you. That's something I cannot do."

Sarah considered these revelations.

He gave her a few seconds to mull things over before interrupting her thoughts. "There's something I've been meaning to ask. When did you first realize you had these abilities?"

She blinked a couple of times as she came back to the moment. "Uh, pretty early on, three, four years old."

"What could you do?"

After some hesitancy, she said, "I've never spoken of this with anyone but my husband, Conrad."

"I didn't mean to pry—"

"It's okay, James. It's only, well, thinking of that time brings back memories and emotions that are…difficult."

"I'm sorry I asked."

"No need to apologize. Really." She took a deep breath, stared out the window, and allowed herself to journey back to a never-forgotten childhood. "The way I remember it is that, somehow, I sort of knew what would happen in the near future, in the same way that I knew where my room was or the color of the sky. It came naturally to me. I didn't think about it, it simply happened. I could see and hear ethereal beings around me, and I sensed—not sensed, but somehow *witnessed* things that happened to friends and family when I wasn't present."

"Powerful indeed," James said after a deep breath. "I can't even fathom what that must've been like. What happened to make you withdraw?"

"At age six, in the middle of a friend's birthday party, I blurted out that her uncle had molested her. I didn't use those exact words, but the effect was the same. They called me an evil liar and labeled me a witch. It got so bad, my parents felt compelled to move me away."

"And your well-meaning parents forced you to hide your gifts."

Sarah nodded. "I suppressed them my entire life, until a couple of years ago."

"How did you regain them?"

"Angela, my husband's long-deceased grandmother, who possessed many of the same attributes I have, brought me from Pasadena to Winthrop. It's a beautiful place in the midst of the Cascades in Washington State."

"What was she after?"

"As it turns out, the family had a long-standing secret. She needed her grandson—that's my husband, Conrad—and his family to learn the history of their ancestors. He and I live, along with our children and grandchildren, in two beautiful Queen Anne style homes known as the twin houses. They were built in the 1800s and they're exactly the same."

"Interesting. Why did Angela choose you?"

"She met me in a dream. She was a psychic herself, and it turned out that we had something in common."

"Really?"

"It's a long story, it'll bore you."

"No, trust me, it won't."

"Well, short version, I helped a young boy who'd lost his hearing after a fall."

"You were a teacher?"

"I was. Fortunately, I discovered he could hear certain tones, and he was fitted with specialized hearing aids. As it turns out, Angela knew his parents."

"I hope to hear the details of that story, someday, but now I understand the connection."

Sarah crossed her arms and leaned on the table. "Your turn James. Tell me about you."

"Fair enough. I also realized I was different from an early age. Unlike yours, my parents were delighted. As you can well imagine, where I was born and raised had a lot to do with that. Here in Eureka no one took it as odd."

"Everyone knew you were a psychic?" she asked with an inquisitive tilt of her head.

"We didn't call it that—special, was the word."

"What could you do?"

"I cohabitate in both this and the spirit world."

"All the time?"

"Yes. For me it's like living in two alternate worlds. One is right here in front of me with a table, utensils, a delicious breakfast and coffee, while the other hovers about, as if a cloud has descended and enveloped that other realm of reality to help me distinguish between the worlds I experience."

"You've lived like that since you were little? Existing in both?"

James nodded. "I've never been alone. No idea what the feeling of being alone is like." He laughed. "Don't be so serious. It's quite all right."

"Are you married?"

"No. Never been. Every time I tried to develop an intimate relationship with a woman, her ancestors stepped in and made it difficult."

"Oh, James." Sarah reached for his hand.

He emitted a half-hearted chuckle. "Don't get me wrong, Sarah. I've had several long-term relationships. I'm not celibate or virginal by any means. Been in love and enjoyed all that comes with it. It's simply that when the time came to commit, the ancestral—let me find the best way to put this delicately—well, the ancestral baggage turned out to be too heavy."

"Ancestral baggage? What on earth do you mean?"

"The ancestors of any bride-to-be made it abundantly clear that, if I married, they would move in right along with her, and I didn't care to live with all of them day in and day out."

Sarah laughed. "Please forgive me, James. I'm not laughing at you. It's just that the image you painted is, well, it's comical. It would make a great movie."

James chortled. "Yeah, imagine the title on the marquee: *Me, my Bride, and Her Dead Relatives*."

"It must've been confusing when you were little to live in these two worlds."

"Not really. That was my reality and I enjoyed it."

"I take it you're retired?"

"You're curious about what I did to earn a living."

"And if you ever left Eureka."

"An attorney. That's what I did, criminal law to be exact. And yes, I left Eureka for many years, and yes, the ability to live in both worlds followed me everywhere. Guess where I went."

Sarah stared into his deep blue eyes and squinted in a mock attempt to read his mind.

"C'mon Sarah. It can't be that hard for you." He took a deep breath and exhaled. "Let it seep in. Allow the whisper to penetrate."

Sarah's eyes widened in surprise. "You also feel the whisper?"

"The private whisper that speaks deep within us."

"All right," Sarah sighed and closed her eyes. "You went back east…To D.C., and after that to Europe. The Hague." She sat back, her eyes wide open. "Oh! You're *the* James Horton."

"Well done, my dear. You've read about me, then."

"Well, of course. Who hasn't? You were the golden boy of the courts. My father idolized you. He used to read your arguments aloud and we'd discuss them in detail." She shook her head. "This is amazing, I'm sitting with *the* James Horton."

"Your father was a lawyer?"

"He was in corporate law, mind you, but he was fascinated by many court cases in The Hague. He truly admired you. You were infallible."

"I've put my gift to good use."

"I'll say you have. Oh, my goodness. I'm in shock. I can't believe I'm friends with *the* James Horton."

"Simply 'James' will do. All that is in the past. These days I'm a happily retired resident of Eureka, well, actually Ferndale, who volunteers at the Booklegger bookstore, and helps the cops here and there."

"You're a legend, James."

"Enough, Sarah. Really." He snatched up the bill, rose to his feet, and extended a hand to help Sarah up. "Let's get a bit of fresh air. How about we take a stroll around Old Town Eureka?"

# 4

# THE DECISION

"Eureka's Old Town," said James as they strolled down Second Street, "is listed as a National Historic and Cultural Arts District. It's the touristy spot of the area. The rest of Eureka is like any other town, nothing special. But here, as you can see, it has retained much of the flavor of its Victorian architecture, and is full of gift shops, museums, antique stores, and restaurants, all within walking distance. And of course, the famous Carson Mansion, which is an absolute masterpiece of Victorian splendor. All in all, there are more than 1,000 Victorian homes in Eureka and Ferndale. I'm lucky enough to live in one of them."

"I'd love to see it." She hesitated a moment. "Gee, I didn't mean to invite myself to your home."

"Don't be silly. Of course you must visit. Only I'm fearful that your whole purpose for being here could be derailed if you do. The force within and around your book is quite adamant against it. Maybe later, when things settle down. When do your friends arrive?"

"Later this evening."

"Well, maybe after they leave. My only advice is to keep the book to yourself. Don't share it with them. It might disturb the communication."

"How is that possible?"

"I get the feeling the entity, or entities, attached to this book are shy, or afraid, or insecure. I'm not exactly sure what it is, but it emanates those kinds of emotions."

"Can you see them?"

"No, not at all," he said, with a hint of frustration. "I can only feel the energy."

"Why do you suppose that is?"

"Who can say? But it's clear they're hiding something."

"Hiding something? How can you tell?"

"The on-again-off-again manifestation and disappearance of the story is a bit of a clue."

"A clue..."

"They're sharing information with you, but at the same time they're fearful or timid about what you might discover."

Sarah inhaled deeply and walked in silence for a good while. James respected her need to process the information. She slowed her steps, glancing over at him. "Are you familiar with a woman named—"

"No names, Sarah." He smiled and strode on.

She caught up and walked alongside him. "Okay. How about this, is there a lake nearby?"

"Yes, Ruth Lake, a couple of hours southeast. It's actually the reservoir of the Mad River."

"The Mad River, what a name! Where did it come from?"

"The story goes that the men who found the river, back in the nineteenth century when it was a mere stream, argued about its exact latitudinal position. Anyway, a heated argument ensued, and given the anger expressed by both sides, they named it the Mad River."

"Anything special about the lake?"

"Special, as in beautiful? Yes, it's lovely. Otherwise, it's an ordinary lake."

She frowned. "It's puzzling. I can't make sense of the story or what it wants from me."

"Don't rush it. Let it develop at the speed it needs. Have you experienced anything similar before?"

"Nothing exactly like this, no. I've witnessed life stories emanating from old photographs, all enabled by Angela. I also read, or watched, a screenplay in my mind."

"A screenplay? That's a new one for me. How come a screenplay?"

"Alexander, the spirit behind it all, had written a screenplay about a series of events that had traumatized a young boy. He insisted I needed to read—well, watch—the movie in my head to understand and help the boy, who by then was a man. Alexander needed his forgiveness."

"Did you help?"

"Yes."

"Did the entire screenplay appear in your mind?"

"Yes. Or rather, the entire movie played out."

"Slow process I would imagine, one or two scenes at a time."

"Yes."

"A screenplay is long. Movies last around two hours. So you've had practice waiting and letting the story develop."

She shrugged. "I have, although I was very impatient and on edge most of the time. My husband had his hands full trying to keep me calm."

"I can imagine. One more question, have you ever had an out-of-body experience with a living person?"

"You mean when I become someone else?"

"In a way, except you remain who you are. You simply enter the other person's reality. You experience what they are undergoing as it's happening."

"Yes, only once. For a few hours I experienced what an amnesiac was enduring. Why?"

"I suspect it may happen to you again."

Sarah stopped in her tracks and turned to James. "Why?"

His eyes became fixed on some distant point and he shook his head. "I'm not sure, but there's a very strong pull around you. As if someone is trying very hard to pull you away from me, away from here. I don't sense evil in the intent, only fear and deep, deep sadness." He faced her and took her hand. "Be aware."

Sarah hesitated. "Of what?"

"Not sure, but keep your guard up. Let the information come through, but don't react impulsively."

She placed her hand over his. "James, meeting you has been extraordinary. Your comfort with all these events that surround us is so admirable."

"I'm simply used to it. Don't worry, you'll get there."

"I wish I could bottle you and take you with me."

"That would be quite a feat." He laughed. "In the meantime, I suggest you go back to your hotel and give the book a chance before your friends get here. If you ignore it for it too long it might get upset, particularly if the story has pressing matters to attend to."

Sarah acknowledged his advice with a smile, and they silently embraced before going their separate ways.

Once ensconced in the comfort of her room, Sarah sat by a window that overlooked the town. It seemed clear to her now that not a single word of the disappearing story had actually been written. The entire tale of *Jackal in the Mirror* was being created inside her mind, courtesy of the entity sharing the information.

"Very well, if that's the case, let's run with it." She opened the book.

# DISCERN

Karla, dressed in a two-piece royal blue suit, briefcase in hand, swung open the glass door to a high-rise building and marched in. She crossed the bustling marble lobby to one of eight elevators, and briskly entered a moment before the doors closed behind her.

She burst from the elevator and headed a short distance down the hallway to a double door displaying in bold gold letters the words: *WOA – World of Art – The International Magazine of Art.* Underneath, in smaller letters, was, *Gerard Simonet – Founder.* Karla pushed the doors open and sauntered through.

The huge reception area was carpeted in white, punctuated by chrome and glass furniture with white cushions. At the center, a narrow translucent desk encircled an attractive receptionist who busily handled a phone bank and an oversized desktop computer. She recognized Karla and nodded. "Good morning, Miss Jordan. They're waiting for you. Your tea is ready."

Karla smiled in appreciation. "Thanks, Linda."

She strode down a narrow hallway toward the end office and opened the double doors.

"Welcome, *mon chou.*" Gerard, a thin, blonde, elegant man of forty-four completely dressed in white sat on a white armchair next to a glass and chrome coffee table.

"*Merci*, Gerard. How are you?" Karla asked, and kissed him on both cheeks.

Testimonials to Gerard and the magazine, as well as imposing paintings, sculptures, and photographs that covered every available surface, glamorized the otherwise monochromatic office.

Occupying an armchair next to him sat Nicole, a slender, exquisite woman in her late twenties, dressed in a revealing fuchsia silk dress that totally clashed with the dominant white and chrome motif of the office and its owner. She lounged coquettishly, cradling a china coffee cup in her hands, and stared at Karla with poorly disguised disdain.

Karla tactfully kissed Nicole on both cheeks, sat across from Gerard, picked up her cup, and sipped her tea.

Gerard tossed a pile of photographs onto the coffee table. The top photograph was of Andrew. "I am very proud of you, *mon chou*, for getting this story. Although I'm disappointed that he refused permission for us to print his photograph."

"It is said you managed to acquaint yourself with him quite intimately," Nicole said in a snide tone.

"Well, Nicole, your sources are always far more crafty than mine."

Pouting at the obvious jab, Nicole leaned over and caressed Gerard's hair to assert her control over the man.

"Karla," Gerard interjected, pushing Nicole's hand away, "do you have any photographs of his statue in the park, the one with the jackals? I'd like to show their eyes in particular. The image could help punctuate the article's comments about the inner life you observed in his art."

Karla flipped open her briefcase and thumbed through the photographs, found the one she was searching for, and pulled it out. "How about this one?" She handed it to Gerard.

The photo had been taken at sunset. The life-size bronze sculpture depicted two jackals, with one animal seen in the background through the snarling fangs of the other. Their eyes vibrated with life and an intense mixture of pleasure and anger.

"*Merveilleuse*! This is perfect, my dear."

Nicole attempted to create a sense of secrecy by leaning in toward Karla and whispering. "Tell me, *chérie*, what is he like? Intimately?"

Karla raised her cup to her lips and shrugged.

"Never mind all that," Gerard scolded as he patted Nicole's knee. He shifted to the front of his chair and leaned across the table toward Karla. "You wrote nothing about his family, education, childhood. Why? That is what our readers are most interested in."

"My research uncovered absolutely nothing about his life prior to his debut as an artist. He categorically refused to discuss anything at all regarding his past. He only agreed to do the story if it centered exclusively on his work. What is 'real and lasting,' as he put it."

"Why?" Nicole said. "Is he hiding something?"

"I'm not sure."

Seeing a chance to attack, Nicole's eyes narrowed. "But you should, shouldn't you?"

"Later, *ma petite*," Gerard said with obvious condescension, and gently brushed Nicole's cheek with his hand. "Karla, there's one more thing. I have three pages to fill in the upcoming issue with something witty and bright on the Chinese miniature exhibit at the Asian Art Museum. Can you manage something?"

"What's my deadline?"

Gerard rolled his head from side to side. "I need it in four days. Only you can do it."

"Flattery will get you anything, Gerard," Karla said with a sly grin. "But it's going to cost you."

"You're worth every penny, my dear. Send me the bill."

Karla smiled as Gerard returned his attention to her photographs of Andrew's work.

"It's imperative that you get something personal on Andrew—if not from him then from his acquaintances. Although it doesn't look like anyone has befriended the recluse."

"I'll give it a go. But don't hold your breath. It's been hard enough to get what I do have."

Karla closed her briefcase and rose to her feet. She bent down to kiss Gerard on both cheeks, ignored Nicole, and headed for the door. "*Adieu.*"

"*Va bien, mon cher.*"

She closed the doors and made her way back toward the ever-smiling receptionist.

"How did it go, Miss Jordan?"

"Fine, Gerard shot me some extra work. Oh, Linda, give me a line on the phone over there, would you, please?" She indicated a phone on a table across the reception area, between two large chairs.

"Sure, Miss Jordan."

"Thanks." She rested her briefcase on the floor, picked up the receiver and dialed. She allowed the phone to ring several times, haltingly replaced the receiver in its cradle, picked up her things, and with a worried look etched on her forehead, left without saying good-bye.

Sarah looked up from the book and sighed. "Is the story about Karla? Is she in danger?" She set the book down, stood up, and ambled about the room to stretch a bit and loosen her joints. "The birthmark on Andrew's hand clearly points to him as the one who caused Martha McKenzie to fall down the stairs. But he didn't appear to be violent or…deviant in any way when he was with Karla. His art is unusual, powerful, and somewhat disquieting, no doubt about that. It's intriguing and certainly eye-catching. But what if he is the one? Tossing Martha into the lake was despicable." She shook her head. "However, his rapport with Karla was tender and loving. Sincere." She glanced at the clock. "Well, Book, we have one hour before Iris and Sonia arrive." She returned to the window and opened the book. "Let's get on with it."

# FLASH

Karla roamed through the exhibit of Chinese miniatures from the Han Dynasty. Signs displayed the dates going as far back as 206 CE, and identified the objects encased in protective glass and individually illuminated. The room was crammed full of visitors, staring, speaking in hushed tones, and enjoying the unique exhibit. As she turned her attention to one of the display cases, she caught a glimpse, from across the room, of the back of a man who looked like Andrew. "Andrew?"

He disappeared behind a case.

Karla pushed her way through the crowd. "Excuse me, please. I'm sorry."

The man sped away.

"Andrew!" She continued to push through the visitors. "Excuse me."

The man rushed out of the museum, the large front doors closing behind him.

Karla emerged onto the busy street, searching everywhere for him, but he'd disappeared into a sea of unfamiliar faces and foot traffic. Frustrated, she trotted down the museum steps and headed up the street.

Sarah blinked as the words on the page dissipated, leaving only the poem behind. "Looks like we're done for the day." She waited a moment. "So be it. Let's read the poem."

### COME BACK

*Somehow*
*The breeze is different when you're gone*
*It doesn't kiss the leaves*
*In passing by*
*It throws them in its fury*
*Here and there*
*It doesn't sing of far off lands*
*It cries*
*Like loneliness and fear*
*It doesn't give relief*
*To a hot and moistened brow*
*It lashes out*
*Against the heart*
*And tries to freeze the skin*
*Come back*
*And help the wind*
*To be a breeze*
*Again*

# 5
# THE FRIENDS

Restaurant 301, located on the ground floor of the Carter House Inn, cast a warm glow over the three friends, as they enjoyed a delicious meal of crisp garden-grown vegetables accompanied by fresh seafood, and exquisite wine.

"C'mon Sarah, tell me more about this James fellow," said Iris.

The changes the last couple of years had produced were, in Iris's case, quite noticeable. Several pounds heavier since Sarah's wedding, Iris chose to accentuate her curves by wearing bright colors with festive designs. Tonight she'd chosen a rainbow skirt, an aqua blouse with multicolored butterflies, bright orange hoop earrings, and a matching necklace. A myriad of white strands ran through her dark brown hair, and her lipstick perfectly matched the deep red polish on her nails.

Sonia, always more demure in comparison, had aged more subtly, though a pair of rectangular frameless eyeglasses now rested on the bridge of her nose. She'd allowed her white hair to grow down below her ears into a soft wave that encircled her neck, and, though she still avoided full makeup, she'd added a touch of rouge to her cheeks and lips. She'd changed from studs to small hoop earrings, and continued to wear comfortable, practical clothes in muted tones that matched well with her complexion.

"I've told you everything. He's brilliant."

"And he's like you," added Sonia.

"We both have…skills, that's all."

"Skills? Really? Is that what you call it?" Iris asked. "No need to play coy with us, missy. I bet you he's head over heels for you. And, who can blame him? I mean, how in the world can you look even more beautiful today than when you got married?" Before Sarah could attempt an answer, Iris went on. "As far as I'm concerned, I've come to the conclusion that life is too short to allow myself to be miserable, so if I get fat, so be it. I'm no longer going to deprive myself of anything." She giggled and leaned into the table. "Between us, the hubby is tickled with the new voluptuous and freer me." She wriggled as she slid her hands down the sides of her body, and they all laughed.

"But enough about me. Conrad must continue to tickle your fancy. You look like you've blossomed into a gorgeous flower." She reached for Sarah's hair. "Look at this, Sonia—shiny, wavy, auburn hair with mere whispers of white here and there. That cinnamon skin of yours would be the envy of every beach bunny in the country, your hazel eyes stand out without any need of makeup, and to top it off, you're more svelte than ever. Conrad must possess some serious magic for you to look this good."

Sarah blushed and shook her head.

"There you go, Iris," Sonia protested. "See what you've done? You embarrassed her."

"Nonsense, she's always blushed easily, and done that crumply thing with her forehead. That has never changed. Probably never will."

"C'mon, she does much more than that."

"Yeah, let's not forget that she talks to spirits, too. And, this place is supposed to be filled with them. I'm so excited to hear what they have to say." Iris rubbed her hands, clearly ready for an adventure.

Sonia held up her hands. "Whoa. Let's not get carried away, Iris." She turned to Sarah. "Where do you suggest we start tomorrow? How about some kind of easy intro so we can keep Iris in check?"

Sarah nodded. "We should start by exploring Old Town. There's a narrated walking tour we can do and, after that, we'll be on our own to browse about the place."

"Will they tell us about the haunted houses?" asked Iris.

"Take a sip of your wine and ease up," snapped Sonia.

Sarah laughed and both her friends looked at her.

"What's so funny?" asked Sonia.

"It's like old times. The two of you arguing while I sit back and watch."

"Except that now your secret is out," retorted Iris, "No escaping that."

"It wasn't a *secret*." Sarah shook her head. "I simply wasn't ready."

"Well, missy, you're the expert, so we're going to put you to good use in every haunted house we can find."

"Iris," interjected Sonia, "we are not doing that. Leave Sarah alone. We're here to have fun, not to impose on her." She turned to Sarah. "I would like to meet this James. From your description he's my kind of hunk."

"Now, look who's talking. You're a married woman, Miss Sonia." Iris turned to Sarah. "Not that I wouldn't like to meet him, too. Married or not, we can always enjoy the view." She winked and raised her wine glass. "Right?"

The three laughed and all raised their glasses.

"How about going to the Booklegger after our tour? Hopefully he'll be there and you can both take turns embarrassing him," Sarah suggested.

"Works for me," Iris said with a wink.

Later that evening, after coaxing her friends to their respective rooms, Sarah sat by the fireplace with the book on her lap. She picked up her cell phone and speed-dialed her husband.

"That was a long dinner," Conrad said with a smile in his voice. "How did it go?"

"We had fun. I'd forgotten how much they like to argue. Those two are at each other's throats every other sentence."

"I remember. They're more like sisters than friends. Their husbands get a kick out of it and, to be honest, so did I."

"Yeah. It's interesting to realize how different I am now than back in our teaching days."

"*You* are the same, but you perceive the world differently."

"Thanks, I needed to hear that. I do wish you were here."

"No, no, no. This is your time to spend with your friends. Make the best of it."

"They desperately want to meet James."

"So?"

"I'm insecure about that."

"Why? From what you've told me about him, he'll be delighted to meet them. I can't fathom any problem with that."

Sarah heaved a deep sigh. "I suppose you're right. I'm being egoistic."

"Boy, are we back to the fancy words after a few hours with your buddies? I hope you don't get an attack of circumlocution."

She laughed with heartfelt amusement.

"Sarah, you are far from trivial. But you're right; maybe sharing him with them isn't in the cards at the moment. You've met an extremely unusual man who shares your abilities—a first for you. And to top it all off he turns out to be someone your father greatly admired. It's natural that you'd like to keep him to yourself."

"How selfish you make that sound."

"Maybe so. It is what it is."

"My dear Watson, you are replete with existential sagacity today."

"I aim to please, Sherlock, I aim to please. What about the book?"

"You're up to date. I'm about to open the book and find out what it offers."

"Good luck. Call me if you need to bounce something off me. I'm at your beck and call."

"Okay. Good night, darling. Thanks for cheering me up."

"Sweet dreams, sweetheart." She ended the call and picked up the book.

# HARMONY

Karla stood by an open balcony peering out over the bustling city. Behind her was a crowded studio, smaller than Andrew's, with paintings of portraits, landscapes, and delicate nudes strewn throughout.

Jeremiah, a stringy-looking man in his late fifties, stood in the middle of the studio touching up the background on a large painting. At this point, the canvas portrayed the vague outline of a woman, and the background itself was a shapeless mass of light and shadows ranging from salmon to a dark maroon. It was evident, however, that the woman had long hair and was looking over her shoulder while holding an object in her hand.

The artist boasted a long salt and pepper beard that covered most of his t-shirt. The beard flowed directly from under equally long hair that he'd abandoned with complete disregard to the occasional spatter of paint. He gazed intensely at his work from under bushy eyebrows that resembled large gray caterpillars. His bright blue eyes provided a surprising dash of color to his otherwise pallid appearance. Possessed with obvious sensuality, Jeremiah was without a doubt an artist with a strong affinity for the female shape.

He spoke to Karla without his eyes ever leaving the canvas. "Little info is known about the guy. Bumped into him here and there, but we're not buddies. I'm clueless about whether he's got any pals. You asked me for help and I set up the meet. End of story."

Karla left the balcony and wandered around the perimeter of the studio toward Jeremiah. "Can't you give me something? You artist guys always have the skinny on each other."

"Not Andrew. He's never hung out with any of the cats that I run with. He's a loner with a capital 'L', as you're well aware. The few times I ever crossed paths with him was at a couple of local watering holes. Folks on gallery row may be able to tell you more than I can."

"But, people talk. Haven't you come across anything about him? Friends, models—"

"Have you?" Jeremiah peered at Karla from beneath his unkempt brows. He placed his brush in a can and his paints on a stool and beckoned Karla to join him. "Let's get ourselves a drink. My alcohol tank is running on empty."

He moseyed over to a spiral staircase and descended a floor. Karla followed.

His apartment was a page—or rather a volume—from the sixties, a veritable bohemian lair. A collection of serapes lay tossed over aging sofas, and a myriad of candles in all shapes and sizes, along with a wide variety of crystals, crowded the tables and multicolored shelves. Orange crates, stacked against the wall, housed a makeshift bar and a handful of books.

Two posters, one of Bob Dylan and another of Joan Baez, were respectfully framed and hung in a place of honor above the stereo. Jeremiah crossed to the bar and took out a bottle of Tequila and, from a small refrigerator, a bottle of *Sangrita*.

Karla shook her head, plopped down on the sofa, and sighed. "I always get a kick out of this place."

"Hey baby, there's hope for you yet."

Jeremiah joined Karla with the bottles tucked under his arms, and two shot glasses in each hand. He set the bottles and glasses down on a small table by the sofa. He poured Tequila into two of the glasses and *Sangrita* into the other two.

"Tequila and *Sangrita*—otherwise called *Widow's Blood*. Discovered this chaser in Mexico."

"Oh, yeah, sorry, I forgot to ask you. How did it go?"

"Sold out. In less than a week."

"All the pieces? How many?"

"Twenty. Came back with a request for twenty more."

Karla reached out to hug him. "Congrats!"

He pushed her gently away. "You're going to get paint all over your nice dress. I'll have to sign it and put it in a frame."

"Yeah, you're a mess."

"Thanks, badge of honor." He winked. "Anyway, this is how you do it. First, Tequila…I like silver to avoid the seepage of the casks in the gold, gives a purer taste." Jeremiah sipped the Tequila. "Then, the *Sangrita*." He sipped the other glass.

With a grimace of reluctance, Karla followed suit. A moment later, she licked her lips. "Hey, that's not bad. What's this *widow's blood* made of? It's both sweet and savory."

"This one's my concoction. In Mexico it's much better, but I haven't been able to find it here. I make it with tomato juice, orange juice, Tabasco, some secret stuff, and lots of love." He took another sip and dropped onto the pillows on the sofa.

"This, and a shoulder to cry on—from a distance, to avoid the paint—are about all I can offer, I'm afraid. Could give you a sermon on the dangers of getting romantically involved with your subject, but coming from me, it would be a bad joke."

Karla set her glass on the table and leaned on Jeremiah's chest. "Forget the paint. I can use the shoulder."

He put an arm around her. "So be it, my beauty."

"He couldn't have simply vanished. There's got to be an explanation. He's been gone for over a week."

"Weren't you after his life's story? Now you've contributed to it."

Visibly upset, Karla sat up, tousled her hair, and stared at the floor.

"I'm sorry, Karla. Didn't mean to sound so prickly."

"No, you're right. I spent several rather intense weeks with him and I learned virtually nothing personal about him."

"Who was the woman in the paper?"

"No idea. An heiress, apparently. It's unclear if she has anything to do with his disappearance. I've looked her up, but came up empty-handed. I can't make the connection."

"Have you asked around the galleries?"

Karla shook her head. "Not yet. Jer, I think something's happened to him."

"Is that what you told the police?"

"Hah! They wouldn't even listen. Lover's quarrel, they said."

Jeremiah poured another round, took a couple of swigs, and collapsed onto the pillows. "Tell *unca* Jerry the truth. Are you in love with this guy?"

Karla glanced at Jeremiah and hesitated. "I'm not sure. I've never done anything quite like this before. I was in the sack with him the first day I met him. I don't usually—"

"Oh, I'm sadly aware you don't."

Karla kissed him softly on the cheek. "Maybe I should've taken you up on it. At least you're reliable."

"And boring. Not old, mind you, just boring."

Karla snickered. "I'm attracted to—"

"Weirdos."

"He's not weird. He's passionate, and formidable, and...scary."

"My point exactly." He pulled her to him and tickled her.

She laughed. "Stop it! I'm trying to be serious."

"But I'm not. You're so ticklish, I love it."

She giggled, giving into his game.

Jeremiah stopped tickling her, and sighed as he leaned back on the cushions. "You do love this dude."

Karla caught her breath. "I'm not sure. Really. There's something about him that's irresistible, and a bit terrifying. Plus I've never been in love—true love, so I have no point of reference." She cocked her head. "Sad. But that's the truth. That's why I'm not sure I'm in love with him. It's not in my nature."

Jeremiah raised his prodigious eyebrows.

"Okay, okay. Let's agree that there is something I do feel. What *it* is, I have no clue. But I couldn't get enough of him, and maybe that's love. Or maybe I'm simply fixated on him."

"Sex. When it chants for you it can be intoxicating. Like the Siren's song."

"And, it did chant for me."

"However you slice it, my dear, you're hooked." He leered at her playfully.

"It's not about sex, Jeremiah. It's more than that. Plus I can't walk away from this. Something's wrong, and it's eating at me."

Lovingly, Jeremiah embraced her. "Tell you what. You check out the galleries and I'll check out the suppliers. Deal?"

Karla leaned her head against his chest. "Thanks, Papa Smurf."

Sarah placed the open book on her lap, waiting for the story to disappear, but the words remained. She turned the page expecting a poem, but to her surprise the story went on without a title for a new chapter. Intrigued by this, she continued to read.

Art galleries, shops, and an assortment of businesses lined the hectic avenue, vying for the attention of the endless stream of passers-by.

From a narrow alley across the street, an unseen observer watched as Karla entered one of the galleries, wearing a trim two-piece mauve suit with a pink silk blouse, and red high heels with a matching purse. She appeared tired and irritated. After a few minutes, she emerged and marched down the street.

She entered the CK Contemporary Gallery. Through the glass windows the observer watched her speak to a tall, impeccably dressed middle-aged art dealer, who listened attentively. When she was done speaking, the art dealer pondered for a second, and shook his head. She nodded at him and emerged from the gallery.

She headed decisively across the street toward the Martin Lawrence Gallery, where she repeated the exercise. A few moments later she exited listlessly.

Two men and a woman called to her from across the street, then maneuvered their way through the traffic and joined her. The concealed observer watched patiently as they chatted for a few minutes, shook their heads, and moments later embraced good-bye. The three made their way back while Karla continued down the street. Half a block later, she entered the Weinstein Gallery and soon after emerged even more crestfallen.

She rolled her head around in a clear effort to relieve some tension as she made her way to the Franklin Bowles Gallery. A tall woman dressed in a brown suit met her at the gallery door. They spoke briefly until Karla shook the woman's hand and went on her way.

The observer stayed with her, keeping a safe distance.

Karla headed down the street and entered Lefty O'Doul's bar. The ever-popular eatery and bar had only a dozen or so customers at this time of day. Its walls displayed an array of photographs of the most famous baseball players of the twentieth century, along with other memorabilia.

Karla dragged herself past the plaster statue depicting Marilyn Monroe's famous *Seven Year Itch* scene until she reached the end of the bar and climbed tiredly onto a stool. The vast array of beer tap handles always brought a smile to her face.

Joe, a jolly bartender with a handlebar mustache approached her. "Hey, Karla baby. Long time no see. Where've you been keeping yourself?

"Oh, around."

"Usual poison?" She nodded and Joe moved over to prepare her a dry vodka martini. "You shouldn't work so hard, kid—you look like shit. "

"You really know how to flatter a girl, Joe." She reached down and flipped off her shoes. "Unfortunately, that's exactly how I feel."

"Working on a new story?"

"Actually, it's an old one." Karla reached down and rubbed her feet. "Hey, has Andrew Stuart been in lately?"

Joe handed her the frosty martini and squinted in an effort to explore his memory banks. "No, not since the last time you guys were here. About—what was it, three, four weeks? You didn't finish his story?"

"No," she lied. "Been out of town for a while. Got back today. I'd like to talk to him. Any idea where I could find him?"

Joe placed a bowl of peanuts close to Karla. "You might try Hoo Wang's or Lady's."

Karla looked at him inquisitively.

Joe snorted. "Way beneath you, baby, they're a couple of bars out near China Town. He mentioned them once or twice. Not that he'd go there. Could've been looking for models."

A group of noisy customers sauntered into the bar.

"Give me a second, Karla, be right back." Joe walked out from behind the bar toward the newly arrived patrons.

Karla sipped her martini and looked around the bar. At the opposite end of the long bar, she noticed a woman in her mid-forties sitting alone. She had long, tinted, bluish-black hair, and was heavily made-up. Her bright pink lipstick matched the color of a sheer scarf that adorned her neck. She wore a striped black and white T-shirt, two or three sizes too small, which made her large breasts very evident. Her brassiere, also too small, made deep indentations in her flabby flesh. She was flirting with a couple of younger men, a few stools away, who were obviously delighted with her coquettish teen-age antics.

Joe returned to Karla. She gestured toward the woman. "A regular?"

Joe glanced toward the corner of the bar. "Molly? Sure, she is. A model. She's posed for most of the artists around here at one time or another. Used to be a real looker. Time's a bitch."

Molly laughed loudly, slid off her stool and exited the bar, followed by the two men.

Karla watched them leave the bar, and finished her drink. "Thanks for the pick-me-up. What do I owe you?"

"Today, a smile."

Karla smiled and patted Joe's hand. "Deal. Thanks, Joe."

"Take care of yourself, Karla, and come back more often like you used to do. Okay?"

Karla slipped on her shoes and made her way toward the door. "You got it."

Lost in the tale, Sarah realized she was staring at the flames in the fireplace, the book resting quietly on her lap. She glanced down. The story had disappeared and the poem patiently waited for Sarah's attention.

### *MISSING YOU*

*There are days like today*
*When I sit all alone*
*And the world and I meet*
*Face to face*
*But I always lose*
*When I'm here without you*

*For the world is just a noise*
*Faces passing by*
*A cry*
*A sigh*

*A song*

*And the noise insults my ears*
*When I can't hear your voice*
*The faces come to nothing*
*If none of them is yours*
*The cry and the sigh are me*
*And the song is my soul*
*Missing you*

# 6

# THE TOURISTS

"Okay, ladies, I've done a ton of research." Sonia produced several pages from her purse as they strolled down 2nd Street in Old Town toward the Tourism Center on G Street. "I downloaded an article from the *Lumberjack,* the newspaper for Humboldt State University."

"No need for that," Iris countered. "We'll learn all about Eureka on our tour."

"Yeah, but what if they don't cover all this stuff? Or worse, what if they don't take us to these places?"

Sarah chuckled. "I, for one, am all ears and ready to learn from your research."

"C'mon, Sarah. Don't humor her. First we take the tour, and after that, we go to wherever Sonia chooses."

Sonia frowned. "Fine. But at least listen to this tidbit. It says here, and I quote: 'Things seem to be going bump in the night all throughout Old Town.' Which means we need to go walking about the city at night instead of in the morning."

"We're going on the ghost tour *tonight.*" Iris rolled her eyes. "Can you chill a bit?"

"Speaking of which, it also says here that the guy who gives that tour is a history and social science teacher at the local High School. Right up your alley, Iris."

"So?"

"Soooo, you can ask him sciencey-type questions, get on his good side, and ask him for special favors."

"What are you talking about? What special favors?"

"Well, this article says that there was a system of underground tunnels connecting a bunch of saloons and brothels back in the nineteenth century, so that the high-powered patrons could travel anonymously. I doubt he'll show us the tunnels on the tour, but if you befriend him, he might be persuaded to give us a private tour. *Comprende*?" She winked.

"You're impossible." Iris shook her head. "We'll have to wait and see, won't we?"

Sarah listened to her friends, but found it impossible to enjoy their repartee. The book and its bewildering story remained a constant presence in the back of her mind.

After their guided tour through the many landmarks of Old Town, they stopped at the Oberon Grill for lunch. The building had once housed a brothel and, according to legend, played host to several spirits who'd perished during the 1932 earthquake.

"The waitress told me," Iris whispered excitedly, "that one of the cooks saw the ghost of the woman who lived upstairs. She said that sometimes her spirit shows up in the bathroom. I'm going to check it out. C'mon Sarah." She got up and dashed off in search of the ghost.

Sarah and Sonia remained seated.

"Wow, did you read the letter in the menu?" Sonia asked.

Sarah glanced over at her friend. "Uh, no."

"The novelist Jack London became involved in a fight with another patron in 1910 right in this very room. This says they argued over politics and started throwing punches."

Sarah opened the menu and read the letter. "Oh, and the bartender closed the doors to the Oberon so that Jack London and the other fellow could finish the fight."

"They went at it for one hour! Can you imagine?"

Iris returned and plopped down on her chair. "Nothing," she said, with obvious disappointment. "Not even a whisper. And why didn't you come, Sarah? You might have been able to coax her into showing up."

"I didn't need to go."

Sonia burst out laughing.

Iris glared at her friend. "What are you laughing at?"

"Read the letter printed in the menu. Not everything is about you."

After lunch they perused the various shops around town until it was time to join Eric, the teacher and ghost-tour guide. After a brief introduction about himself, and his approach to the tour, he led them through several historic buildings where he regaled them with stories of the ghosts detected or sensed by the current and past owners of the various establishments in Old Town. They learned about the decapitated man who lost his head on the train tracks on First Street, and all about the famous spirit of Sarah Carson, who sits in a rocking chair staring out of one of the windows of the Carson Mansion.

By the time they returned to their hotel, the chill of the evening had descended, and they were anxious to rest their feet and enjoy some much-needed nourishment. Dinner at their hotel became a whirlwind of chatter about their day, what they'd experienced, what they liked or didn't like, and what they wished they could visit again.

Sonia's biggest disappointment was that Eric didn't take them through the underground tunnels, which she blamed on Iris's lack of enthusiasm to engage him. Iris felt deflated because Sarah had failed to summon a single spirit.

"Did you at least catch a glance of any ghosts at all today?" Iris pleaded.

"Sorry, I'm afraid not."

"C'mon, Sarah, can you try a bit harder tomorrow?"

"Sorry, Iris. It doesn't work that way for me. I can't summon the spirits. Trust me, I've tried. They appear at their leisure and on their own terms."

"Could you at least try to get *something*?"

Sarah patted Iris's arm. "I'll give it my best."

"Well, one thing I noticed," Sonia chimed in, "is that you never suggested for us to go the bookstore and meet James."

"Oh," Sarah blushed, "It must've slipped my mind."

"Tomorrow we'll definitely go see him," Iris demanded.

"All right. Tomorrow, for sure." Sarah yawned. "Listen you guys, I'm beat." She rose from the table and kissed them both good night.

After she disappeared down the hallway, Iris turned to Sonia. "She was a big disappointment. I mean, I thought we'd encounter at least *one* ghost. What a let-down."

"C'mon. It's not easy for her. I'm sure she feels bad that she couldn't please us."

"You're right." Iris sipped the last of her drink. "Let's call it a night. Maybe tomorrow the spirits will come knocking."

Relieved to be back in the quiet surroundings of her room and the comfort of her nightgown, Sarah relaxed in the armchair by a warm fire.

As much as she'd enjoyed spending the day with Iris and Sonia, she felt ill at ease the entire time. What disturbed her most was not her failure to fulfill her friends' expectations of witnessing their own personal ghost fest, but that she had not perceived a single life force whatsoever. That, in and of itself, denoted a clear departure from her usual instincts, and also appeared to confirm James's assessment that the energy emanating from the entity or entities surrounding her book were actively blocking any other type of communication.

Tired as she was, she pulled the book onto her lap and opened it. "Let's find out what you have in mind this time."

# DANGER

Andrew's studio had been ransacked. Smashed sculptures lay strewn about the space, tables were overturned, paint splattered everywhere, paintings defaced or slashed, and all the women depicted in the oils smeared with red paint.

The studio teemed with police officers and forensic personnel. Bizarre elongated shadows created by a lamp knocked upon the floor, produced an eerie effect on the walls and ceiling as the men and women moved about the room.

Detective Austen, middle-aged and lethargic, wrote information on a small pad as he questioned an elderly man outside the entrance to the studio.

"Woke up when I heard the racket, 'bout two in the morning," the old man said. "I came over and pounded on the door, but it didn't do no good, they kept goin' at it. I went back to my place to call you guys, and that must've been when they got away."

Karla climbed the stairs and attempted to push through the door past the two men.

"Whoa, Missy. May I help you?" Austen blocked the way.

"Sorry. The policeman downstairs said I could come up. I'm Karla Jordan. Are you Detective Austen?"

"Yes I am. I appreciate you coming on such short notice, Miss Jordan." He turned to the old man and opened the door wider. "Thank you, sir, you can go."

As the old man exited, Austen ushered Karla inside the studio.

She froze, stunned by the violent destruction.

Caught off-guard by her abrupt stop, Austen bumped into her. "Sorry."

"My God. What happened?"

"I was hoping you could tell us."

Shaken, Karla took in the brutal devastation of Andrew's work. "This is appalling."

Austen followed her as she inched her way about the studio. "We're dusting for prints, so, please don't touch anything." He hesitated. "I'm sorry we didn't pay attention to your earlier call about his disappearance."

Karla spun to face him. "And now look at what's happened! He could be dead!" Tears welled in her eyes and she turned away from Austen, wiping her face with her sleeve.

With a deep breath, she turned her attention back to the studio and ambled through the chaos, searching, scanning the debris, unable to accept such violence. She glanced at the large easel in the center of the studio, which now stood uncovered with its back to her. The table with the newspaper article and the knife remained intact. Step by careful step, she advanced toward the easel.

Austen followed her, trying to decipher her every move, her every glance.

When she reached the easel and faced it, the color drained from her face. Immobile, she recognized the portrait of Martha McKenzie, the only painting in the room that portrayed a woman without an animal. A stunning rendition, it was also the only piece illustrating a woman that had not been smeared with red paint. Instead, the canvass had been slashed across her throat.

"Were you acquainted with Martha McKenzie?"

"No."

"Was Mr. Stuart?"

"I have no idea." She couldn't stop herself from staring at the slashed painting.

Austen observed her. "What is it, Ms. Jordan?"

"This painting…he wouldn't show it to me—and it's so different. He doesn't paint portraits. This is entirely different from his usual style."

"It's a good likeness. There appears to be some connection between Mr. Stuart and her."

"I agree. Unless he's working on commission for this particular painting." She turned toward the detective. "I'm sorry I can't help you. I have no idea who could have done this or why." She placed her hand on his arm. "Please try to find him."

Austen nodded.

With tears welling up in her eyes, she fled the studio.

The detective watched her disappear, then turned his eyes to the bedlam around him, and shook his head.

Sarah closed her eyes and sighed. "Am I supposed to find Andrew? Is he the one in danger? Or is it Karla?"

Sensing no response, she continued reading.

Karla burst into Jeremiah's studio. "Jer! I need to talk." She dropped her purse by the door, shed her jacket, and kicked off her high heels.

As if completely unaware of her presence, he continued painting.

"Jeremiah!" She paced back and forth.

He remained unperturbed.

She stopped next to his painting and stared at him. "Please, listen to me."

"Relax, Karla. Pour yourself a drink and sit down. I need to finish this—"

"I can't relax."

He continued to paint.

"Andrew's studio has been destroyed!"

Stopping mid-stroke, Jeremiah looked up.

"And that's not all. He was painting a portrait of the dead McKenzie woman. The one in the newspaper that had been pinned with the knife."

"A portrait?" His expression reflected incredulity.

"Exactly! A portrait! No animals, a simple—no, an utterly realistic portrait. Not his style, at all. Jeremiah, something is terribly wrong."

Jeremiah put down his brush. "Karla, please calm yourself. Sit down."

"Someone slashed the portrait right across her throat."

Jeremiah approached her and took her into his arms. She gave in to his embrace. He held her hand and guided her softly downstairs to the sofa. He tossed some rags aside and sat her down, then stepped to his makeshift bar and grabbed a glass and a bottle of brandy. He poured a glass and handed it to her.

She shook her head. He sat next to her and held the glass to her lips. "You're in shock. This will help. C'mon."

She took a sip and grimaced. "Why did he disappear that morning? Why wouldn't he show me the painting? Who is this woman to him? Where is he?"

Jeremiah encouraged her to take a few more sips then wrapped her in his arms. "You're a bit obsessive about this guy."

"Obsessive? I'm not obsessive about him! I—"

Jeremiah held her at arm's length and stared into her eyes. "What do you call what you're doing? Fun? You can't work—no—you don't *want* to work. You spend your days, and probably your nights, pretending to be Ms. Detective Extraordinaire. And you're trying to rope me into being your cohort. That alone tops it all."

After another sip of brandy Karla turned to him with a heartfelt sigh.

"That's my girl. Let's dissect what's really going on here." He settled back into the sofa. "First, you need to admit you don't like being dumped without an explanation."

Karla blushed.

Jeremiah burst out laughing. "Ah, hah! We've pinpointed that female pride is in play."

"Yes, I admit that at first that could've been the case. And yes, I find him extremely attractive. But there's much more to it than that. The allure started with the mystery surrounding him—the secrecy surrounding his whole life. Where did he come from, what's his real name? I doubt that it's Stuart. Why this fixation on jackals or wolves or whatever they are? Why refuse to reveal anything about his past? Add to that the mystery about his sudden disappearance, the knife stabbed into the newspaper article, and now this...this desecration of his work. All these unanswered questions irk me. I can't let go. I need to get to the bottom of this."

"There you have it. That's the Karla I love. You've rekindled the fire within. So get your ass out there and use your considerable wits to dig it all up."

"I will."

"Let's toast to all the jilted women who won't let go."

Jeremiah held up the brandy bottle and Karla raised her glass. "Now my dear, you must leave, I have a deadline and so do you. My advice is to center yourself, do the reporter writer stuff you do so well, and research the hell out of this McKenzie woman. By the way, not a single vendor in the whole city has been in contact with Andrew in a while."

"Thanks, Jer, I needed that." She got up and kissed him. She slipped her shoes on, grabbed her jacket and purse, and headed out.

"For the record, Jeremiah," she said as she opened the door, "you make a splendid cohort."

Sarah placed the book on the table. "It's Karla's story. But it's tied to Andrew's. The next step is to find out why their stories are interlaced with the poems." When no response came forth, she continued to read.

From the shadows of the corner building, Karla's unseen observer watched her emerge from her car, lock it, and trudge down the steep sidewalk toward her duplex.

Focused on searching in her purse for the house keys as she walked, she failed to hear the footsteps behind her until they drew closer. Reluctant to look over her shoulder and signal her awareness, Karla hastened her pace. Abruptly, she stumbled and fell to the concrete. The contents of her purse spilled to the sidewalk. She scrambled to collect her things as footsteps drew nearer. Karla looked up as a policeman squatted down to help her collect her belongings.

"May I help you, ma'am? Sorry to startle you, but I noticed a man following you and I rushed over. He took off when he saw me."

"Thank you, officer. I must've stepped on one of those cracks, and my heel got caught."

The officer helped her to her feet and finished collecting the spilled contents of her purse. He stuffed them in her bag and handed it to her, touching the brim of his cap. "I'd be happy to walk you to wherever you're going."

"Thanks. I'd appreciate that. I'm going to the next building."

The officer looked her over and noticed her leg. "Looks like you'll need a Band-Aid or two on that knee. Are you sure you're okay? This is a steep hill."

Karla looked at her scraped knee and ripped stockings. "Yes, I'm fine. Thank you." She removed both shoes, and allowed the officer to escort her down the hill.

Across the street, the observer slipped through the darkness, concealed from the policeman and Karla as they made their way to her duplex.

Karla opened the front door, thanked the officer, and stepped in. The policeman looked around casually and headed across the street toward the onlooker, who stepped back into the shadows for a moment and re-emerged after the policeman passed by.

Sarah turned the page, but the story had disappeared. "You have a knack for keeping me in suspense," she sighed. "So be it. I'll read the poem."

### *ANOTHER NIGHT*

*It's that time of night again*
*When the darkness says the things*
*It shouldn't*
*To my soul*

*I'm looking through the windowpane*
*At the dark and lonely night*
*Asking*
*Where you are*

*I can't hold back the jealousy*
*Or the pain of knowing*
*That someone else might see*
*The things that made me love you*
*Unless I'm there to say*
*Your love belongs to me*

# 7

# THE DREAM

Sarah sat up, wide awake, her body bathed in a cold sweat, her heart pounding as she struggled for breath. She turned on the light, jumped out of the bed, and headed to the table where the book rested. She grabbed it, steadied her trembling hands, forced herself to open it, and read.

## RELEASE

Molly lay in the center of the wooden floor, the sheer pink scarf tied loosely around her neck, the black and white striped t-shirt discarded indifferently in a corner of the room. Her brassiere, skirt, and underwear were missing. A circle of votive candles around her provided the only source of light, their flickering shadows almost masking the imperfections of her worn-out body. Her lipstick had lost its luster and the sparkle in her eyes had been dulled by death.

Youthful, masculine hands softly caressed her limp body, the tips of the fingers lovingly stroking her.

Tenderly, they untied the scarf and glided it off, stroked her hair, and removed the stray curls from her face. The left hand, red birthmark clearly visible, reached for her eyes and gently closed them.

His face concealed by shadows, he leaned in to kiss her cheek, curled up next to her corpse, and wept.

Crickets chirped in the distance as a rhythmic paddling gradually broke through nature's sounds. The nude body of Molly lay lifeless in the stern of the old rowboat.

The small boat slid easily across the water.

The rowing stopped and the oars were shipped. The moonlight shined on the birthmark on the back of one hand as the man hefted Molly's corpse and slipped it overboard.

Clasping the edge of the boat, he waited until she sank into the dark water. When the ripples subsided, he grasped the oars and rowed away.

There it was, word for terrifying word.

She slammed the book shut and set it down.

"I dreamed this entire scene." Sarah returned to the bed, grabbed her cell phone and dialed.

"You all right?" a sleepy Conrad answered.

"Oh, I'm sorry. I didn't realize what time it is."

Alarmed by her voice, he asked, "What happened?"

"I had a horrible dream. The man with the birthmark might have killed a woman and dumped her in the lake."

"You dreamed it?"

"The same exact version showed up in the book, word for word. I dreamed it first, and then I read it. The same lake and boat as before." Shivering, she drew her knees up to her chest.

"Did you see his face? Who was the woman?"

"No, I didn't see his face. What I get are flashes of his hands, his actions, and he always has his back to me. But I have seen the woman before. She was in the bar where Karla went to look for Andrew. The bartender said she was a regular and a model for the artists."

"Can you at least tell when these events are taking place?"

"Not exactly, but I have a strong feeling that the story is about Karla and that she's the one in danger."

"From Andrew?"

"Part of me says yes. After all, the birthmark is quite a telltale." She sighed. "But what about his studio? He couldn't have done that to his own work. Could he?"

"He could if he's lost his mind."

"You've got a point."

"What about James, have you asked him?"

"He refuses to hear a word about the book or the story. He says it isn't meant for him, so I can't ask him anything about it. It's clear that it's okay for me to share it all with you, but apparently not with James."

"He can't have the details, I get that. But what if you ask him questions about the places you've read about? You have the actual names of the galleries Karla visited."

"Yeah, I've looked them up. They're in San Francisco, but some are also in other cities."

"Describe the house by the lake to him. Maybe he's familiar with it. How about the bar? You said he works with cops—maybe he's crossed paths with Austen. I can ask Sheriff Williams here to track him down."

"Boy, oh boy, Dr. Watson, you are amazing. None of that occurred to me."

"As, always, I aim to please."

"You please me plenty." She sighed and realized that her body had returned to normal. "These horrible images are so unsettling that I can't think straight."

"Plus you have Iris and Sonia to deal with. Don't allow the book to interfere with your friends. Try to enjoy the next couple of days. After that, maybe James can guide you, or once you come home we can look more deeply into it. Can you stop reading it and stay away from the book for a couple days?"

"It seems that if I don't read it, I dream it. Frankly, I'd much rather read it than be shaken awake with disturbing visions."

"I can understand that. Wish I could help."

"I'll be okay. Sorry I woke you up. Go back to sleep."

"Are you feeling better?"

"Yes. You have no idea how much."

"Good. Call me later today after your explorations with Iris and Sonia."

"I shall. Love you, Dr. Watson."

"Goodnight, sweetheart."

She hung up and pressed the phone to her chest. "I do wish you were here."

She glared across the room at the book. Moments later, she turned off the light, and pulled the covers over her head.

But the book beckoned and sleep refused to come.

After tossing and turning for half an hour, she reluctantly turned on the light, crossed the room, snatched up the book, and returned to bed. "All right, you win." After a deep breath, she braced herself and opened the book.

# COUNTERPART

A kettle whistled in the kitchen as a shoeless Karla emerged from the bathroom wrapped in a terrycloth robe, drying her hair with a towel. She crossed to the kitchen and made a cup of tea.

Holding the teacup, she sauntered to the living room and snuggled into the sofa where a pile of mail awaited her. She blew lightly on her tea and sipped it while examining the mail. She flipped through several bills, a couple of letters, and some magazines.

Close to the bottom of the pile, one envelope caught her eye. Addressed to her in hand-printed letters, it had no stamp and no return address. Intrigued, she set her cup down and tore open the envelope, only to find what appeared to be a copy of a magazine article. The photographs in the article had been carefully cut out and were missing. She avidly read the article and examined the envelope, but found no clues about its sender.

She opened her laptop and soon found what she sought. "I'll be darned." She grinned.

Moments later she hurried to her bathroom, blow-dried her hair and put on makeup. She slipped on a navy blue pinstriped three-piece suit, a green blouse and green high-heeled shoes. Checking her image in the wall mirror she smiled. After transferring the contents of her purse into a matching green one, she hurried out the front door.

Twenty minutes later, Karla found herself waiting in an opulent private reception area. The wall directly in front of her was emblazoned with *Aldercrest Corporation,* written out in large bronze letters.

A middle-aged man sat across from her with an attaché case on his lap. He kept glancing toward the double doors to his right, while his legs jiggled up and down, and his fingers tapped fitfully on his attaché case.

Karla noticed sweat trickling down the man's neck and collecting in his shirt collar.

An attractive, impeccably dressed woman in her late twenties emerged from the double doors. She left one door open and glanced toward the man.

"Alright, Mr. Dawson, he's ready to see you." She crossed the reception area and took a seat behind her desk. "Please close the door behind you."

The man exhaled audibly as he rose to his feet. "Thanks, Susan, wish me luck." He took another deep breath and walked decisively through the open door, closing it behind him.

Susan smiled uncomfortably and glanced toward Karla. "Sorry, Miss Jordan, but he had an appointment."

A young man entered the room through a door behind the receptionist toting a stack of letters and magazines. "Hey Susan, I got two tickets for the concert Saturday. How about it?" He stacked the mail in an in-basket at one end of her desk, leaned forward, and faced her. "Come on. I had to move mountains to get these." He flashed a pair of tickets.

She gave him a condescending smile, slid out from behind the desk, and walked toward a bank of file cabinets on the opposite side of the room. "Sorry. I have to go visit my parents this weekend. Why don't you ask Lisa? I bet she'd love to go."

Melodramatically disappointed, the young man leaned against the wall, staring at his tickets. "Lisa's so young."

"Precisely."

He glanced at Susan and sighed, then exited the office the same way he had entered.

Susan cocked her head when she noticed Karla smiling. "I'm sorry you've had to wait so long. Are you sure you can't come another day?"

"I have to meet with him. It could save someone's life."

Jarred by the comment, Susan glanced at Karla and discerned sincerity in her eyes. "I understand." She returned to her desk and glanced discreetly at the appointment book.

The wooden double doors opened and Dawson emerged, back first, addressing someone inside. "I'll get on it right away, sir." Visibly shaken, Dawson closed the door and heaved a deep sigh. After a moment, he looked at Susan. "I should've broken a leg and stayed in Aspen." He wet his lips, sighed once more, and walked off, an invisible burden upon his shoulders.

"Like I said, it isn't a good day. Let me try once more."

"Thanks, I appreciate it."

Susan tapped the door lightly before slipping inside, closing it behind her.

Karla glanced at her watch and got to her feet. After stretching her neck and back, she ambled about the reception area. At the entrance, she glanced through the glass doors that looked out into a sprawling workplace. The floor had been split into three parallel walkthroughs, each framed by offices hidden behind square or rectangular partitions, and bordered by secretarial desks. She noticed no loitering or chatting as in most offices. Everyone's attention was focused on a task.

Karla turned around as the wooden double doors opened behind her. Susan glanced at her. "Ms. Jordan, he will meet with you now. Please come in."

Karla picked up her purse, and walked toward her. "Thank you, Susan."

Susan stepped aside to let Karla in. "He's on the phone at the moment, but have a seat and he'll be right with you," she said, and closed the door behind her.

The formidable, elegant office was bathed in soft sunlight coming through floor-to-ceiling tinted windows that bordered two sides of the room. Behind an immense desk, a man sat with his back to Karla facing the city below, and holding a phone.

Subtle hidden lighting fell directly on paintings, sculptures, and mementos scattered about the enormous space. Across from the desk, at the opposite side of the office, a large leather sofa stood against an art-covered wall, a coffee table in front, and leather armchair on each side.

Karla's breath caught for a moment when she realized that one of Andrew's paintings hung on the wall behind the sofa. It depicted a family of jackals, two adults and two snarling cubs ready to pounce.

"That's my favorite painting. Do you like it, Ms. Jordan?"

Karla jumped at the sound of the man's voice. Startled she spun toward him. "Andrew?"

The man holding the phone laughed—Andrew's laugh. "No, Ms. Jordan, I'm Daryl."

Daryl was the spitting image of Andrew—clean-cut and far more elegant, but identical nevertheless. He allowed her to stare at him in silence for a few seconds.

After a long pause, Karla found her voice. "But—"

"Andrew is my twin brother."

"I noticed the resemblance when I found your photograph online, but your voice..."

"We're identical twins." His demeanor changed as his eyes looked down to the papers on his desk. "Yes, that's correct," he growled into the phone. "Call back with the final number." He hung up and came around the desk, his hand outstretched, and a smile across his lips. "I'm Daryl McKenzie, and you're Karla Jordan. Correct?"

Stunned, Karla hesitated. "Yes." She stretched out her hand.

He shook it firmly. "Judging from your reaction, I presume our voices are the same."

"Presume?"

"I haven't seen Andrew in...well, a very long time." He motioned for Karla to sit on the sofa while he took one of the armchairs.

"What can I do for you, Miss Jordan?"

"I am...well, was...Andrew's friend." She reached into her purse, took out her business card, and placed it on the coffee table. "I've been writing a piece about Andrew for WOA magazine. Are you familiar with that publication?"

Daryl glanced at her card and smiled—Andrew's smile.

Karla stared at him in disbelief. "I'm sorry about your mother."

For a moment a dark cloud flashed across his face. "Thank you. My assistant said something about life and death. I'm very busy, Miss Jordan. Today is a bad—"

"Yes, I'm aware of that. This won't take a moment." She frowned. "Andrew has disappeared. Someone ransacked his studio, and there was a painting of your mother there. An unfinished portrait."

Daryl hesitated for a moment. "I wasn't aware Andrew painted portraits."

"You're correct. Never portraits."

"Is that right? You say his studio was ransacked?"

"Yes. The police are looking into it. "

Daryl cocked his head. "Go on."

"I was sent an article in the mail about you and your corporation."

"Yet you were surprised when you saw me."

"The article didn't include photographs."

"That's not unusual, is it?"

"No, but what's curious is that in this case the photos were all cut out intentionally. I can see why. Whoever sent it intended to shock me."

"Is that so?"

"Why else?" She studied his solemn expression for a moment. "But getting back to Andrew, has he contacted you?"

Daryl sat erect in his chair. "I haven't heard from Andrew in twelve years or more. What makes you think he'd wish to talk to me?"

"Because he's your brother. I had no idea he even had a brother, let alone a twin brother. Now he's disappeared and I have no idea why. But we need to find him. All I have is your mother's portrait, the newspaper article about her death, and this mutilated article about you. I simply followed a lead. I'd never even heard the McKenzie name. When I researched your mother, I couldn't find any connection to Andrew."

There was a long pause. Karla hung on to the silence with the expectation of a response. Daryl leaned forward and studied her.

"Miss Jordan—"

"Call me Karla, please."

"As you wish, Karla. Maybe Mother's unfortunate death brought back some memories and Andrew simply needs to be alone. Like I said, it's been a long time since we've been in touch. But I'll see what I can do. Let me make some phone calls."

"Thank you. You have no idea how much I'd appreciate it."

Daryl stood and helped Karla up. "I'm sorry I can't give you more time today. But let me assure you that I'll look into it. If you and I join forces it might be easier to find him. How about getting together for dinner tomorrow? We can compare notes."

"Terrific. Where?"

"The Big 4 at seven o'clock. Do you know where it is?"

"Yes. I'll be there."

"Very well. I look forward to it." He extended his hand.

Karla reciprocated. He gripped it a bit too firmly for comfort, but she slid her hand out of his grasp and headed for the double doors.

"Allow me." Daryl moved past her and opened the door for her.

"Until tomorrow." She went out.

"Indeed." Daryl shut the door behind her and crossed his office in a couple of strides. He reached for the phone. "Susan, cancel the rest of my appointments for today. Ask Furnell to find out anything he can on Karla Jordan."

"Yes, sir."

"Top priority."

"I understand, sir."

"Get me a copy of a magazine called WOA. Can you find it?

"Yes, sir. Is it W, O and then A?"

"It could be. You'll have to research it."

"Very well, sir. Anything else?

"Tell Furnell to look into that magazine as well."

"I shall."

Daryl hung up, turned toward the city, and sighed. "Andrew, what have you done?"

The loud ring of the hotel phone startled Sarah. Book in hand she reached for the handset, "Yes?"

"Sarah, we're waiting. What's going on?" Iris said irritably.

"Sorry. I had a bad night and…never mind. I'll take a quick shower and meet you downstairs in a few." Without waiting for a response she hung up and glanced at the book.

A poem waited to be read.

### WHAT REMINDS ME OF YOU

*What reminds me of you*
*Is not the way the sun*
*Catches your hair*
*Or the way your eyes reflect me*
*It isn't the way that you smile*
*Every morning*
*It isn't your hand holding mine*
*Or the kiss of your sweet tender lips*

*What reminds me of you*
*Is not your warmth next to me*
*And isn't the things that you say*
*It isn't the fact that my*
*Dreams all come true*
*Every time that you're in my arms*

*What reminds me of you is that*
*When you are gone*
*My life and my dreams are gone too*

# 8

# THE OBSTRUCTION

"Sorry ladies, James isn't here," said the woman behind the desk at the Booklegger bookstore. "Had to go on one of his job calls. He's out of town for a while."

"When do you expect him back?" asked Sarah.

"In a while."

"But what's a while? Is it a day, a couple of days, a week?" asked Iris impatiently.

She shrugged. "When James leaves, it's always for a while."

"Do you mind leaving him a message for me?" Sarah suggested.

"I can give you his cell number and you can leave a message there. Hard to imagine when he and I will cross paths, so no sense in leaving it with me."

"I've got his number. Thanks."

The three friends headed out the door.

"Well, that sucks," said Iris.

An hour later they strolled through the Clark Historical Museum, taking their time viewing the displays of the rich history of the county. The docent had told them all about the local Native American cultures, the gold rush settlements, the success of the lumber industry, and the thriving ranching and farming trades, as well as those livings wrung from the sea. The period room gave them an enjoyable glimpse of Victorian elegance, its remarkable craftsmanship seen in everyday work, home life, and play.

"A psychic visited the museum eight years ago and sensed four spirits in four separate locations throughout the building," the docent told them. "Four years later, the Humboldt Area Paranormal Society found the same four ghosts in the same locations."

"There's a society that studies ghosts?" Sonia shook her head in disbelief.

"They do investigations to scientifically identify or debunk paranormal sightings."

"No kidding." Iris could hardly contain her enthusiasm. "Can we visit with them? Do you have an address or phone for them?"

The docent shook her head. "No. I'm told they can be found online on Facebook. I'm not into social media, so I can't help you."

"I'll look them up," Iris said. "I'm on Facebook."

"Good. I'm happy to guide you through the museum and answer your questions, but that's as far as I can go. Can you guess in what rooms the ghosts reside?"

Sonia and Iris turned to Sarah, expecting her to impress the docent with her perceptive powers, but Sarah shook her head and shrugged.

The docent giggled. "Not to worry, honey. You've got to have pretty special psychic powers to sense them. These ghosts passed on a long time ago."

"How come they're here?" Sonia asked.

"During the 1870s the museum was the Bay Hotel, and Eureka's Chinatown was up the street. One of the ghosts is believed to be a young girl. Her true identity is yet to be determined, but it's possible that she could be the daughter or wife of a merchant named Kwan Sing Long. The ghost resides in the museum's basement where he used to store his goods. Apparently she's not interested in leaving."

"Can we go down there and meet her?" asked Iris.

"I'm afraid not, dearie. Unfortunately visitors can't access the basement. It's not safe for the public. "

"From a hotel to a museum?"

"Well, not quite. In 1911, the Bay Hotel was reconstructed into the Bank of Eureka. The museum currently occupies the same reconstruction footprint as the bank. I'm sure you noticed the bank teller windows when you first came in."

"What about the other ghosts?" Iris asked.

"Another female ghost haunts the lounge outside the second floor bathroom. A psychic claimed the woman was angry because she didn't have a place to sit after the reconstruction. The museum puts out a folding chair every night to keep the ghost happy." She giggled.

"We can go by that one, right?" Iris asked.

"No, we don't allow visitors there either. Sorry." She smiled. "The third spirit is a child that loves the piano in the Victorian room. It is said that every once in a while, a couple of piano notes can be heard."

"Have you ever heard them?" inquired Iris.

"No, not I, but my colleagues have." She winked. "I've already told you all about the Native American wing of the museum, but what I didn't tell you is that the bear costume is home to a spirit that is said to protect the museum from unfriendly energies. That's why this museum and its ghosts are friendly to visitors like you."

Sarah frowned, frustrated at her inability to sense any of these entities, thus thwarting her friend's hopes of an in-person paranormal encounter.

"I'll leave you to it, dearies. You can wander about and check all the exhibits at your leisure, if you wish." She looked at Sarah, "When you're done here, you might enjoy visiting the Humboldt State Historic Park Museum. It houses some wonderful displays of the former U.S. Army Fort that operated from the1850s to the 1870s, and shows the interactions between European Americans and Native Americans. It's a couple of miles down Highway 101, on a bluff overlooking the bay. A beautiful view."

"Thank you," Sarah said, as the docent walked away.

"Thank you," Iris called out.

The docent turned to them and waved.

"Why don't we go to the fort?" Sonia suggested.

"In a bit." Iris held Sarah's arm. "Sarah, c'mon, call the ghosts to come and chat with us."

"I'm afraid I can't. They won't come near me."

"Why not?"

Sarah hesitated a moment. "They can't."

Iris frowned. "Why?"

"Because I'm—unreachable at this moment."

"Make yourself reachable, then." Iris insisted.

"Iris, stop harassing her. If she's not reachable, she's not. C'mon." Sonia took Sarah's hand and led her toward the exit.

An irritated Iris shook her head and followed.

After a short drive up Highway 101, they wandered through the grounds of the fort and the museum at Humboldt Park.

"So, you're telling me you can't sense *anything*?" Iris had run out of patience.

"I'm afraid not." Sarah responded apologetically. "Listen, as much as I would like to, it's not likely to happen. Sorry."

"How come?" Sonia's curiosity was aroused.

"As I told you earlier, I found a book of poems at the Booklegger, and apparently it…well, it needs all of my attention."

This bit of news stopped Iris in her tracks. "Attention for what?"

Sarah shrugged. "I'm afraid I'm in the dark about that at the moment."

"So, how did you conclude that it needs you?" wondered Sonia.

"It's difficult to explain, but it insists on being with me. It screams if I try to—"

"Whoa," Iris exclaimed. "It screams? A book?"

"Only I can hear it, of course. It demands all of my attention and interferes very aggressively with any communication from other spirits. I'm useless except to the entity attached to that book. It kept me awake most of the night. That's why I was late." She glanced at Iris. "So, can you please cut me some slack?"

Iris blushed. "Jeez, Sarah, sorry. I didn't mean to push you. It's very cool to have a psychic friend and—"

"Don't fret, Iris. It's my fault. I shouldn't have been so secretive. It's normal for you to expect me to sense all the spirits that roam around Eureka. And normally I should've. That's what we all expected. But it's not to be. The energy connected with the book has seized me. I should've told you a lot sooner. Please, forgive me."

"Is it talking with you now? The ghost, I mean." Iris looked around.

Sarah laughed. "No, it's not here. At least I don't sense it. It chooses when and where to show up, but keeps everything else at bay." She shrugged apologetically.

Iris frowned. "When it shows up, tell him he's a pain in the ass for messing up our holiday."

"What if it's a she?" Sonia winked.

"Same thing. Bothersome all the way." Iris squeezed Sarah's hand. "I'm so very sorry. What a pain I've been."

"Yes, you have, but then, you always are," Sonia interjected, "We're used to it. Frankly, it's your nagging that pushed us to do better year after year. It's what made us the best of the best as teachers. So, no pity party here. Anyway, now that that's settled, what should we do next?"

"I'm really curious about a small town not too far from here called Alderpoint. On the way back we can drive through the Avenue of the Giants. The giant redwood trees are the tallest trees in the world and some of the oldest. How about it?" Sarah suggested.

"Sonia, didn't Steinbeck call them the 'ambassadors from another time?'" Iris asked.

"Yeah, he did."

"Okay," said Iris. "Let's do the time-traveling trees. I'll drive."

# TURMOIL

Outside of an opulent reception area, a black marble wall pierced by ornate elevator doors bore bright brass letters that announced: *ALDERCREST CORPORATION.*

Directly below, a bronze bust was labeled *Robert McKenzie Jr. – Founder.*

Activity in the offices appeared subdued. Music played softly in the background. The voices of the employees were muffled by the partitions or glass doors so that only the mechanical tapping of computer keyboards stood out.

One of the elevator doors opened and Daryl, briefcase in hand, burst through, followed by an obese man in his early forties. Daryl greeted the receptionists, and darted through the central corridor toward his office. The man desperately tried to keep up with Daryl, who smiled in every direction as he greeted his employees.

"Mr. McKenzie, I told them the type of improvements you expected. I told them you had personally pointed them out to the staff when you were there in February, that you had ordered them finished by April, that after months of delays and excuses we needed to have results."

Daryl abruptly halted his frantic pace, raised an arm to stop the man behind him, and slowly walked toward one of the secretaries. The woman slightly chubby and in her mid-twenties, looked embarrassed by Daryl's attention.

"Well, well," Daryl said with a broad smile. "If it isn't Miss Motherhood herself. How are you, Sheryl?"

"Fine, Mr. McKenzie. Thank you."

"How do you like being a mom? Is it as good as you imagined it would be?"

"When I'm back to getting a full night's sleep, I'll like it better." She giggled nervously.

"Give yourself time. Don't try to overdo it yet, either. If you need more time at home, take it. Simply ask."

"Thank you, Mr. McKenzie, but I'm ready, and willing to work. It's a nice respite, to be honest. I leave the baby in the office nursery downstairs where I can feed him and be with him as often as I need to. It works out great."

"What did you name him?"

"Uh-oh, I was afraid you'd ask that."

"My God, what did you name him?"

She blushed. "Daryl—Daryl Jonathan."

Daryl burst out laughing and addressed everyone within earshot. "Ladies and Gentlemen, we have a lunatic in our midst. Not content with hearing my name all day long, she lays the curse on her own son."

Everyone laughed politely and went back to work.

Daryl looked at Sheryl whose cheeks had turned crimson. "Nasty thing to do to a child. But I'm honored to share the name, and I thank you."

"We're very grateful for the lovely presents. I really didn't expect—"

"That's the whole point, isn't it?" He winked.

"It is indeed, sir."

"Enjoy motherhood." He resumed his pace toward his office, followed by the big man who picked up right where he left off.

"Of course, they gave me all kinds of excuses, but I told them they would have to answer to us and that I had already filed in Superior Court. I said the matter was out of our hands."

Daryl pushed through the glass doors and entered the reception area of his office, where several people were waiting. He walked by acknowledging each person politely.

Susan opened his office door and Daryl hastened through without stopping. Susan stopped the man following Daryl. "A minute please, Mr. Lawrence." She closed the doors behind her, staying just inside the door.

"Good morning, Susan. How are you today?"

"Fine, Mr. McKenzie. How are you?"

"All right, thanks. Only one coffee for me, please. Let Lawrence in."

Susan opened the doors, ushered Lawrence in, and closed the doors behind her.

Daryl placed his briefcase on the floor next to his desk and pointed to one of the armchairs as a cue for his employee to sit down.

Lawrence obeyed, placing his briefcase on his lap and gripping it tightly.

Daryl sat on the edge of his desk as his jovial demeanor shifted to stern. "Correct me if I'm wrong, but I have the distinct impression that you're trying to say you need my approval so you can file a lawsuit against Richardson Wineries."

"That is correct, sir. After examining the procedures followed by this company in the past, it was evident that it's our only recourse. I told them that I had already filed it, but, of course, you need to approve such a move. Ogilvie is ready to file. I have it right here, ready for your signature." He opened his briefcase and produced the papers.

Daryl stared at the man from across the room as Susan entered with a cup of coffee, placed it beside Daryl, and left. "Mr. Lawrence, you are the perfect example of why I'm always reluctant to retain the attorneys that work in the companies I buy." Daryl sipped his coffee and glared at Lawrence. "My father didn't build this company on the smoldering ashes of others, Mr. Lawrence. The reason Aldercrest is as big as it is, is because instead of devouring the makers of products we're interested in, or the wineries we acquire, we nourish, encourage, and propel them into greatness. We actively help them to become more profitable, which makes us more profitable."

Daryl set his coffee on the desk, and approached Lawrence like a predator moving in for the kill. He yanked the papers from the man's hands, and tore them in half. "If you had researched Aldercrest—as you claim you did—you would've found that we don't simply own two hundred and forty-six companies and wineries outright. We are engaged with them. We have a symbiotic relationship with them. What you have done is not only going to cause me a great deal of expense and wasted time, but also, a great deal of embarrassment."

Daryl towered over Lawrence, watching him squirm in the armchair. He tossed the papers at him and returned to his desk. "Now, you will call Ogilvie and tell him to cancel all action against Richardson Wineries. After that you will call Lionel Richardson, tell him personally that this was your mistake, and apologize for the inconvenience. And last, but most definitely not least, have your letter of resignation on my desk before lunch today. Good-bye, Mr. Lawrence."

Lawrence collected his briefcase and papers and gradually recovered from his bewilderment. His fear slowly turned to anger, and by the time he reached the door, he'd gathered his courage. "You haven't heard the last of this."

Without so much as a glance at him, Daryl said coldly, "For your sake, I hope I have."

Lawrence stormed out, slamming the door behind him.

Daryl sipped his coffee and picked up the phone. "Susan, let Furnell in. Apologize to the others for the brief delay, please."

He drank from his cup as he turned toward the city that stretched out at his feet.

After a knock on the door Susan ushered Furnell in. A former army criminal investigator, Furnell was an imposing man, tall, muscular, and with a swagger reminiscent of John Wayne.

Daryl turned toward him and placed his coffee cup on the desk. Then, he placed his briefcase on the desk, opened it, extracted a pink sheer scarf, and handed it to Furnell. "Find out who has been placing these—items in my briefcase. This is not the first time, but it had better be the last. Whoever is playing these childish pranks is to be fired. Take care of it."

"Very well, sir. May I have access to your calendar, both private and business?"

"Yes. I'll inform Susan."

"Were the materials on Ms. Jordan satisfactory?"

"What?"

"The background you requested on Ms. Karla Jordan, was it all right?"

"Oh, yes. I'd almost forgotten. Big money, huh?" Daryl rummaged through the papers on his desk looking for the file.

"It appears so."

"Remind me how?"

"Her father inherited the family firm, and turned it into one of the largest construction and engineering firms in the country. She got a nice chunk when her trust came due."

"Respected in her own right, though?" He opened and closed several drawers in his desk. "Where in God's name did I put that file?" he muttered.

"Yes, indeed. She started writing in college, and worked in the UK after that. She's got a flair for words and, apparently, a good eye for art."

"She got that from her mother, if I recall."

"Her mother is an avid collector of art, particularly modern art. They have quite a collection in their homes."

"Her place is in…"

"Pleasant Street, in Nob Hill, a high-end duplex. Lives on her own."

"She owns?"

"Outright."

Frustrated, Daryl slammed the drawer closed. "I give up. I must've left it home." He came to his feet and extended his hand. "Thanks, Furnell. Well done." After they shook hands, he escorted him to the door. "Find out about these damned scarves. Ask Susan to come in, please."

"I will, sir." Furnell closed the doors behind him, and Daryl returned to his desk.

Susan entered the office, closed the door, and approached him, holding out a piece of paper. "I prepared Mr. Lawrence's letter of resignation. If you approve, all it needs is his signature. Is there anything you wish me to follow up on?"

He took the letter and read it. "It's fine. Ensure that everybody adheres to all the customary procedures. I need him gone today."

"Yes, sir."

"Give Furnell full access to all my calendars."

"Very well. Shall I ask Mr. Gibson to come in?"

"Give me ten minutes."

Susan nodded and left.

Daryl slumped into his chair, leaned forward, and rested his head on his hands. "Andrew, this has to stop."

"Is that why we're going to Alderpoint?" Sonia asked.

Sarah, her head resting against the car window, remained silent.

"Hello? Earth to Sarah!" Iris called out as she drove.

Startled, Sarah straightened up and looked at Iris. "What?"

"Sonia's telling us about this place from her research and asking questions, as she always does."

"Oh, I didn't hear." She turned to Sonia. "What did you ask?"

"I read that the Rancho Sequoia area of Alderpoint is called 'Murder Mountain,' on account of the Carson serial killers in the eighties. The question was whether that's why you suggested we come?"

"Oh. Sorry. I must've detached."

"No kidding, you've been in a world of your own ever since we left. Anyway, are we here because you wish to connect with whoever has been killed in this area?" Iris eyed Sarah in the car mirror and winked.

"Iris, what on earth do you mean?" Sarah asked.

"Why are we here? I mean, look around. This is a really small town and very isolated. So, what's so special about it? Other than the Carson murders Sonia told us about, why did you suggest we come here? I hope it's to chat with the ghosts."

"No, only curiosity," Sarah said absentmindedly. She hastened to add. "I read that this town attracts people who want to escape the intrusions of modern life. I thought it could be interesting."

"Sorry, but it looks desolate and frightening to me. Appalachia meets Humboldt County," Iris said. "And that's without taking into account the curve-packed and horribly-marked road that you conveniently spaced out on. I don't like it."

"This part is locally referred to as the Emerald Triangle for its principal crop. Guess what that is."

Iris arched her brows. "Sonia, you've missed the boat on this one. There's nothing around here that even remotely looks like a farm."

"No I didn't, but in any case we shouldn't stop and get out of the car. It looks much too unwelcoming. I vote that we skip this place," Sonia said. "Okay with you, Sarah?"

"Sure. This is not where—" she stopped herself. "I mean…this doesn't look like I'd imagined it. And it doesn't have a lake."

Iris and Sonia glanced at each other. "A lake?" they asked in unison.

Sarah shrugged. "Somehow I pictured houses or cabins around a lake, and small docks with rowboats tied to them."

"Well, your imagination tricked you this time," Iris muttered.

"If we head west and join Highway 101 we'll be on our way to the Avenue of the Giants in no time," Sonia suggested.

"Sounds good to me," Sarah answered.

"Then let's get out of here." Iris gunned the engine and sped off down the road.

"You haven't guessed what they grow here."

"Okay, I'll try." Iris rolled down her window and sniffed the air. "Wow! Is that what I think it is?"

Sarah rolled down her window. "Oh, my gosh. You can really smell the marijuana."

"That's because pot is the main industry here. It replaced lumber as the number one crop. They've grown and sold marijuana here for personal medical use since 1996."

"Where exactly are we?" Sarah closed her window.

"North of Garberville. Maybe it's where the Gerber baby food got started," Iris asked.

"*Garber*ville not Gerberville, silly," Sonia replied. "The postmaster, a guy named Garber, gave the town its name back in the 1800s."

"And now they're all pot farmers." Iris laughed.

"They take it seriously in terms of the healing powers it provides. They even have a cannabis college."

Iris couldn't restrain a chuckle. "Oh, c'mon, Sonia, you've got to be kidding."

"Well," Sarah said, "nestled in the middle of the Redwood Forest is the perfect location."

"When do we get to the Avenue of the Giants?" Iris impatiently asked.

Sonia checked the GPS. "We're at the Southern entrance."

"How long did you say the Avenue is?" Sarah asked.

"A little over thirty miles. But there are lots of interesting spots along the way. I'll tell you all about them as we get to each location."

"Why skimp on the information? Inquiring minds want to know," Iris protested.

Sonia rolled her eyes with irritation. "I'm not skimping. But it's silly to tell you about it ahead of time only to repeat it when we get there. Sarah, you have no idea how lucky you are to live far away from this ogre."

Sarah laughed. "I'm enjoying her input."

"Only because you don't have to live with it all the time."

"C'mon, Sonia, it's not like we live together, for crying out loud."

"Dealing with you at our book club, golf, church charities, and bridge is more than enough."

Sarah smiled. "C'mon you guys, you love it, and I'm thrilled to be reliving our years together. It makes me realize how much I've missed it."

"Anyway, these huge trees that line the road are called Coast Redwoods."

"Look at this," Iris said, indicating the views in every direction. "Isn't it gorgeous how this road winds along the Earl River?"

"How did you figure out it was the Earl River," Sonia asked.

"There was a sign back there. You're not the only one who can read."

Stunned by the beauty that surrounded them, the three remained silent a long while.

Sonia broke the spell. "Iris, the famous tree house is coming up."

"Oh," Sarah said, "that should be fun."

Iris pulled off the road and followed the signs into a parking area. The simple act of emerging from the vehicle, stretching their arms and legs while they inhaled the forest air, invigorated them all.

"What a fabulous place," Iris said.

Sarah pointed. "Looks like it's that way."

As they approached the house, Sonia took the lead. "This famous tree house was built within a giant redwood."

"We can see that, Miss Smarty Pants." Iris threw her arm around Sonia and kissed her on the cheek. "I do love you. It baffles me as to why, but God help me, I do."

Sonia kissed her back. "Me too, Miss Irritating."

Sarah threw her arms around her two friends. "And I love you both."

They made their way into the house through the hollow trunk, and found themselves inside a cavernous room.

"A living tree..." Sarah whispered.

"Yep," Sonia said. "The original cavity was caused by a forest fire, and the Native Americans and trappers used it as shelter for years. In the early twentieth century a man named McCleod came in here and carved out the room. Amazing, huh?"

They toured the surrounding area, and the fresh air and nature enthralled them. Half an hour later they were back on the road and ready for more.

Their next stop was the Immortal Tree, located in the northern half of the Avenue of the Giants.

"Look at that tree," Sonia exclaimed. "And it's not the oldest redwood in the forest, even though it's over 950 years old. It's around 250 feet tall, but originally it was much taller."

"How so?" Iris asked.

"A direct lighting-strike removed forty-five feet off the top. This amazing tree has survived the hardships of time, fire, and floods. Not to mention man."

"Look at that." Iris pointed to the markers visible on the tree.

"You can tell where the loggers' axes tried to cut it down." Sarah pointed out several indentations. "How sad."

"Not for the tree." Iris winked. "Because obviously they failed."

Sonia leaned forward to examine it closely. "And this has to be the line where the floodwaters covered the tree."

After a half-mile hike on a self-guided trail admiring not only the trees, but also the wildflowers and native shrubbery, they were ready to head back to Eureka. Iris took the wheel while Sonia continued to read from the information booklets she'd gathered at their hotel. Sarah rested her head against the window to take in the sights and allowed her mind to wander.

# TWINS

A group of five businessmen opened the door to The Big 4 restaurant and split into two groups as Karla walked through. Taken by her striking appearance, they turned to eye her and whisper appreciative remarks amongst themselves. The curves of her alluring body were revealed by an exquisite silk turquoise dress, which she'd embellished with bright yellow shoes and a matching purse. Her hair cascaded down to her shoulders, bouncing with every step.

The restaurant, named in honor of the "Big Four" businessmen who built the Central Pacific Railroad, retained its elegant early-California décor. Rich green leather chairs, dark wood bar stools, sparkling beveled glass panes and mirrors surrounded an incomparable collection of Gold Rush and western railroad memorabilia.

Karla marched up the stairs, past the piano player who performed requested oldies for the patrons that filled the swanky old-world bar. An elegant maître d' welcomed Karla. "Good afternoon, madam."

"Thank you. I'm here to meet Mr. McKenzie."

"Mr. McKenzie has not arrived yet. Would you prefer to wait in the bar or at your table?"

"At the table, please."

The maître d' acknowledged her request with a slight bow. "Right this way."

Karla followed him into the elegant dining room. The tables were placed far enough from each other to allow for considerable privacy and relaxed comfort. The maître d' guided her to a table at the far left corner of the large dining room. He pulled out the chair on the right side of the table, leaving the other chair, which faced the entire restaurant, open for Daryl.

"Would you like an aperitif?"

"A dry vodka Martini, please. With onions."

"Very well, madame."

As Karla leaned back to examine her surroundings, Daryl approached the table. "I apologize for being late." Daryl slid in. "I hope you haven't been waiting long."

"No. Just got here myself."

"You look stunning." Smiling suggestively, Daryl extended his hand and Karla proffered hers in return. He leaned forward and gallantly kissed it, allowing his lips to linger. "Your eyes are…captivating."

Karla smiled politely as his gray eyes locked onto her, and then pulled back her hand.

A slim middle-aged waiter with a competent air of experience approached the table and handed them menus. "Good evening, Mr. McKenzie. Shall I get you the usual?"

"Hello, Ron, nice to see you."

"Same here, sir."

"To answer your question, yes, thank you. Would you like a cocktail, Karla?

"The maître d' already took my order."

"Very well." The waiter bowed and left.

"Ron has worked here for over twenty years." Daryl winked at Karla. "He's a good guy."

"You come here often?"

Daryl scanned the room with a satisfied look. "My father's favorite. We used to come here together. It's an old-fashioned place with a friendly, modern approach to service and food."

A busboy brought a plate of tiny hors d'oeuvres. "Compliments of the chef, Mr. McKenzie."

"Thank him for me."

The busboy bowed and left.

"I have asked them not seat anyone near us so we can talk freely."

"You can do that? Won't they lose money?"

"I've taken care of that. Don't worry." He adjusted the silverware around his plate, shifted the salt and peppershakers an inch to the left, and straightened the napkin on his lap. "Do you wish to begin our talk about Andrew?"

"May I be very blunt?"

"Go right ahead. You're famous for being so. Aren't you?"

Ron returned with a small tray and set a dry Martini in front of Daryl, another before Karla, then walked discreetly away.

"Every time I come here," Karla said, "I get a kick out of these small old-fashioned Martini glasses. I feel as I've stepped into a 1920s black and white movie. They're the perfect size for a pre-dinner cocktail."

They sipped their Martinis.

"They're also very well balanced," Daryl added.

"What did you mean when you said I'm famous for being blunt?"

"You have a reputation for straight forward honest articles about your subjects." Daryl paused to sip his drink. "Why should you treat me any differently?"

Karla gave him an incredulous look. "You've read my work?"

Daryl raised his glass. "Let's say that, not only do we have the same taste in drinks, but I also like what you do and...how you do it." He lifted his glass slightly, as if to toast her.

Karla hesitated before she raised her glass and toasted. "How—"

Daryl raised his eyebrows inquisitively. "What?"

"Andrew said the exact same thing to me not long ago."

"That's interesting. Never thought my brother and I could have anything in common. Go on, be blunt."

Karla scrutinized him for a second, looking directly into his eyes. "Why do you hate Andrew?"

"I don't hate Andrew. We merely...can't get along."

"Would you mind telling me why?"

"No, not at all. But all I can offer is my hypotheses. He never told you why?"

"Until yesterday I didn't even know he had a brother. As far as I was concerned, his name was Andrew *Stuart*, not McKenzie and—"

"Andrew Stuart?"

Karla nodded and sipped her drink.

"Andrew Stuart the painter?"

"And sculptor. Why the surprise?"

"It's impossible. Really? My twin brother is *that* artist?"

Ron silently approached the table ready to take their order, but Daryl signaled that he should wait.

Karla eyed Daryl in amazement. "You mean to tell me you were not aware that the painting in your office was your brother's?"

"No. My father bought it about two years ago..." Daryl shifted his gaze, grabbed his drink and gulped it down. "Right before he died."

"I'm sorry, I don't mean to bring up—"

"No problem." Daryl opened the menu and thumbed through it avoiding Karla's gaze. "Father died of a heart attack."

"Did he have a history—"

"No. His death was unexpected and unwelcome."

"That must've been—"

"Let's get back to Andrew. You were asking about the painting and I started to tell you that I found my father staring at it one day. He told me that the painting was telling him something, and that he'd been striving to understand what that could possibly be. He never figured it out. I've been wondering the same thing."

"Your father was unaware that the painting was by his son?"

"Completely. He didn't connect the two, any more than I did. Mother had no idea, either..." He paused and closed his eyes. A second later he glanced at Karla and forced a smile. "Or maybe she did. Mother was good at keeping secrets." He looked down at his menu.

He raised his hand, and in an instant Ron materialized at his side. "Shall we order? Have you decided what you'd like?"

"This is your rodeo. I'll leave it up to you."

"Ron, please tell Chef that I would appreciate if he prepared a special, off-menu meal for us reminiscent of my father's favorites."

"I'm sure that won't be a problem."

"We'll have Avocat au Caviar, Chateaubriand, rare, and…" he looked at Karla, "would you like wine with dinner?"

"I'd love some. How about Clos de L'Oratoire?"

Daryl regarded her with admiration. "An excellent choice indeed. A Châteauneuf du Pape would go perfectly with the meat. But I have a surprise for you." Daryl nodded to Ron. "The Chanteuse, please."

"Indeed, sir."

Daryl turned his attention back to Karla. "Well, let's answer your blunt question. Andrew always complained that my parents preferred me to him. I have no clue how that idea got started, but he was quite convinced it was true. We used to fight about it all the time. He always accused me of destroying his drawings of those darn dogs or wolves or whatever they were. He cared for them more than for me—I should say *us*, his family. Then one day, when we were fifteen or so, he said I'd burned all his drawings and broken his new fishing rod. He told my father I'd smashed it against a tree or something. All I remember is that he jumped me and beat me until I lost consciousness."

Karla noticed a subtle gleam of anger in his eyes as he paused for a moment, but he recovered immediately and continued. "That's the last time he ever spoke to me. He changed a lot after that. He didn't talk to anyone really, except Mother." Daryl looked down, deep in thought.

Karla shifted nervously. "I'm sorry to make you dig up these painful memories."

Daryl grinned, back in control, his eyes fixed on her. "Hey, it's okay."

Unable to withstand his intense stare, Karla glanced away.

"All that matters is that you're trying to find Andrew. And, regardless of what has happened in the past, he's my brother." He took her hand in his. "And we're going to find him. You and I."

She tried to pull her hand away, but Daryl refused to relinquish it, his grey eyes boring into hers. His resemblance to Andrew unnerved her, but it also filled her with inexplicable fascination. Smiling, Karla retrieved her hand. "So you're telling me that since the age of fifteen or there about, you have not talked to your brother?"

Daryl shrugged and looked away.

"How is that possible?"

"After that incident and Andrew's subsequent brooding period, the rift in the family became too painful for my mother, so they sent him away to school. And then, I suppose he went to college."

"And you?"

"I remained at home for a couple of years, and eventually went off to college."

"Did you ask about him?"

Daryl's charming stare became stern. "No. And he never ask about me."

"How could all of you not have seen any photos of Andrew?"

"Have *you*?"

Karla frowned. "No. You're right. He always shied away from that."

"There you have it."

Ron removed the appetizer plates and the cocktail glasses, then gave them to a busboy. He took the Avocat Au Caviar plates from another busboy and placed them before Karla and Daryl. He removed a couple of aperitif wine glasses from the same tray. "May I serve you Chanteuse sparkling wine with your appetizer?"

"Please."

Ron set the glasses down and poured the bubbly.

"Thank you, Ron," Karla smiled as he left. "They treat you like royalty."

Daryl winked. "That's because I am."

"Tell me about Aldercrest. Where does the name come from?" she asked, taking a bite of her appetizer.

Daryl beamed with pride. "The name is a creation of my father's, using references to the lake town where we grew up. Father had a soft spot for alder trees."

"This is delicious."

"I thought you'd like it. Take a sip of the sparkly."

She savored the wine. "It's perfect. Great selection." She took another sip and licked her lips. "So, tell me, what's so special about alder trees?"

"These particular trees release high amounts of nitrogen into the soil, because of an important symbiotic relationship with bacteria. The bacteria grow in the root nodules, and the result of this mutual relationship is extremely fertile soil in the area where the alders grow." Daryl studied her carefully. "Andrew really didn't tell you anything, did he?"

She shook her head.

"Not surprising," Daryl said with a smirk. "Andrew turned out to be a loner; he used to hide out in the forest around the lake for days, sometimes weeks. Maybe that's where he is, come to think of it. That forest is pretty big, wild, and mountainous, with lots of valleys and plenty of trees to hide in. Andrew is quite familiar with that countryside."

"Sounds like a beautiful place to grow up."

Daryl turned suddenly pensive. "Everything always looks better from the outside."

Karla stared at him for a moment. "What do you mean?"

"Just that."

"Weren't you happy growing up there?"

"I was. Not sure about my brother."

They ate and sipped their aperitif in silence for a while.

Daryl's mood shifted unexpectedly as he raised his glass. "The role of an aperitif is to stimulate the appetite for the meal that follows. The name derives from the Latin *aperire* 'to open.' Did it tingle and refresh?"

"I wouldn't have chosen those words, but yes, it did."

The instant they finished their appetizers and drinks a busboy removed their plates and glasses. Ron replaced them with wine glasses. "Shall I serve the wine, sir?"

"Please show Ms. Jordan the bottle first."

Ron handed her the bottle.

"Chanteuse, that's the same label as the sparkling wine, isn't it?" she asked Daryl.

"Yes."

"I haven't come across this wine before," she said as she examined the bottle.

"That's because it's a special reserve." Daryl glowed with pride. "It's our wine."

"Yours?" Karla returned the bottle to the waiter.

"My grandfather went into the wine business right after Prohibition. He started with several vineyards around the lake, which we still own. My father expanded what was already a lucrative business into a corporation when we moved to Napa and acquired more vineyards."

Daryl gestured to Ron. The waiter opened the bottle and poured the wine into a splendid crystal decanter and swirled it.

"You seem to appreciate your wines. Did the sparkling wine remind you of anything?"

"The subtlety of a Dom Pérignon."

"Thanks for the compliment. In a way it's very similar. We specialize in mixing grapes, just as the brilliant old Benedictine monk, Dom Pérignon, did back in the 1600s."

Ron poured the wine, then served the Chateaubriand. He straightened up and proffered a subtle nod. "Chef sends his regards and hopes you'll enjoy your meal."

"Thanks Ron. I'm sure we will." Daryl raised his glass, sniffed the wine, and tasted it. "Give me your honest opinion." He winked at Karla.

She sipped the wine and closed her eyes. "It's delicious. A hint of Tempranillo?"

"I'm impressed. It's a blend of Carignan grapes from France, our own Napa Syrah grapes, with a nice combination of Tempranillo and Graciano grapes from Spain."

"And the name Chanteuse?"

Daryl's eyes darkened and his jaw tensed. "Father fell in love with my mother when he heard her sing. She had a beautiful voice and loved to sing. He named his first vineyard Chanteuse to honor her. I've considered changing the name, but we're too well established and it wouldn't be wise. From a business point of view." He looked away from her and focused on his meal.

Perplexed, Karla followed suit, wondering why he disliked the label. After a few moments, she looked up to find him staring at her. In spite of herself, she blushed.

His morose mood had dissipated and he flashed her another one of his Andrew smiles.

"Sarah, Sarah..." Sonia whispered softly as she gently nudged her friend. "We're back, honey."

Sarah blinked. "What?"

"We're back at the hotel. Are you all right? You were out of it, staring out the car window, stiff as a board," Iris said.

Sarah nodded hesitantly. "Yes, I'm fine."

"You were real quiet all the way back, wouldn't answer our questions or engage in conversation. We couldn't decide whether you were taking the whole experience in or had simply fallen asleep. Anyway, we let you be, but since we got back we've been trying to...well get you out of your trance. But you didn't react. You simply sat there," Sonia said sheepishly.

"Trance?" Sarah asked meekly.

Iris grabbed her hand and pulled her out of the car. "C'mon, what you need is a stiff drink and some food."

"We all need both." Sonia reached for Sarah's free hand.

"We promise not to interrogate you about what happened or who cast the spell on you." Iris winked.

"That promise might be a tall order, Iris." Sonia giggled. "Your record on keeping promises is not stellar." Sarah grinned.

"I will this time," Iris protested. "We figured that maybe the book spirit got into your head and you went visiting with him, or her—or them. To tell you the truth, watching you like that turned out to be enough paranormal stuff to last me a lifetime. I can't imagine how you can cope with all this shit going on in your head."

"It's surprising at times." Sarah cocked her head. "And, frankly, very annoying when it zaps me out of reality."

"Well, you're back with the living, and we won't talk anymore about spirits. We're done for the day—or days. First a warm bath, followed by a nice meal," asserted Sonia as they marched arm in arm into their hotel.

Sarah rushed into her room, went straight for the book and opened it. "Seriously, you give me a poem?" She stared at the book in frustration. "Where are the scenes in the Aldercrest offices?" She flipped through the book but all she found was page after page of poems.

Exasperated, she tossed the book on the bed, removed her shoes, shed her blouse, and stomped into the bathroom. She ran hot water in the tub, and poured in some bubble bath for good measure. She cast off her remaining garments, snatched the book, and eased into the tub. "All right, let's take a look at the poem."

### NIGHT

*The moon was singing*
*The other night*
*And the stars*

*Joined in the chorus*
*Their music*
*Spoke of happiness*
*Of loneliness*
*Of multitudes*
*And dark*
*Of watching sheep*
*That flock together*
*Of reflections in a mirror*
*And the sound of*
*Crickets in the breeze*

*They loved the things*
*That night provides*
*The silence cool*
*The quiet calm*
*The nightingales*
*The June bugs*
*And the tide*

*But*
*When I asked*
*If they*
*Liked roses*
*Humming birds*
*And honey bees*
*When I spoke*
*To them*
*Of children playing*
*The changing colors*
*Of the leaves*
*And mornings by the sea*
*They stared at me*
*Bewildered*
*And simply said to me*

*Day*
*May have the golden sun*
*Flowers bees and kids*
*But night's a time of living peace*
*The time when lovers*
*Love*

# 9

# THE CHAMELEON

"A trance?" Conrad's concern came across loud and clear.

"That's what they said. They were quite worried."

"I can't blame them. What did you say?"

"I described what I went through last year with Alexander. They loved that story. At least it kept them entertained. We never went back to my so-called trance, or *spell* as Iris labeled it."

"Spell?"

"She's concluded that the ghost in the book had cast a spell on me. It's her way to grasp what's going on."

Conrad laughed. "She's not that far from the truth. How are you feeling?"

"Anxious. I have absolutely no recollection of the drive back to the hotel. Somewhat similar to what Alexander put me through. At least I wasn't driving."

"Alexander actually wrote the screenplay he played in your mind. Could the woman whose voice you sense be the author?"

"No, not likely. I'm miffed at this psychotic book, though."

Conrad laughed. "Psychotic book. What a description."

"Well, it is."

"You must admit that the image of a book being psychotic is quite funny."

"Nonetheless, it's psychotic."

"Who do you suppose is the author?"

"I have no idea. Which makes it even more frustrating."

"And no sign of James?"

"None. I left him a voicemail, but he hasn't called back. Did you find out anything from Sheriff Williams?"

"He didn't find anyone by the name of Austen in Eureka. He's searching nearby cities."

"Ask him to try San Francisco."

"Why there?"

"The Big 4 restaurant, the galleries, and the bar Karla went to, are all in San Francisco."

"Okay, I'll ask Williams to check San Francisco."

"I'm getting the impression that the book, or the story, is getting impatient."

"How come?"

"The person behind the book is showing me what's happening now, and I'm expected to do something about it."

"How did you arrive at that conclusion?"

"Gerard, the art magazine editor asked Karla to write about the Chinese miniatures, remember? So I looked it up. There's currently a Chinese miniatures exhibit in San Francisco. I'm pretty sure that means that the McKenzie woman must've died fairly recently."

"It makes sense. By the way, I haven't found a thing about an artist named Andrew Stuart."

"Me neither. I also asked around here, but nobody's heard of him. They don't recognize the name Aldercrest either, although I thought it might be the town that's located south of Eureka, the one called Alderpoint, and the book might have changed the word *point* to *crest*. But there's no lake there and it's a very isolated, unwelcoming place. "

"All these names could be fake."

"Why use fake names?"

"Maybe so you don't get distracted looking them up and reading about them online. From what James told you, this entity needs to be in control."

"That certainly makes sense. I haven't been able to find anything online about the art magazine she works for either."

"It appears as if you're getting glimpses of real events, real places, and even real people, that are somehow hidden in some elaborate maze."

"James said that maybe whoever is communicating all this is ashamed or afraid for some reason. That somehow Karla is in danger. The look and demeanor of this new twin is creating some serious internal conflicts for her."

"What's your take on Daryl?"

"He appears to be all right—unyielding and decisive in his business, kind to his employees, and in complete control of his life. He's definitely full of himself, though."

"Interesting."

"What?"

"You speak with fondness about Andrew, although there are clear indications he might be the killer, but your tone is a bit dry and reserved when you describe Daryl."

"Mm…" Sarah paused. "It could be that I've only now met Daryl."

"You only glanced briefly at Andrew."

"True, but that glance gave me more of a clear sense about him. So far Daryl has offered a rollercoaster of emotions. He's much more difficult to read. Curious, isn't it?"

"Yes, it certainly is. Listen, it's time for you to get some rest. We'll chat tomorrow night. Maybe I'll have some news for you by then and James will have called you back. Enjoy the time with your buddies tomorrow."

She switched off the lights, curled up in bed, and drifted off to sleep.

# ABERRANCE

Inside a seedy hotel room, a woman in her mid-twenties lay totally nude on the cracked linoleum floor, a pink sheer scarf tied loosely around her neck. A circle of small white candles in dainty crystal cups surrounded her. Her unblinking eyes focused on nothing.

Masculine hands gently caressed her inert body, the tips of the fingers stroking it with sensuous pleasure, the red birthmark visible on the back of the left hand.

He slid the scarf from her neck, closed her eyes, straightened her hair, and curled up beside her to nuzzle against her neck.

Sarah, heart pounding and sweat dotting her upper lip, shot upright in bed and glanced about the darkness apprehensively. She caught sight of the clock on the bedside table. "It's four in the morning! What the hell?"

She jumped out of bed and ran to the bathroom. Trembling, she gripped the rim of the sink. She plashed cold water on her face and the back of her neck, slumped onto the edge of the bathtub, and buried her face in a towel.

"This is too much. Whoever you are and whatever it is that you have in mind, I cannot be witnessing these things. They're macabre. You're transferring your pain and anguish to me—It aches... deeply." Tears flooded her eyes. "Please, stop."

She forced herself to regain her composure, took a long shower, and allowed the water to wash away the nightmare. She dried off and turned the television to the early morning news. She removed the towel from her head, and shook her hair loose.

"We've received many calls, as well as Twitter, and Facebook messages," the news anchorman announced, "requesting a replay of last night's report, given that many viewers missed the late evening news coverage. So we're pleased to rerun it throughout our morning coverage. Here is Armando Garcia."

A young reporter in a suit and tie, microphone in hand, appeared on the screen. "Good evening, we're coming to you from the California Medical Facility in Vacaville," he announced, "where Dr. Clarion, head of the State prison's psychiatric unit of the California Medical Facility, held a press conference late last night to show the filmed interview of John Rand's twenty third personality. As reported earlier, the name John Rand is the pseudonym given to him in order to protect his victims. John is also the name of one of the many personalities of this man, who escaped from the medical facility two weeks ago, and is yet to be apprehended. By releasing this last interview with John, Dr. Clarion and the Medical Board wish to offer the public a glimpse into this man and his illness. They also hope that someone might recognize him and lead authorities to his recapture."

A crude video image of two men sitting at a table in a small stark room flickered into focus. Dr. Clarion, a smallish man with tiny wire-rimmed glasses wearing a physician's white coat a couple of sizes too big, appeared on the left of the screen. A disheveled middle-aged man in hospital green pants and t-shirt sat on the right. The man twirled his hair around the index and middle fingers of one hand while shaking his head rhythmically. He had a blank stare, but somehow, also appeared fearful.

"John," Dr. Clarion got his attention. "I'd like to speak with Cameron, if I may. Would that be all right?"

John answered almost inaudibly. "Yeah, yeah. That would be okay."

For a moment, nothing happened. Then, John's head dropped. It moved in a circular motion that continued until his head was erect once again. He took a deep breath, blinked a couple of times, and opened his eyes into a fierce stare. His facial expression took on a threatening look for a second, then his eyes rolled, and he took another deep breath. His eyes popped open, this time with an expression of infantile surprise.

"Hi, Doc." His voice had a high-pitched childish quality. "Will you let me do some drawings today? I haven't done any for a long time."

"Hello, Peter, I would like to speak with Cameron, not with you at the moment. Maybe later you can do some drawing." Dr. Clarion called out, "Cameron, stop hiding. Only cowards hide behind children."

The man let out a loud grunt. He rose to his feet, lifted his chair above his head, and brought it down solidly onto the table. The chair clanged against the metal table. He then tossed the chair aside, and stood with his hands on his hips, head cocked in defiance.

Unperturbed, Dr. Clarion remained seated.

The man took a menacing step toward Dr. Clarion.

"Who da hell d'ya think yer callin' a coward? If you don't let me outta dis joint, I'm gonna rip yer damn little head off!" He pushed the table away and grabbed Dr. Clarion by the neck.

"If you kill me you can never get out," the doctor cried out.

"Fine." He eased his grip. "Let's walk out together, ya little shit." He yanked Dr. Clarion up from the chair and propelled him against the door.

Dr. Clarion yelled, "Cameron! Help! I need you, Cameron!"

The man froze in his tracks. For a second, John's body turned limp and his eyes rolled as if he were about to faint. As abruptly as before, he straightened up, opened his eyes, and looked about the room, appraising the situation. He spotted the chair on the floor. "My word." He shook his head. "Hello, Dr. Clarion." His voice had become several tones deeper and was cloaked in an impeccable British accent. "I notice you have met our boy, Paul. You are none the worse for wear, I trust?"

He helped Dr. Clarion up, then dragged the table to the middle of the room, picked up the chairs, placed them on either side of the table, and sat down calmly, resting his hands on his lap. He indicated for Dr. Clarion to sit.

The doctor sat across from him rubbing his neck. "Thank you, Cameron. Paul makes twenty three, doesn't it?"

"Indeed."

"Are you aware of any more?"

"No. As I have mentioned before, although I am aware of the lot, some may wish to hide from me. Not all appreciate my," he sneered, "ability to control. Paul, as you've witnessed, is quite volatile."

"Why hadn't you introduced me to Paul before?"

"My dear chap, it's obvious, isn't it?"

"Not to me."

"We are ashamed. He is, after all, the reason we got pinched. Isn't he?"

"When did he first emerge?"

"It's quite evident. Isn't it?"

"I'd like for you to enlighten me."

Cameron leaned back in the chair with a smirk on his face. "When he killed Mommy and Daddy, of course."

Dr. Clarion's eyes widened. "You," he hesitated, "you never told me…" he shook his head. "He couldn't have. You were, what—six years old? The carnage was—all along it's been assumed that some unknown perpetrator committed the crime."

"Oh, he did it, alright. And the boys gave him a standing ovation. Even our girls enjoyed it. Afterwards, quite cleverly, Louie emerged and took charge. He organized the lot as best he could and hid the entire horde behind John, who of course, to this day, has no recollection of what happened."

"But you never told me he had killed your—"

"I only found out a few months ago, and only because I caught them plotting."

"Plotting?"

"Yes. Paul said he had had enough of this place and planned to get rid of John. He solicited Louie's assistance. I overheard them and, as you can well imagine," he jutted his chin with pride, "I put a stop to it. Paul came after me, but I have managed to garner a great deal of support amongst the team, and I sincerely hope that we put an end to that absurd plan. It's safer for us here."

"Why didn't you tell me this before?"

Cameron cocked his head and grinned. "Because, dear boy, we prefer not to tattle. Instead we thought it best to give you a glimpse of our bad—no, no—our *worst* boy."

The filmed interview flickered off, and the reporter reappeared on the screen. "Paul, the twenty-third recorded personality of John Rand, is assumed to be the one that planned and executed the escape. As reported before, Dr. Clarion surmises that John split, or, disassociated personalities at the age of three as a result of severe physical and sexual assault by his parents. It was Dr. Clarion's testimony and filmed interviews with the various personalities that caused Mr. Rand to be incarcerated for life in a mental hospital. This last revelation by Cameron closes the case of the heinous murders of Mr. Rand's parents. However, it is also what propelled him to escape. We'll bring you more details on this bizarre case as they unfold. For Channel Three News, this is Armando Garcia at the California Medical Facility in Vacaville."

As the three friends ate their breakfast, Iris couldn't stop dissecting the televised interview "Didn't Sybil have fifteen or sixteen personalities?" she asked as she took a bite of her pastry and sipped her sweetened coffee.

"Yeah," Sonia answered, "at least that many."

"How awful life must've been for that guy, Rand, as a kid, just as it was for Sybil."

"Yeah, but he's out there, and there's no telling what trouble or violence he might be causing."

"He must be very clever to have escaped," said Iris. "You'd expect the staff to be more careful with him."

"Who knows how those mental institutions are run." Sonia sighed and sipped her coffee.

Iris looked at Sarah. "What do you think, Sarah? You're awfully quiet this morning."

"Am I? Sorry, had a bad night."

"That's 'cause you read——"

"Iris!" Sonia interjected.

"Oops, sorry. No mentioning of the darn crazy book allowed."

Sonia scowled and shook her head. "You're impossible. Anyway, what are we doing for our last day here?"

"I'd like to go shopping," Iris answered. " I'm done with the tourist stuff, given that our psychic pal is otherwise engaged. Plus, I have family and friends that expect me to bring them something from spooky Eureka."

"I'd like to explore the museums a bit slower," Sonia said. "We breezed through them looking for the ghosts."

JACKAL IN THE MIRROR

They turned to Sarah who shrugged. "I'll kick back and—"

"You're going to read your crazy book, aren't you?"

"Iris," Sonia scolded. "You promised."

"Sorry," Iris said. "Okay, how about the three of us meet up here for a late lunch? Let's say one thirty?"

They agreed.

"Sarah, if you hear from James, will you tell us?"

"Of course. Go on, enjoy yourselves." She watched the two leave while she finished her coffee.

Back in her room, Sarah eyed the book that sat on the small table in front of the fireplace. Resolutely, she picked it up. "If you need me to do something, stop playing games. Guide me for a change. I've had my fill of these bizarre images. Is Karla in danger? Is that why you keep showing her? Please, give me some answers."

She settled into the chair by the small table and opened the book.

# ECHO

"Furnell, who the hell is placing these scarves in my briefcase? Why can't your people find out what's going on?"

"I'm sorry, Mr. McKenzie," Furnell responded sheepishly. "We placed a tracking device in your briefcase to monitor its whereabouts. You've had your briefcase either in your home or here in your office the entire time and we have not seen anyone tamper with it."

"How can that be?" Exasperated, Daryl slammed his fist on his desk. "You may leave." He massaged his fist with his other hand as Furnell exited the office. "Susan!" he yelled.

"Yes, sir?"

"Get me some ice and a towel. Please."
"Right away, sir." She scampered out.

Sarah's cell phone rang, startling her. She reached for her purse and extracted it. "Hello?"

"Hey, Sarah, James here."

"James, I'm so glad you called."

"Sorry I haven't answered your messages, I've been helping some folks with a—never mind. What can I do for you?"

"Lots, I hope. Are you back?"

"No. I'm consulting away from Eureka. I usually don't allow interruptions when I'm working. It interferes with the flow of things."

"Oh, I'm so sorry, James. I didn't mean to interrupt you."

"Don't worry, my dear, anything for you. Having trouble with your book?"

"Serious trouble, I'd say. May I ask you a quick question?"

"Shoot."

"I now understand that the story from the book is entirely in my head. There are no appearing and disappearing pages."

"Yeah, I figured as much."

"You did?"

"I got the feeling early on that the person in need of your assistance is in some type of danger. Serious danger, I'd say. And the entity attached to your book is trying to help. But the exchange is difficult. I told you that I sensed reluctance, serious fear, maybe even guilt."

"The problem is that I'm detaching from the here and now when the images play in my head. To tell you the truth, I find it distressing"

"Remember, I warned you about entering into another person's reality. When you do that, you relinquish control."

"That's not—"

"Sometimes it's better for spirits to communicate by allowing you to experience what's going on."

"Yeah, I understand that, but I'm not experiencing being in someone's reality. I perceive the story as if I were reading it, witnessing the goings on. When the story takes over, I'm there and not here. When it releases me, I have no recollection of getting from point A to point B."

"I understand."

"This is new for me. In the past, even though I witnessed the events related to me by the spirits, I retained some control over my surroundings and my actions."

"And you don't want to lose control?"

"I most certainly don't. It's terrifying. Plus, why feed me this drip of stories I can't interpret? Why not tell me what I need to do to help?"

"Well, it might be difficult for this particular entity to do so."

"But if someone is in imminent danger, why not point me in the right direction instead of wasting valuable time?"

"My dear, I'm truly sorry I can't be there with you. You sound scared."

"I am, James. I saw on television about the Rand man with multiple personalities and—"

"You're afraid it's about him?"

"It could be. The Paul personality—"

"Yes, Paul is dangerous, but only to those who try to harm him. Do you sense anyone in the narrative you're witnessing that might harm Paul? Has he appeared in the story?"

"No. But the face of the most dangerous character in the story eludes me. If it's him, he'll likely harm others."

"Those you fear he could harm, do they pose a danger to him?"

"No, I don't believe they do. At least not so far."

"I don't wish to impart advice that's going to put you in harm's way. All I can suggest is that you listen to your instincts and follow them. But frankly, I can't imagine the Rand scenario playing out near you."

"Why do you say that?"

Sarah could almost feel James struggling with his response. "He's been on the loose for a couple of weeks. I don't sense anything about him in connection with you. I hope that helps."

137

She took a deep breath. "I'm being paranoid, aren't I? Any idea when you'll be back?"

"Not for a while. You'll probably be gone. When are you heading back home?"

"Tomorrow."

"I'll give you a call when I'm done. Maybe I can come visit with you, if that's okay. I'd like to visit your twin houses. And I'd very much like to meet Conrad."

"Consider it a date."

"Remember, Sarah, trust your instincts. They'll never let you down."

They rang off, and with great reluctance, Sarah turned her attention back to the book.

A love poem welcomed her.

### *LOVE*

*As the sun declines*
*And hides beyond*
*The night*
*I look*
*Forward*
*To the quiet times*
*With you*
*The candlelight*
*The wine*
*The tender*
*Smile*
*That says so much*
*The knowing that*
*Your hand is*
*Safe*
*In mine*
*We can watch the shadows*
*Dancing*
*As they rush along the walls*

*Or*
*Hear the breeze that's singing*
*All our memories*
*Not letting us forget*
*The way we loved*
*And love*

# 10

## THE SHIFT

Conrad sighed. "You're right, it's a stirring poem. Whoever wrote this book loved profoundly."

"Difficult to imagine that such a beautiful book of poems can be connected to the dreadful story of *Jackal in The Mirror*. To show me that title in the first place, and convince me that I'm reading a book that doesn't exist, is downright exasperating."

"But that's not what you need to focus on."

"Pray continue, Dr. Watson."

"It's clear to me, from what James told you, that someone is in serious trouble and you're being used to somehow offer that person help. Don't try to make sense of how it's presented, instead listen and learn as much as you can. Who needs your help?"

"Karla, or maybe Andrew."

"From what you've told me, that makes sense."

"You suspect that Rand guy might be the one?"

"No, I agree with James that this Rand fellow doesn't appear to be the one that's out to harm her. Watching that interview was simply a coincidence in my opinion."

"But what if he is the one cuddling up to those women after he kills them?"

"Did he have the birthmark in the clip you saw?"

"I didn't notice any."

"There you have it."

"So... who?"

"You'll have to wait for that."

"And Rand?"

"You're asking me if he can harm you?"

"Yes."

"No."

"That's pretty definitive."

"First, he's far from where you are. Vacaville is way south."

"Yeah, near San Francisco. And Karla."

"C'mon. Vacaville is almost sixty miles north of Frisco and he'd have to cross the bay. That's quite a trek for a mental patient who's running away with every law enforcement officer in the state on his tail. On the other hand, there's a lot of difficult terrain around Vacaville that's perfect for hiding."

"Boy, you're well informed."

"Yeah, I looked it all up." After a long pause, Conrad continued. "Anyway, I'm with James. You shouldn't fret about Rand. You want me to come join you?"

"No. One way or the other, I'm driving home tomorrow after the girls leave. I'll stop in Oregon for the night and be home the next day."

"What are you going to do this afternoon?"

"After lunch we'll probably hang around, I suppose. We've done about everything around here. Did you find out about Austen?"

"I haven't gotten a call back. Your pal the sheriff must be busy."

"How about Aldercrest or the McKenzie family?"

"Nothing. I'm pretty sure they're not real names. I did find a State Park named MacKerricher South of Eureka. The owners of the land that became the park were farmers and the town was created as a result of the railroad."

"Hold on, someone's knocking at the door." Phone in hand Sarah walked to the door and opened it.

Iris stormed in followed by Sonia. "What are you doing, we've been waiting for you?"

"Sorry, I took a nap and I've been on the phone with Conrad."

"Oh, let me say hi." Iris took the phone. "Hi there, handsome."

"Iris, I'm told that you've had a ball down there, even though Sarah disappointed you."

"Nonsense. She didn't disappoint me, quite the opposite. I'm in awe of her. I don't understand how she can do what she does. I would've liked for her to chat with some of the local ghosts and get the skinny on why they're here, and their lives, and all that stuff. But the book spirit is selfish and obsessive. A real pain in the ass. Anyhow, we've done a bunch of other interesting things. How are you?"

"I miss my wife, but other than that, all's well here."

"Hold on, Sonia would like to say hello." She handed the phone to Sonia.

"Conrad, hi. How about the kids and grandkids?"

"All well, Sonia. Are you taking care of Sarah? Iris can get under her skin and with—"

"Yep, I've got it under control, don't fret. Give the family hugs and kisses from all of us."

"I shall."

She handed the phone to Sarah.

"What was that all about?"

"Just banter."

"Okay, I'll call you tomorrow when I'm ready to hit the road. Love you."

"Enjoy your last day with the girls."

After she hung up, Sarah noticed that Iris had grabbed the book, opened it, and was reading. "Iris, what are you doing?"

Iris looked up. "These are exquisite poems. Listen to this one.

### *LOVELIGHT*

*Any kind of light*
*Is right to watch you by*
*Any kind of night*
*Is right for lullabies*

*So singing you to sleep*
*And seeing starlight in your eyes*
*Gives every single night*
*The greatest kind of light*
*For loving you*

Such beautiful images." Iris smiled. "Sarah, what do you make of it all?"

Sonia took the book from Iris, closed it and set it back on the small table. "C'mon you two, I'm starving. I found a place for lunch you'll both love. It's called Café Nooner. I found it on the web yesterday and it was featured on the Food Network show Diners, Drive-Ins and Dives."

"I love that show," Iris chimed in.

"Anyway, apparently the owners dropped their corporate jobs, and with zero experience in the restaurant business, they opened this very successful café. They serve some type of Mediterranean-Creole-fusion style food using all local and organic produce."

They left the room and Sarah closed the door behind them.

After lunch, while waiting for change from their bill, Sonia withdrew a paper from her purse. "I discovered another thing we can do this afternoon that'll help shed at least one ounce of the pounds we just put on."

"I'm certainly up for doing something after this meal," said Sarah. "What is it?"

"A tour on the historic *Madaket*."

"What's that? Sounds like a market or something." Iris said.

"It's the oldest continuously operating passenger vessel in the country. Their website says that we'll learn the history of Humboldt Bay and Eureka's waterfront during a narrated cruise. It travels along the shores of the bay and the captain explains the local history, points of interests, and wildlife."

"Lead on, Macduff," Sarah said.

The three exited the restaurant and headed toward C Street, pausing from time to time for window-shopping or to view some local handicraft.

Down at the dock, they purchased the boarding passes and headed to the front of the boat.

The *Madaket* departed, and moments later the captain welcomed everyone aboard. After the cursory safety reminders and emergency procedures, the narration began. "The *Madaket* is the last remaining vessel of a seven-vessel fleet that once transported families and workers around Humboldt Bay. There were mill workers and longshoremen…"

Sarah closed her eyes to enjoy the fresh breeze of the bay while the vessel followed the contours of the shore and the captain's narration continued.

## DEPARTURE

Karla, in designer blue jeans and a long-sleeved white shirt, got on her knees, and dug deep in the back of her closet. The search produced a pair of hiking boots, which she tossed onto the floor. She crossed the room to a chest where she found two pairs of thick socks in a drawer. She slipped one pair on, followed by the boots. The other pair was tossed into a carry-on suitcase along with extra clothing. Karla headed to the bathroom and gathered up her essentials. She closed her suitcase and headed to the living room, where she dropped it by the front door.

At her desk, she picked up her briefcase, packed her laptop, a notebook, and a couple of books. She grabbed her cell phone and examined it closely, wrote something on a small pad, tore it off, and stuffed it into her shirt pocket.

Carrying her purse and both her bags, she stepped outside, slamming the door behind her.

After loading everything into her car, she took off through the streets of San Francisco. She headed north across the Bay Bridge, leaving the city behind.

*Sarah, you must leave. You must help Karla. You must leave, right now!*

Sarah spun around in search of the source of the voice, even though she knew it wouldn't be there. She escaped to the back of the ship.

Puzzled by Sarah's sudden departure, Iris and Sonia glanced at each other and followed.

Once they reached her, Iris touched Sarah's shoulder. "What's the rush?"

"What? Oh. No rush. Got tired of being upfront. Anyway, we're about to get off."

Sarah's phone crackled. "What's wrong with my phone?" She fished the phone out of her purse and pressed the answer button. Through piercing static she perceived the words.

*"Sarah, you must leave now!"*

"You look a bit pale," Iris noted with concern. "Are you okay?"

*"Now!"* The screeching voice shook Sarah's entire body. *"Now!"* it yelled again. *"Now, now, now!"*

Sarah covered her ears and shut her eyes.

Sonia reached for her. "Sarah, what's wrong?"

Sarah opened her eyes, shut off the phone and dropped it in her bag. "Nothing, a horrible headache."

"I'll get you something to drink, I have some aspirin," Iris said as she moved towards the center of the ship.

"Don't bother, Iris," Sarah called out.

Sonia wrapped her arms around Sarah and guided her toward an empty seat. "C'mon, sit down. You're white as a sheet. Are you dizzy? Seasick?"

"No, just a bad headache."

Iris returned empty-handed. "No drinks. We're docking."

The captain announced that the docking procedures were about to start, and thanked the passengers for their patronage. Once the ship was docked, the friends exited the vessel and headed back to their hotel.

Sarah apologized when they reached the lobby. "Sorry to be such a party pooper. If you don't mind, I'm going to go lie down. I had very little sleep last night. I'm beat."

Without waiting for a response, she hurried back to her room.

Moments later, Sarah snatched up the book and frantically scanned its pages. She slammed it shut. "Nothing but poems."

*You must help her, Sarah! Now!*

"Stop getting into my head! To help her, I need more than poems!" Sarah yelled.

She pulled her cell phone from her purse and stared at it. With reluctance she turned it on and waited. When the phone remained silent and free of static, she ventured a call.

"All done?" Conrad asked, with optimistic cheer.

"No. I'm hearing voices."

"Voices?"

"Well, *the* voice. The woman's voice."

"You've heard her before."

"Yeah, but now she's screaming at me through the phone."

"What does she say?"

"That I need to leave immediately and help Karla."

"Leave where? Eureka?"

"Where else?"

"Where does she want you to go?"

"I have no idea."

"And the story in the book?"

"A glimpse of Karla leaving San Francisco headed north, then the woman's voice yelling that I needed to go. I open the book and find only the poems."

"At least you've confirmed that San Francisco is where Karla is."

Sarah sighed. "Yeah, but she's gone. No idea where." She closed her eyes and shook her head. "This entire trip has been a fiasco."

"It has not. You've spent some time with Iris and Sonia, you've visited some interesting things, and seen some beautiful scenery. And, don't forget, you've met James."

She took a deep breath and forced herself to calm down. "You're right, as usual."

"Give yourself a break."

"It's not me. The woman is hysterical. She yells at me with this incredible urgency that I need to go and help Karla, but she doesn't tell me where. Her screams tear into my head. It hurts and it's nerve wracking."

"I can only imagine what's it like. But it's not surprising. Remember she's pure energy."

"Which is affecting my phone."

"How?"

"Loud crackling, and when I turn it on, screeching static along with her screams."

"What an effort to release so much energy."

"I get that...oh..." she sighed, "she's so real to me, I forget she's dead."

"C'mon, maybe together we can figure out where Karla's heading? Any clues?"

"The last bit of story had her leaving across the Bay Bridge."

"That's a start. Once you calm down—"

"How can I? I'm supposed to rush off to *somewhere* in search of a woman whose real name I don't even know."

"Yeah, that's what you're going to do."

"And I suppose you're fine with me gallivanting all over the California countryside."

Conrad chuckled in a conscious effort to bring some levity to the situation. "Gallivanting, huh? No, I don't like it one bit, but I'm a realist. You can't stop yourself when you sense that someone's in trouble. You're going to do whatever it takes, no matter what. I'll fly down and meet you and we'll work this out together."

"No, no, Conrad, please don't."

"Tom can handle the store without me and—"

"No, I'll be okay. It's plain stupid to lose control and call you over nothing."

"Nonsense, Sarah. I can tell this has you pretty rattled. I'll check on flights to Eureka—"

"No, *please*, no. All the flights we found were expensive and went to San Francisco first. You'll lose an entire day trying to get here."

"Let's make a deal—we meet in San Francisco. We can look around there. Later we can drive back home together. I'd like to stop in Eureka on the way back and maybe meet James."

"You spoil me."

"Let's hope so. I'll call you when I have a flight booked. Hopefully I can get there tomorrow. I'll book us a room in San Francisco and we'll take it from there."

"See you tomorrow. I love you," she whispered as she hung up.

She stared at the book for a moment, shook her head, and strode to the bathroom. She filled the tub, testing the water until it reached a perfect temperature, added an aromatic bubble bath, and got undressed. She slipped in, closed her eyes, and allowed her body a chance to relax.

# THE SPARK

The room, suffused in the dim light from three beeswax candles in a brass candelabrum that sat on the desk, embraced the couple in a cocoon of comfort. The mountain cabin stood silent save for the natural evening lullabies that hummed in the wilderness surrounding it.

The young man wrote in a small notebook. He glanced at the woman asleep in the bed, her nude body caressed by the sheets. He smiled as his eyes traced every inch of her. He stopped and lingered on her lips, the memory of their union fresh in his mind and body.

Even with her eyes closed, she knew he was looking at her, and enjoyed the awareness that she pleased him.

A few hours earlier, she'd arrived at the cabin and waited for him, afraid and reluctant, but despite it all, anxious to welcome his embrace. They knew it was wrong to surrender to their long-concealed emotions and the desire that burned inside them, but awareness of right and wrong had not stopped them from consummating their love.

Now, she reveled in the memory of how he'd pulled her to him, his mouth hungry for hers, his arms sliding over her chilled shoulders. Could the same memory be traveling though him, she wondered?

At the same moment, he savored the recollection of how she'd trembled under his embrace and her complete surrender to him, her body welcoming his. He'd kissed her with such need, such desperate ferocity, that she'd whimpered, and he'd pulled back, but she reached behind his neck and drew him to her, reciprocating his hunger.

Now, even as he wrote down the emotions she inspired, he smiled, reminiscing how he'd undressed her without his lips ever leaving hers, and gently lowered her onto the bed. How his eyes had devoured her body moaning with desire, as he'd shed his clothes and descended toward her. "Martha," he'd said, his voice low and deep as he slipped inside her.

She'd placed her slender finger over his lips. "I don't wish to hear who I am, or who you are," she'd whispered into his mouth, "let's be us."

When he'd joined with her at last, the endless years of restraint, of distance, of denial, had erupted into a frenzy of kisses, bites, and strokes that craved full possession. Their passion, finally unbridled and free of restraint, had been spontaneous, irrepressible, and honest. Their union had lasted mere minutes, but reflected an eternity. They knew that by having allowed their passion to materialize, nothing would stand in its way.

He set down his pen and turned toward her. He watched her breathe and his tongue ran over his lips, the taste of her still palpable, her scent lingering. He sighed and returned to his notebook.

She opened her eyes and smiled, comfortable in the realization that her mind was one with his, and as such, could savor the poems he wrote for her.

Sarah's eyes popped open. "Martha…" she whispered. "Your lover wrote these poems for you. Who is he?"

Silence.

She emerged from the bathtub and dried herself.

"I understand why you're apprehensive. I'm sure it must've been difficult for you to engage in this relationship. But, why be so coy about it? This must've happened in your twenties? Surely it doesn't matter now?"

Silence.

There was a knock at the door. Sarah slipped into the terrycloth robe and opened the door. Iris pranced in followed by Sonia.

"You look much better," Iris said. "Headache gone?"

"Yes. Took a nice hot bath."

"Can we get you something? Maybe bring you dinner?" Sonia asked.

"I'm not hungry, only tired. You guys go ahead, I'm going to turn in early tonight."

"Only if you're sure."

"I am. We'll have breakfast in the morning. Nine...ish?" Sarah asked.

"That's sounds good." Sonia hugged Sarah and kissed her on the cheek. "I hope you have a restful night. Call us if you need anything."

Iris joined in, hugging both women. "Call us even if you don't need anything. That's what friends are for. We're just down the hallway."

"Thank you. Love you both."

They departed in a flurry of gentle bickering, and Sarah shut the door behind them. She approached the table where the book lay and picked it up.

"This illicit affair is the reason you're changing the actual names and not giving me the full picture. Tell me if I'm wrong."

Silence.

"No dialogue with you, a one-sided conversation except when you yell at me." She paused. "Yeah, I get it, your way is to give me the book of poems, and offer me bits and pieces of Karla's story and glimpses of your past."

She slid into her nightgown and got in bed. "Okay. Let's read the poems he wrote for you that night." She opened the book.

### *YOU*

*As questions rise*
*And then subside*
*To reappear some other time*
*A constant flow*
*Of unknown thoughts*
*Of feeling*
*Strong as life*
*Emerge as nonsense words*

*Despair and love*
*Within one phrase*
*Cannot a man's true feelings*
*Say*
*And yet*
*When all is done*
*When all is said*
*The feeling still remains*
*So new*
*So fresh*
*And if words could stand alone*
*With words I'd build the highest walls*
*Pave the straightest road*
*And find the brightest light*
*And with the world locked out*
*A road to you*
*And the sun to light my way*
*The wall I'll make*
*The road I'll build*
*But*
*The light*
*Is always*
*You*

**THEN and NOW**

*What have you done to me*
*What chord's been struck*
*What tune's been played*
*Composed and sung*
*Since first we met*
*What sun rises*
*What moon shines*
*Through what door*
*Did indifference leave*

*And love arrive*

*I know before*
*When I peered inside*
*There was a night*
*Of darkest black*
*No stars*
*No sun*
*No here I am*
*No take this hand*
*And be my friend*

*What I recall*
*Is an endless end*
*A spiral going nowhere*
*Now*
*Flowers grow*
*And children laugh*
*And birds have wings*
*To fly*

# ALDERCREST

Karla drove along a winding mountain road nearly obscured by a blanket of thick fog.

She passed a road sign shrouded in low-hanging clouds that distorted its information. She squinted as she leaned forward in an effort to read. "Did it say Clear Lake? Oh, hell!"

Karla continued carefully down the narrow mountain road, the fog allowing forty feet of visibility at best.

At long last, a handful of dim lights broke through the gloom. "God, I hope this is the right place." A small scenic village emerged, surrounded by lush mountain greenery. Fog seeped through the trees and floated across the buildings in waves, its tiny drops of water clinging to the day's dust and dirt.

Spotting a motel, she pulled in, parking directly in front of the office door. Karla stepped out of the car and stretched to release the tension of the drive. She waved her hands through the moist air and rubbed her damp fingers. "Talk about a heavy fog."

She reached for her purse, shut the car door, and climbed the steps toward the illuminated door facing the parking lot.

The office consisted of a small room with a desk and a bell next to a sign that read: *Ring for Service.* Karla followed the instructions.

A door behind the desk creaked open and a plump woman in her late fifties emerged. Her unruly white hair had been tied in long braids adorned with leather straps. She wore tattered slippers, jeans, and a tie-dyed T-shirt that did nothing to disguise her stout shape. She sported a broad smile and kind eyes. "Hi there. Welcome to the beautiful Mountain Lodge. I'm Judy, how can I help you?"

"Is this Aldercrest? The fog is so thick I'm not sure I read the road sign correctly."

"Yes, ma'am, you're in the right place. This fog though, is real strange for us. We don't get much fog around here. The mountains tend to keep it out, or in this case, in. Glad you found us. That fog bank is like driving through whipped cream." She giggled.

"I'd like a room, please, if you have any vacancies."

"Lake view?"

"Uh, sure. That would be great."

"How long are you staying?"

"I haven't decided." She pulled a wallet from her purse, and handed Judy a credit card. "Could you keep it open?"

Judy turned the registry around. "Sure thing, no problem. Write your particulars right here."

While Karla entered her information, Judy processed her credit card.

"What brings you out here? Vacation?"

"Not exactly. I'm a reporter and I'm writing a story on the McKenzie family. Do you know them?"

Judy returned Karla's credit card and turned the registry around. "Well, I know *of* them. It's said they put the town on the map. In fact, our main street is named after them."

"Really? Are there any members of the family still living around here?"

Judy squinted in an effort to recollect. "Don't think so. I've only been here for five years, though. You should ask Elisa, the waitress at Pines, the local diner. It's a few blocks down McKenzie Street."

"Where is that?"

"Yeah, right, the fog. Nothing to it, if you go out of our parking lot and hang a left, you'll come to McKenzie Street. You missed it 'cause of the fog, but it's not far from here at all."

Judy opened a drawer under the desk and handed her the room key.

"Thank you."

"Sure thing, honey. Your room is down at the end, facing the lake." She pointed to her left. "You can leave your car parked where it is if you like, or you can move it right in front your door. Parking is not assigned. Enjoy your stay."

"Thanks, Judy. I will."

Karla closed the door behind her, stepped down to her car and attempted to spot the end of the motel. The thick fog covered the entire lot, so she decided to leave the car put. She grabbed her briefcase and suitcase, and walked the length of the porch to her room.

She opened the door, and switched on the light. "Well, at least it's not a dump."

The room had a queen-sized bed with a plush comforter, plenty of pillows of varying sizes, and a beautiful carved redwood headboard. The bed was framed by two matching redwood night tables with large lamps shaped like pinecones. A deep sofa with lavish multi-shaped cushions occupied one corner, while a desk and office chair stood in the opposite corner. A redwood credenza with a small refrigerator faced the bed, and was topped by a coffee maker and bar accouterments. A large flat-screen television had been installed on the wall above it. Paintings of the lake and its surroundings adorned the walls.

She unpacked quickly, left the lodge behind, and turned onto McKenzie Street. The main street showcased curiosity shops of all types and sizes, an arcade with electronic games, and a bowling alley. Between the shops and a parking lot, a red, white, and blue flashing neon sign read, "Pines: Best Diner in Town."

She stepped through the door and entered a large, rustic, log-cabin-type room with tables in the center and booths along three walls. The fourth wall had a counter lined with stools and access to the kitchen behind it. The diner was empty at this hour, except for an elderly couple parked in a corner booth. The old man played checkers solo as his companion snoozed, her head bobbing, quietly snoring.

A fiftyish waitress—red-haired, heavily made-up and clearly hoping to look thirtyish—sat cleaning her nails and humming. She looked up and spotted Karla standing by the door. She shoved the nail file into an apron pocket and flashed a well-practiced smile "Welcome to Pines. Pick a place and make it your own."

"Thanks." Karla found a table that overlooked the entire place and sat down.

"Menus are on the table."

"What do you recommend?"

"Beef stew."

"Okay. Beef stew, please."

"To drink?"

"Iced tea."

"Coming right up."

The front door of the diner flew open and a large middle-aged man entered. He'd been working hard at something that induced heavy sweating, and it showed. He cheerfully greeted everybody with a tip of his cap.

"Hey, Darlin'," he said to the waitress, "yer baby's home and he needs some o' that good ol' mother's milk. Ice cold and foamin'." He ambled over to where the elderly man sat and immediately picked up on the game of checkers. The old woman didn't stir and continued snoring.

The waitress slammed a bottle of beer down on the counter and yelled. "Ned, come and get it if you want it."

Ned strutted over to the counter. "Sure thing, my Elisa. Anything you ask, darlin'." He reached toward her, but she spun away and strode toward Karla with the glass of iced tea, which she placed in front of her.

"Thanks."

"Don't mention it. Stew will be right up." She sashayed back toward the kitchen, swaying her hips with the clear intention of enticing Ned.

"You keep that dance up, Darlin'." He winked and returned to the checkers game.

Moments later Elisa emerged from the kitchen carrying a bowl in one hand and a breadbasket in the other. She set them in front of Karla. "Anything else, honey?"

"No, thank you. But maybe you could tell me where I could find the McKenzies."

"Which ones do you mean?"

"The McKenzie family, the one whose name is on the main street."

"Are you a relative or something?"

"No. I'm a reporter and I'm doing a story on the town and the McKenzie family."

"You're too late for that. They're all gone or dead. Nothing left of them—except for Mary Ellen. But she ain't really a McKenzie." She waited in silence, expecting Karla to react.

Karla squinted at her with curiosity. "Mary Ellen?"

"She was Martha's babysitter. Jennifer's too. And the boys."

"Jennifer?"

Elisa cocked her head. "Martha's sister."

"Oh, that Jennifer."

"'Course, I haven't seen her in over a year, so could be she's dead."

"You mean Jennifer?"

"No, Mary Ellen," Elisa said impatiently.

"I get it."

"Damn, Ned." The older man banged the table and proceeded to arrange the checker pieces while Ned guffawed.

Startled by the noise, both Karla and Elisa looked toward them.

"Be right back, Jer." Ned stood up, grabbed his beer, and walked toward the two women.

"You looking for Mary Ellen? Oh, she's alive all right. I fixed her water heater 'bout six weeks ago."

"Could you tell me how to get to her house?"

"Sure, if ya really wanna go all by yerself up to that lonely cabin. It's clear at the top o' the mountain. And you're aware what happened up there?"

Karla nodded courteously in the hope that Elisa and Ned would keep talking.

"Those are silly ol' stories made up by a bunch of scared old fools." Elisa smirked. "Mary Ellen doesn't mind. She's lived there all alone for years."

"Yup. All alone." Ned lowered his voice in mock suspense. "Surrounded by ghosts."

Karla ate in silence as Elisa and the man glared at each other.

"She's way smarter than you and your useless lot hangin' around bars and diners." Elisa made a swift turn and marched off with a pronounced sway.

Ned laughed and swatted Elisa as she went by. She giggled.

"Wow! That woman can get me goin'."

"So," Karla said to get his attention, "can you tell me how to get there?"

"Sure. Take the first road to the right off of McKenzie Street. It's called Summit. You can't miss it, even in this weird fog. The road dead-ends at her house."

He winked at her and headed back to his checker game.

Karla finished her stew and walked toward Elisa. "How much do I owe you?"

"Ten fifty."

"Is there a County registrar anywhere near?"

"Yeah, a couple of doors down the street."

"How about a newspaper office?"

"Same place."

"Thanks for everything. The stew was delicious."

She left the diner as a cold evening breeze swept along the main artery of Aldercrest. Shivering, she scurried down the street. As she turned the corner she bumped into a man. "I'm sorry," she said.

"No problem," James answered.

"James!" Sarah sat up in bed. "My, God. James is there." She reached for her cell phone and dialed.

"Mm?" a groggy Conrad answered.

"James is there," Sarah blurted out. "He's there. He bumped into Karla."

"Sarah, please. You realize it's two-thirty in the morning?"

"He bumped into Karla."

"Where—"

"I dreamed it. He's there."

"I get you that James is there. But where is there?"

"Aldercrest. I'm going there."

"Calm down, Sarah. A place named Aldercrest doesn't exist."

"I'm aware of that, but I'll find the real place. Martha finally showed me a glimpse of where I need to go."

"Martha?"

"Yeah, she's the one talking to me through the book. It's her book. Well, sort of. Her lover wrote those poems for her."

"Wow! Lots of information since we last spoke."

"They had an affair and he was a poet."

"How—"

"She showed me a glimpse of their love."

"A couple of pieces of the puzzle have fallen into place."

"James is in Aldercrest—"

"But—"

"I'm well aware that's not the real name. Nevertheless, they're both in the same town, Clear Lake, that's the real name. Karla saw a sign on the road."

"But it could also be a false one."

"No, Clear Lake exists, I saw it on the map when I was looking for—"

"That doesn't mean that's where they are."

"She showed me James, so clearly that's where I need to be. I'm leaving right now. It was nighttime there and it's nighttime here. I have to catch up with them. You don't need to come here. I'll be with James."

Conrad tried to slow her down. "Hold on Sarah, I don't like the sound of this. You need to calm down and figure things out."

"I don't have time for that. I'm checking out. I'll leave a note with my goodbyes for the girls. I'll call you when I get there."

"But—"

"Don't worry, I'll be with James. He'll take care of me. Love you."

She rang off, grabbed the hotel telephone from the nightstand, and dialed the front desk, but there was no answer. "Oh, that's right. No one's there till the morning. I'll leave them a note saying that something came up and that I had to check out during the night."

Her cell phone rang. She glanced at it and saw Conrad's smiling face, but before she could answer, the phone growled, the image disappeared, and static replaced his face.

"Martha," she protested, "don't interfere! Let him through!"

The phone grumbled.

She snatched up the hotel's phone. No dial tone, only static.

Frustrated, she got her suitcase, gathered all her belongings and threw them inside. She wrote a couple of quick notes to Sonia and Iris on the hotel's letterhead, and put them in her purse along with her cell and the book. She dropped the notes off at the front desk, and left.

She got into her car and took off. The streets of Eureka were deserted at that time of night, providing her with a moment to gather her thoughts. "C'mon," she whispered, "time to give me more clues, Martha."

### TIMES

*So strange a thing*
*I seem to feel*
*At times*

*Almost as though*
*I heard myself*
*Then turned*
*And found me*

*Gone*

*And wondered*
*Why I left*

*Sometimes I reach*
*To touch a rose*
*And*
*Though I hold it*
*In my hand*
*I touch it not*

*Somehow I stop myself from*
*Feelings that I feel*
*Or seeing sights*
*That I can see*

*The moon now hides*
*Behind the clouds*
*The mountains roam*
*In fog*

*My clumsy hands*
*Cannot hold flowers*
*And so I go*
*Alone*

"For crying out loud, Martha! The last thing I need is a poem bouncing around in my head!" Sarah drove into the dark, Eureka's lights fading away in the rear view mirror. "I'm on the road at three-thirty in the morning because you need me to help Karla, and I have no idea if where I'm heading is correct. I get the urgency, but a little help won't hurt."

Silence.

"I'm going to take your silence as confirmation I'm heading in the right direction."

# 11

# THE SEARCH

Sarah squinted as she struggled to follow the road through a blanket of heavy fog. "This is ridiculous. Martha, you need to be more helpful. Why did we veer off back there?"

Martha remained silent.

"This fog keeps getting thicker and thicker. You better tell me if we're still heading for Clear Lake or you're taking me somewhere else."

Eventually, the lack of visibility forced her to find a safe place and pull to the side of the road. She grabbed her cell phone, hoping to pinpoint her location, but there was no reception.

"This is your doing Martha, and I don't like it. I can't help if you keep me in the dark." She looked at her watch. "All I can do is wait it out. Sunrise should be around the corner."

She leaned her head back on the headrest, sighed with exasperation, and closed her eyes.

## ENLIGHTENMENT

Karla walked briskly along McKenzie Street until she spotted it, a small sign dangling above a doorway. *Registrar, Notary Public, Printing, Copies. Aldercrest*

*Mirror. Joseph Klass, Editor.* The door itself had another sign: *Open Daily 9:00 A.M. - 5:00 P.M.*

She sighed, turned away, and returned to the lodge. She reached the parking lot in time to catch a glimpse of what looked like Andrew's metallic-blue Jeep Wrangler speeding by. She froze in her tracks, wondering if Andrew might be at the wheel. She ran to her car, revved it and gave chase, but the Jeep had darted too quickly up the road and eluded her. After a few hundred feet, she gave up. Resigned, she turned around and headed off in search of Summit Road.

Minutes later, she turned onto the road and ascended a steep hill. Trees arched overhead, forming a tunnel over the dirt road that twisted and turned incessantly. Wisps of fog cast eerie shadows across the road as the crescent moon shined here and there through the trees.

As if the incessant curves weren't enough, the road made a sudden sharp turn and Karla faced an even steeper incline. She advanced with caution as she climbed the twisting road.

The fog became denser. Karla clung to the wheel, her chest almost touching it. The car's fog lights provided little visibility as she crept along, unable to find even the edge of the road.

Abruptly, the side of the mountain shot up in front of her. She stopped the car and turned off the engine. She peered in all directions but saw only fog, a few boulders, and the occasional tree branch.

"He did say at the end of the road. This must be it."

She pulled a flashlight from the glove compartment, and cautiously exited the car. Unable to discern her surroundings, she crept around the car in search of a driveway or any sign of a house. She found nothing.

Faintly visible through the fog she spotted two dim lights above her in the distance. Gingerly, she trudged up the mountain toward the glowing lights, her eyes on the ground watching every step she took.

Abruptly, the lights went out.

Karla froze.

Other than the beam of light from her flashlight, only darkness, dense fog, and a chilly breeze surrounded her. "Hello? Is there anyone there? I need help!"

No response.

She continued to advance cautiously in the direction where the lights had been, following the beam from her flashlight.

A makeshift stone step appeared. She moved closer, and another appeared immediately above it. She looked about for a structure, but the fog remained so thick that all she could recognize was the rugged mountainous terrain covered by dense water droplets and moss.

She took one cautious step up, and then another, but on the third step she slipped on the wet stone and slid to the ground. She put the flashlight in her mouth, crouched, and climbed the makeshift steps on all fours. Much to her surprise and relief, the next step she found was made entirely of wood.

As her gaze searched upward, the silhouette of a structure, barely distinguishable in the gloom, took shape. She rose and climbed the last few steps until she stood on wooden planking. "A porch?"

She pointed her flashlight first right and then left in search of any sign confirming that indeed her feet stood on a porch. The plank was lined with old boxes and crates stacked on top of each other. She aimed the beam of light right in front of her and, as she inched forward, a door opened and a blinding light burst through the fog.

Startled, Karla stepped back and dropped her flashlight.

"Stay where you are," warned a raspy female voice. "I got two barrels aimed right at your gut." A second later, the shotgun poked Karla in the stomach.

"Oh, my God. Please, please don't shoot. I mean you no harm."

"Who are you?"

"Are you Mary Ellen?"

"I got the gun, I do the asking."

"I'm looking for a woman named Mary Ellen."

"Why? Who are you?"

"I'm a reporter. My name is Karla Jordan. I'm doing a story about the McKenzie family and I was told that you could give me some information about them."

"Who else is with you?"

"I came here by myself."

The shotgun retreated from her stomach, much to Karla's relief. "That was a damn stupid thing to do," the raspy voice said.

"I couldn't agree with you more."

The woman with the shotgun didn't make a sound for several seconds.

All that Karla could distinguish against the blinding light was the woman's small silhouette, as she stood motionless in the open door with the weapon resting across her body.

"Please," Karla said. "I didn't mean to inconvenience you. If you'd like, I'll go back to my car and when the fog lifts I'll leave and come back tomorrow. That is, if you are Mary Ellen."

"What's your interest in the McKenzies?"

"I read some noteworthy stories about the town and my publisher suggested there might be interesting angles to cover."

Silence.

Karla squinted, trying to make out the woman behind the shotgun.

"Interesting angles? Damn the noteworthy stories."

"Are you Mary Ellen?"

"Of course I am, and you sure as hell know I am. Don't imagine for a minute you can pull one over on me, young lady." She snorted. "No sense shivering out here in the cold. You might as well come in."

She lowered the shotgun, turned, and disappeared inside the house.

Karla followed her across the creaking porch.

"Well, thanks for nothing, Martha." Sarah frowned. "Karla is deep in the fog in some godforsaken place up some mountain, and I'm in the same soup, parked on a godforsaken road with no idea where it leads."

The dense fog had not lessened with the sunrise. However, with the light of day, and bolstered by a brief rest, Sarah started the car and continued to follow the narrow mountain road. As she proceeded, she spotted a road sign, but the fog made it impossible to read. Nevertheless, she continued forward. A few minutes and a handful of curves later, she pulled into the roadside motel on the outskirts of a small town.

The motel in no way resembled the Mountain Lodge Sarah had witnessed through Martha's tale. This one consisted of small, isolated cabins that stood parallel to each other, all painted in white with red A-frame roofs. Each cabin had a small driveway leading to the front door and two parking slots next to it.

Sarah pulled up in front of a cabin with a red neon sign that blinked "Office Open." She got out of the car and approached the door. As she reached for the knob, the door flew open. A large heavyset man wearing a Hawaiian shirt and straw hat stepped out, bumping into Sarah.

"Sorry, ma'am," he removed his hat and bowed his head in a sign of contrition.

"It's all right."

He opened the door for Sarah and bowed. "Please." Sarah stepped in and thanked the man, who closed the door behind her.

A petite young woman with very short platinum hair, heavy black eye makeup, and large round glasses stood behind a small counter. "Hi there, I'm Ann. Welcome to Cozy Cabins. You looking to book one?"

Sarah approached the young woman. "I'm not sure if I'll be staying yet. Where exactly am I? The fog made it impossible to read the road signs."

"North Lake."

Sarah sighed. "Could you tell me if there's a sheriff's department nearby?"

"Are you in trouble?" Ann asked with concern.

Sarah smiled. "No, no. I just need to find it."

169

Ann raised her eyebrows. "Are you lost or something? I can call the Sheriff if you'd like."

Sarah tried to ease the woman's concerns. "No, that won't be necessary. I'm perfectly all right. I'm looking for a friend of mine that does some consulting for the police or the sheriff's departments, only I'm not certain which station he's working with."

Ann thought it over. "Well I'd say he'd be with the Chief, wouldn't you?"

"That makes sense. Where would I find him?"

The young woman giggled. "Lakeport, of course."

"How far is that from here?"

"Well, let me get you the address. Hold on." She grabbed her cell phone and typed. She scrolled and tapped a few times, grabbed a piece of paper, and wrote down the address. "Here you go. Do you have a GPS?"

"My phone's been acting up—can you give me a sense of where it is?"

"Nothing to it. I'll write it down for you. Sounds more complicated than it really is." She wrote the directions. "At the traffic circle take the first exit onto Parallel Drive. They're right there on the left." She handed Sarah the paper.

"Thanks. Is there a place for breakfast nearby?"

"Yeah, there's a coffee shop down the street. You can leave your car right here if you like. It's easier to walk down there. Parking can be tough."

"Thanks. I'm Sarah by the way." She extended her hand.

She shook Sarah's hand. "If you decide to stay, make sure you come back here. The cabins are real nice."

"I will. Thanks for all your help, Ann."

"No sweat. Bye."

"Bye."

Outside, Sarah locked her car and made her way toward the coffee shop. As she walked down the street she caught sight of a metallic-blue Jeep Wrangler coming towards her. "Andrew's car," she whispered. The Jeep drove past her and disappeared around the next corner.

She shook her head and continued walking. *Now, I'm seeing things.*

She entered the coffee shop to find a picture-perfect country-style room complete with doilies, wooden chairs with tied-on cushioned seats, matching curtains, and a delicious scent of freshly baked bread.

A young woman who could've passed for Dorothy in *The Wizard of Oz* welcomed her with a smile. "Good morning, I'm Amy your hostess. Breakfast for one?"

"Good morning to you Amy, and yes, thank you."

"Please, follow me."

The coffee shop was full, with only a couple of empty tables. Sarah followed the young woman to one and settled into a chair. The woman handed her the menu. "Would you like some coffee?"

"I'd love some, thanks."

"Curtis will be your waiter, and he'll be here in no time. Enjoy your breakfast."

"Thanks." Sarah had barely opened the menu when her coffee appeared, along with a glass of water.

Curtis, a freckled redhead decked out in a checkered shirt with a bowtie, black pants, and a forest green apron, grinned down at her. "Good morning, I'm Curtis, and I aim to please. Are you ready, or would you like some suggestions?"

Sarah closed the menu. "I'd love suggestions, thank you."

"We bake our own bread and pies as well as doughnuts, bear claws, and all that good stuff that goes real well with our fresh fruits. We make the best pancakes in the area and serve them with our homemade syrups, and anything with eggs is cooked to perfection. Our famous Eggs Benedict are mouth watering."

"Well, Curtis, you've done a superb job of tempting me. From that marvelous list, what would *you* choose?"

"For the eggs I'd go with the Benedict, but if you prefer pastry, I'd say a sampler basket with our fresh-picked berries and a side of cream."

"The sampler with the berries and cream it is. You're well versed on the food—you make it all sound delicious."

"I should. It's my folks' place. Amy, the hostess is my little sister. My mom is the chef and my dad does the business stuff. I'm hoping to train as a chef and follow my mom. Sis likes the business side, and schmoozing with the guests. So, we're here to stay, it looks like. "

Sarah smiled. "Well, Curtis, I wish you all the very best."

"Thanks. I'll be back with your food in no time."

Sarah sat back and prepared to enjoy her cup of coffee.

# RECURRENCE

The familiar rhythmic paddling broke the near-stillness of the lake, the crickets chirping in harmony with the oars. The weathered rowboat slid across the water under low-hanging clouds.

The nude corpse of yet another woman lay irreverently in one corner of the boat. The rowing ceased and the oars were brought in. The shadow of the man lifted the woman's body and slipped it overboard. When the ripples subsided, the boat moved away, a dark silhouette bent over the oars.

# 12

## THE CONTACT

"**M**a'am? Are you all right?" Curtis stood next Sarah. She didn't respond, staring instead into the cup of coffee she held in one hand. "Ma'am?" Curtis reached and placed his hand gently on Sarah's shoulder.

She jerked back and looked up at a concerned Curtis. "What?"

"I brought you your food, but you looked—well, you were pretty distracted."

"I'm sorry, Curtis. I got to thinking about something and lost myself there." She looked at the plates before her. "This looks marvelous, thank you."

"Hope you like it." Curtis turned, and walked away. "Hi, guys," he said to a couple of sheriffs as they entered, "your table's been waiting for you. What did you do with Amy?"

"No need for her to walk us here. She sent us this way, and here we are." They sat down two tables away from Sarah.

"Well, Dad said—"

"Don't sweat it, Curtis. It's okay."

"Alright. The same as usual?"

"You got it."

Curtis walked away and moments later Amy brought two cups of coffee and placed them in front of the officers. "Here you go P&P. I'm gonna hear from Curtis about this, aren't I?"

"Hope not, darling. Send him to us if he gives you any grief."

She grinned and walked off.

Sarah watched the exchange with interest. One of the officers noticed her staring and nodded. Sarah nodded back, and turned her eyes back to her food.

She glanced at them furtively as she ate, while they were served breakfast, hoping they wouldn't catch her watching them.

Curtis came to pour her another cup of coffee as the men were finishing their eggs.

"Are those officers from Lakeport?" she whispered.

"Never asked. They're regulars. P&P, we call 'em, on account one is Patrick and the other is Peter."

"I wonder if you'd do me a favor. Would you mind asking them if it's all right for me to ask them a question? I'm looking for a friend who does some consulting work with the authorities."

"No, don't mind at all. Hold on." He walked over to them. "That lady there," he looked in Sarah's direction, "asked if you'd mind if she asked you a question. She's looking for someone."

They both looked over at Sarah. She smiled apologetically.

"I got this," said Patrick as he stood up. "Thanks, Curtis." He walked up to Sarah, both thumbs tucked into his belt, and dipped his head in greeting. "Ma'am. I'm Sheriff Patrick Terrence."

"Nice to meet you. I'm Sarah Thompson. Won't you sit down?"

They shook hands and the sheriff sat. "Curtis tells me you're looking for someone?"

"Yes," Sarah leaned forward. "His name is James Horton and he consults with some of the local authorities. Have you heard of him?"

"May I ask why you're interested in finding this person?"

"He's my colleague."

"Colleague?"

"We…sort of do the same work. Have you met him? I understand he's in these parts, only I'm not sure exactly where."

"Have you tried to reach him?"

"Yes, but he's not answering his cell. He doesn't like interruptions when he's working."

"That should tell you something."

"You're right, only it appears that what I'm looking into is related to what he's looking into, and he's not aware of it. I myself found out only recently."

Sheriff Terrence stared pensively at Sarah. "Let me talk with my partner." He rose and returned to his table.

Sarah sipped her coffee while the two officers spoke in muted tones.

She took a deep breath, opened her purse and took out a card, resolutely stood, and went to their table. They started to stand. "No, please. I just came over to give you the telephone number of Sheriff Williams in Okanogan County. That's in Washington State where I'm from. I've worked with him. If you're concerned, please speak with him. He'll vouch for me." She handed the card to Patrick. "If you find James Horton, please inform him that I'm here—staying down the road at the Cozy Cabins—and that it's important I speak with him as soon as possible."

"That's good of you, Mrs. Thompson," the sheriff said, "We certainly will follow up."

Sarah returned to her table and finished her breakfast.

Moments later Curtis came over with more coffee. "Thanks, Curtis, but I'm done. The check please and extend my congratulations to your mother. Her pastries are outstanding."

"Sure thing." He searched his bib pocket for the check and handed it to Sarah. "Are you sure you're okay?"

Sarah nodded. "Yes, I'm fine." She opened her purse and took out her wallet. "Sometimes when I'm working on a problem I tend to concentrate so hard on it that I sort of detach. Thank you so much for your concern." She handed him the check and money. "I don't need any change."

Curtis took the money. "Thanks! Be sure to come back. We do great lunches, too."

"I most certainly will. Thank you, Curtis."

Sarah rose from the table and nodded goodbye to the officers.

After exiting the restaurant, she made her way back to the Cozy Cabins and booked a room. Once settled in, she grabbed her phone, but even before turning it on static erupted from it. She set her phone on the table and reached for the hotel's landline. It greeted her with static as well. "Damn it, Martha! I have to let my husband know where I am."

She left the cabin and made her way to the front office. "Hi Ann, it seems I have bad connections both on my cell and the phone in the room. Could you please place a call for me?"

"Sure thing, Mrs. Thompson." Ann lifted the receiver and immediately pulled it away from her ear.

Sarah could hear the static from across the counter.

"Sorry, the lines must be down. Hopefully they'll be back up soon."

"Thanks for trying. "

Sarah walked out of the office. "Martha, if you weren't already dead, I'd..."

Back in the cabin, exhaustion hit her. She fluffed the pillows and leaned back for some much-needed rest. But her frustration kept her tossing about, and soon it became obvious that sleep would be impossible. Moments later Sarah opened the book and read.

### *NOT ALONE*

*I find that*
*When I'm all alone*
*My thoughts run faster than my life*
*If yesterday*
*I was fifteen*
*Today*
*I'm sixty-five*
*I spend a lifetime*
*At your side*
*Away from you*
*And*

*Back again*
*Nights and days*
*Of love*
*And words*
*And dreams*
*Years and years*
*Of life*
*And stars*
*And schemes*
*The clock*
*Has not gone*
*Fifteen times*
*Round and round its face*
*When*
*Fifteen years*
*I've spent*
*By you*
*For you*
*With you*
*And when I know*
*We'll meet again*
*I find I'm not alone*

# CLARITY

A warm fire burned in Mary Ellen's large stone fireplace. To one side an elaborate wrought-iron stand, shaped like a fleur-de-lis, held a set of iron fireplace tools. The pommels on the handles of the fire poker, tong, brush, and scoop were also shaped like a fleur-de-lis. Dry logs were neatly stacked on the far side of the fireplace.

The living and dining areas, as well as a kitchen area, were all situated inside one vast room. Antique furniture gave it a hospitable, homey atmosphere, but it was evident that this old house had once been an elegant, well-appointed manor.

"Sit by the fire, and warm yourself." Mary Ellen set the shotgun on a rack next to the front door, which she closed and bolted.

Karla walked toward the fireplace. Two large armchairs faced a rocking chair across a small coffee table. She stood next to one of the armchairs and turned to study her hostess.

Mary Ellen shuffled over to the rocking chair and turned on a lamp perched on a side table. In the meager light from the lamp and the fireplace, she appeared more ancient than the furnishings in the house. It seemed impossible that her tiny, gnome-like frame had handled the heavy shotgun with such ease.

"Why would anybody want to read about this place? Care for some soup?"

"No, thank you. I just ate."

Mary Ellen sat on her rocking chair. Karla remained standing. "Sit. The armchair won't bite."

Karla sat down and noticed the elegant upholstery. "This fabric is exquisite."

"Indeed." Mary Ellen waved a hand to encompass the entire room. "All this is Martha's doing. She always liked pretty things. Look around. She picked this stuff herself. Every last bit, except a handful of knickknacks I've added over the years."

"This was her home?"

"No. This was her love."

Karla glanced around the cabin. "Every piece is quite handsome on its own. Not a single one is part of a set, yet they all fit together to perfection. That's quite an achievement."

"You have a good eye, young lady."

"I write about art, among other things." Mary Ellen studied her. Karla continued, "Visitors must love coming here. Your home makes one feel welcomed. Some of the knickknacks, as you call them, look European. Is that right?"

Mary Ellen's eyes wandered to the shelves and tabletops. "Yep. They bring back fond memories— mostly gifts from the girls. The others are from this part of the world." She sighed.

"I'm sorry. I don't wish to make you sad."

Mary Ellen looked up, and Karla could almost spot the shadows of memories floating behind her life-worn eyes, before she turned toward the flickering flames. "Nobody comes here anymore. After the McKenzies left, they had no need to visit, no need to come all this way."

"Don't they own land around here?"

"They do. Lots of it. Rolling hills of vineyards off Highway 53 on Old State Highway. Oh, and also off of Lakeview Road. They have more, but I can't remember where."

"You must've been well acquainted with them?"

"I must've. That's why you're here."

"It is."

The old woman stared at Karla. "You're fibbing me, young woman. I don't like fibs. What are you really after?"

"I'm trying to find out a few things."

"If you were a true reporter," Mary Ellen said, with a sardonic smile, "you would've found out a little more about the McKenzie folk before you came here. Whom do you write for?"

Uncomfortable with the lie, Karla turned toward the fire to avoid Mary Ellen's glare. "I was given this assignment at the last moment this afternoon—I haven't had time to prepare."

Mary Ellen stood, grabbed the fire poker, and expertly nudged the logs, causing a barrage of sparks to shoot up the chimney and the flames to burst back to life. "And what are you really interested in, the story of the town—or the McKenzies?"

"Both, of course. But you've piqued my curiosity, so I'd rather learn more about the McKenzies. Are any of them still living in this area?"

Mary Ellen ambled toward the kitchen. In a few steps she reached an ancient black cast-iron stove that stood against the wall. Decorative brass scrollwork around the door castings and handles adorned the range and oven doorframes. The stove sat on four ornate legs that protruded from a stunning brass skirt. Mary Ellen opened the door to a matching shelf above the range and took out a bowl. She set it to one side of the stove atop a sturdy redwood counter, then turned her attention to a steaming pot on top of one of the burners. She grabbed a ladle that sat in a spoon rest in the middle of the cooktop and stirred.

"Nope," she answered at last. "Their cousin Morley was the last one. He died...let's see...about three years ago. The rest of them cleared out of here way back when."

Karla joined Mary Ellen in the kitchen. "I'm curious. If, as you say, this house was Martha's love, how did you end up with it?"

"Faithfulness, I suppose. Although I didn't really deserve it, considering Jenny's death."

"Jenny? You mean Jennifer, Martha's sister?"

"Yep. Been dead for years. But you wouldn't want to write about that."

"Why not?"

Mary Ellen studied Karla for several seconds then turned back to her stew. "You think you're a smart cookie, don't you?"

Karla remained silent.

Mary Ellen ladled some soup into her bowl. "Anyhow, it's Jenny's death has most of the town talking that there's some kind of curse on this cabin, and a curse on the McKenzies on account of the other deaths. Sure you won't join me? I make a mean soup."

"I'm sure. Thank you."

The old woman carried her bowl over to an elegant dining area a few steps from the kitchen and sat at the table. She gestured at Karla to join her.

Karla sat across from Mary Ellen, on one of the stylish age-old chairs that surrounded the table. "Tell me about the sisters."

Mary Ellen looked over at Karla and chuckled. "You'd like that, huh? Well, it won't do no harm anymore, I suppose." She scooped up a spoonful of soup and blew on it. "Martha had two sons."

"Yes. Twins. Daryl and Andrew."

Mary Ellen squinted at Karla, as if this action might provide deeper insight into the young woman across from her. Karla averted her gaze, and looked at the old stove.

Mary Ellen frowned. "You're very aware of some things, and others you don't have a clue about. Why's that, I wonder?"

Karla made a feeble attempt to laugh the question off. "I'm not well informed, just getting started. Please go on."

"Yes, you're right. Twin boys, Daryl and Andrew... he was a strange one, that boy. Least, people around here thought so. Poor soul."

Intrigued by this assertion, Karla leaned forward. "Andrew? Why?"

Mary Ellen slowly got to her feet and headed toward the cupboard. "He used to stroll these forests all by himself at night. During the day, too, mind you." She found the saltshaker and returned to her seat. She shook some salt into her soup and sipped loudly, nodding before she spoke. "You'd spot him walking the roads at night or trudging through the forest during the day. Marching forward like he had someplace important to be, something urgent to do. People said it was his aunt Jennifer's soul that haunted him. She died in this very house. That's the reason nobody comes here at night— they're scared. Most everyone said I was crazy to move in when Martha gave me this here house. Be honest with you, it makes me feel that much safer knowing how scared people are." She chuckled to herself.

"Tell me about Andrew, please."

Mary Ellen squinted at Karla and sneered. "That's it—you're after Andrew's story."

Karla blushed.

"There you have it. This reporter business was a damn poor excuse. You can't even answer the question as to whom you write for. What's your interest in Andrew?"

This time, Karla didn't avoid Mary Ellen's penetrating gaze. "He's disappeared and I'm trying to find him." Tears welled in her eyes.

The old woman was clearly taken aback by this unexpected revelation, but then she frowned. "And? What's he to you?"

She cleared her throat. "He was my lo—my boyfriend for a short while."

"Boyfriend, huh? Now I get it. Have to admit it surprises me, though." Mary Ellen returned to her soup, slurping with gusto. "Have you wondered whether he wishes to be found?

"No. I'm certain he's in trouble."

"I get that."

A long silence ensued, interrupted only by slurping as Mary Ellen ate her soup.

Karla finally spoke. "Why did Martha give you this house?"

"'Cause of ..." Mary Ellen stopped eating and turned toward the fireplace as if someone had called her name.

Karla followed her gaze. "Anything wrong?"

Mary Ellen turned to Karla as if remembering where she was. "Nope." She sipped her soup and took a big bite of chicken.

"You were telling me why Martha gave you this house."

"No I wasn't. You wanted me to. But that's for me to—it's not my secret to share."

"It's a secret?

"Never you mind, missy."

"Could Andrew be around here somewhere?"

Mary Ellen set down her spoon and glared at Karla. "I suppose Daryl told you that."

Karla nodded.

"Well, Daryl would say that, wouldn't he?"

"So?"

She shook her head and returned to her soup. "I doubt he'd come here."

"On account of Jennifer's death? Why? How did she die?"

Mary Ellen seemed lost in her memories. After a few seconds she looked at Karla.

"I blamed myself, at first," she said. "I had to go to my sister Isabella's that week. She was terribly sick. I wouldn't have gone, but she had nobody else to take care of her."

"What happened?"

"I used to take care of the boys, as I'd done with their mama and auntie when they were little girls. They spent more time with me than with their own mothers." She rested her eyes on Karla and waited for a reaction.

"Yes, I knew you were their nanny. The girls grew up in these parts as well?"

Mary Ellen shook her head and continued eating. "No, up north. Ferndale."

"What about their husbands?"

"Ah, yes. The first McKenzie twins."

Karla gasped. "What do you mean, *first*?"

# 13

## THE ALLIANCE

L oud knocking jolted Sarah from a deep sleep. It took a moment to recognize where she was. The Cozy Cabins. She'd fallen asleep on top of the bed while reading the book. A stressful night without much sleep and a nap had left her groggy. More knocking, this time more intense.

"One moment, please," she yelled. She stood up, straightened her clothes, patted her hair down, and went to the door.

"My God, Sarah," James said with a broad smile, "you're a sight for sore eyes. What on earth are you—"

Sarah flung her arms around him. "I can't tell you how glad I am to see you."

James laughed in her embrace. "I get it."

Sarah blushed and pulled back. "I'm sorry. I hope I didn't embarrass you."

"Not at all."

"Please come in."

He stepped in and looked around. "This one is in pastels. Mine's done in fall colors. I wondered if every cabin was different."

"You're staying here?"

"I am. Number 6." He walked about, taking in the decor.

"You're helping them with the murders of the women dumped in the lake."

James halted and gasped as her words sunk in. "Dear God. Your story."

Sarah nodded.

"You have information about these murders?"

"Only what Mar—"

A screeching cry pierced the room.

"Oh, boy." James breathed in as he covered his ears. "No names, Sarah, please."

"Did you hear that?"

"Oh, yeah."

"All right, no names," she said, glancing up. "I promise."

James made his way to one of the chairs around a small table by the window. "Your entity is very protective." He sat with a sigh.

"Can you...oh," Sarah sat in the opposing chair. "I'm not sure if I should tell you if it's a he or a she."

"I can't sense that, but I most certainly heard a female scream. I do sense a ton of energy around you—like I felt back in Eureka—but no one has materialized for me. It's allowing me to be with you, but continues to be very protective of his or her identity and information. I sense an incredibly strong barrier."

"So do I, although I'm starting to understand why. I'm being fed the story and the history, but without the real names or the real locations. It's a bunch of images and information—or misinformation."

"Let's try to glean the facts a bit at a time. Tell me what you've learned as it relates to the murders, without any names. We'll start with that, and hopefully the communication will be permitted."

"The first death shown to me back in the bookstore in Eureka, when I first met you, was of a woman in her mid to late sixties. A man caused her death. I should say, the shadow of a man, because that's all I perceived, except for—" Sarah paused, unsure about whether she could reveal the next bit of evidence. But then she went on, "a birthmark on his left hand."

"Good. No problem with receiving that. Do you have any idea who the woman was?"

Sarah took Martha's silence as approval to go on. "I do, in relation to the story that is being told to me, but it's not her real name or when she actually died. It could've been last week or last year. That part is a mystery. I'm convinced it's recent, but I could be wrong."

James arched his eyebrows. "How did she die?"

"She reached for this man, but he slapped her hand away, and she fell down the stairs."

"An accident?"

"It could be. But his actions afterwards were extremely bizarre." Sensing no opposition, she continued. "He first straightened her limbs and fixed her hair and nightgown, then he carefully carried her corpse into a living room. He placed the body in the center of a circle of votive candles, and then he...cuddled up to her. Afterwards I saw—" she paused to ascertain permission, listening, then said, "I saw him row a boat out onto a lake and dump her body like it was last week's trash."

"Cuddling first, then dumping the body into the lake. Opposing behaviors. Anything else about her?"

"Yes. The poems in the book were written for her."

"Wow. That's interesting, particularly from the point of view of the book itself. Who's the author?"

"I've seen him, but I have no clue of his identity."

"Husband, maybe?"

Sarah shook her head. "Lover."

"Mm. I'm beginning to understand the protective nature that surrounds this entity. Can you tell me about the murders?"

"The man with the birthmark, he follows a ritual. He surrounds the women with votive candles, and—"

"Are they alive when he does this?"

"No. I don't see their deaths. I observe them after they've died. Strangled, I'm guessing."

"With his bare hands?"

"A pink sheer scarf appears to be a significant part of it."

James tilted his head. "Go on."

Sarah took a deep breath. "Once they're dead, he cuddles up to them."

"Cuddles. A pattern. Part of this ritual you mentioned."

She nodded.

James reached over and patted Sarah's hand reassuringly. "What happens next?"

She shrugged. "He rows out and dumps their bodies in the lake. It's so—unnatural, so gruesome. Does any of this help?"

"Actually, it does. You've described to perfection the manner in which these women have died. In fact, the coroner has found that they've been strangled by something tied around their necks."

"Have you identified the women? How many? Hold on a minute—how were they found? He dumps them in the lake to hide them."

"He hasn't weighed them down."

"That's right. He simply shoves them out of the boat. Their bodies sink."

"But soon they come back to the surface. It's almost as if he's taunting us. He wants us to find them. What can you tell me about the boat."

"It's a little, rinky-dink, very old rowboat. It's tied to a small pier at the bottom of a hill, right below the home where the older woman died."

"Her home?"

"It could be. At least I assumed it was. She was wearing a nightgown."

"That might be a very important clue."

"Have any of the dead women come to you, talked to you, I mean?" She glanced around the room. "Are they here?"

James held Sarah's hand. "No, they're not here. And yes, I've spoken with them. They didn't know him. One thought she'd met him, or had worked with him, but in the end she wasn't sure. He didn't behave as she remembered him."

"How can that be?"

"She said he'd changed. He looked like the same man she'd met or worked with, but up close he was completely different."

"I wonder why and how? What about the others?"

"They'd never met him before. Sarah," he tightened his grip on her hand, "they were all paid to have sex with him."

"Oh." She stood up and paced the room.

"What is it?"

"One of them wasn't a…" She turned to face James. "She was a model in a big city that could be San Francisco. But it's all assumptions."

"Really? A model? Like in magazines or fashion runway?"

"No, for artists. For portraits or sculptures."

"How—?"

"She first appeared in a bar where… the person I'm supposed to help was. This person asked the bartender about her."

"Where was this bar?"

"I'm not exactly sure. I'm given names of people or places that may or may not be right. But, in this particular instance, I looked up the names of the bar and the galleries in the story, and actually found them in San Francisco's gallery row on Geary Street right by Union Square."

James jumped to his feet. "Get your purse and jacket, Sarah. We're off to chat with the investigating team."

"I'm not sure I can. It might interfere with my task. I'm supposed to be helping…a person that is or will be in trouble in the very near future. Maybe she's the next victim."

"What do you need to do? How can I help?"

"I'm being spoon-fed the story in bits and pieces."

"But how? You're no longer reading pages in the book."

Sarah nodded. "I've surmised that the entity connected to the book and the story determined that I would accept this *Jackal in the Mirror* tale if it was shown as a book, title and all. It started as the most effective way of communicating with me. Now it pops into my mind or I dream it or…I detach from the present and view it."

"And you feel you lose control?"

"Yes. Conrad said—oh, dear… I have to call him, but the entity is messing with my phone. You'll have to call him for me. He has no idea where I am."

"Tell you what, Sarah. Get your stuff and I'll call him while we're in the car. C'mon."

# DERIVATION

"Are you saying that Martha and Jenny married twin brothers?" Karla asked.

Mary Ellen studied her for a moment. "I don't buy your story that you're 'sort of aware of Andrew and Daryl' yet you don't have an inkling about their history. It all sounds a bit fishy."

"I'm sorry, but—"

"Yeah, yeah, you'll have an answer for that, too. You look all right and you come across as sincere, except for the reporter business, and I trust you're worried about Andrew. Otherwise, I'd have shot you."

"You wouldn't have."

Mary Ellen chuckled. "No, I wouldn't."

"Tell me about the girls' husbands, the McKenzie twins, please."

The old woman pursed her lips and mulled over Karla's request. She took a deep breath and nodded. "Robert married Martha, and Gabriel married Jenny."

"Did the four of them meet in school?"

"Nope. The twins' grandfather, Robert senior, came from Canada some time back in the early 1900s. Big Bob, they called him. He struck it rich in the mines when he was young. He was no dummy and realized what mining did to people, so as soon as he made his fortune he got out of that racket, bought some land, and got into tree farming."

"Tree farming?"

"Orchards, walnuts, pears, all kinds of fruit. Eventually he noticed that grapes found the weather

around the lake to their liking. He started a few vineyards and went into wine making. He was real sharp,
that one."

"And the girls?"

"Well they were home-grown and came from railroad money—and dairy, mind you."

"In Ferndale?"

"Yep, and Eureka."

"How did they meet the twins?"

"Well the girls, they'd come to Clear Lake every
summer and on holidays. They had a real nice home,
not too far from the McKenzie's big house down toward
the southeastern part of the lake in the Buckingham
area. Both homes were right on the water. That's a real
beautiful part of the lake. The whole lake's beautiful, in
its own way."

Karla smiled recognizing Mary Ellen's love for the
area. "So they had a big house and this house as well?"

"Martha didn't care for the uppity high-end society
around there. She liked hills and mountains, so she
made Robert build her this here house. They called it a
cabin." She sniggered. "She called it home. She loved
being up here, away from the racket down there. The
boys enjoyed being out in the woods. So different from
the lake scene."

"The love she invested in this home is tangible.
Please tell me how they met."

"Gabriel met Martha first, when they were in their
early teens, maybe even younger, at some gathering
or other. I don't recall. Anyway, they sort of saw eye-to-
eye right off the bat. After that, they'd get together every

time she was in these parts. That went on for several years. He'd give her some of his poems and she'd turn them into songs. She sang them all the time, even told me how taken she was with this boy poet."

"She sang them?"

"Martha had a beautiful voice. That's probably how Robert fell in love with her."

Karla frowned, confused. "Robert?"

"Don't get your panties in a wad. It's simple really. Robert heard Martha singing in some church choir when she was around seventeen or eighteen. Anyway, he jumped the gun and asked for her hand in marriage."

"You mean he asked before Gabriel did?"

"Jenny was expected to marry first on account she was the eldest."

"You mean to tell me that they forced him to marry the older sister?"

"Not forced, no. By the time any marrying talk was going on, Robert had his mind set on Martha, and Gabriel was off for months in San Francisco working on this poem business. Never wrote or nothing. Martha took that as a sign he wasn't interested in her, and Robert, him being the first-born and heir to the business, jumped to the head of the line. So, when Gabriel finally came back, he married Jenny. It all worked out, mind you."

"But they were twins. They were born at the same time."

"Sure, twins all right, but Robert came first and Gabriel right after. So Robert took priority in everyone's eyes."

"Gabriel lost out because he was born second?"

"Lost out?" Mary Ellen frowned. "Oh, you mean the money."

Karla nodded.

"No, he didn't lose out at all. He got his share. Both boys inherited huge chunks of money. Anyhow, little Robert—Bobby Junior they called him—liked the business and Gabriel didn't. He didn't care for it at all. He had his writing thing."

"They all lived here?"

"No, silly, they couldn't all fit in here." Mary Ellen sipped loudly and spit as she chuckled. "It's gone cold." She wiped her mouth with the napkin, took her bowl to the kitchen, and washed it. She dried her hands, filled a kettle with water, and set it on the stove to boil. "I'm about to have a tea. Would you like some?"

Karla joined her by the stove. "Yes, that would be lovely."

"C'mon, let's sit over here while this old kettle warms up. I'm too old to stand." She wobbled over to her rocking chair and plopped down.

Karla sat in the armchair across from her. "Tell me more about this house. And Jenny's death."

"You had to bring that up, didn't you?" She winced and then shrugged. "All right, no real reason not to tell you, I suppose. Like I said, my sister was real sick and I had no choice but to go take care of her. So, Martha asked Jenny to watch the boys while she traveled to New York with Robert. Jenny hated the big house, so she went and asked them to bring them boys here."

"Why not her house? Where did she live? Where did they all live?"

"Robert senior had moved to Napa, so Robert junior got the lake house when he married Martha. Gabriel was city driven, but eventually changed his mind and bought a big house near his brother's. Jenny didn't go for the life in San Francisco. They both favored being near their siblings, anyhow."

"So why not have the boys stay at her place?"

"Gabriel was away on one of his trips to San Francisco, and their house was too big for her to keep track of two rambunctious boys. With no nanny, she needed to care for the boys on her own and this house was more manageable." She closed her eyes.

Unwilling to intrude on her memories, Karla waited in silence.

The old woman finally opened her eyes and wiped away some tears. "Look at me getting all sentimental. Where was I?"

"You mentioned her house and her need to care for the twins here."

"Yeah, the help at her big place weren't trained to deal with the twins. They were little, and Jenny thought they'd be more at ease in the small cabin they were familiar with and..." She stopped and stared into the fireplace.

The flickering light of the flames danced across the old woman's pained face.

"Jenny died here," she whispered at last, "while her sister was gone." Tears glistened in her eyes.

Karla remained silent.

"The little boys, they were only four, spent days up here, alone with Jenny's corpse." Mary Ellen pointed to the bathroom. "Little Daryl, he was in there when they found him."

Karla shifted her gaze in the direction of the bathroom, and shivered in spite of the warm fire. She rubbed her arms to warm them up. Mary Ellen rose slowly and made her way toward the fireplace. She tossed on another log and stood motionless, staring into the flames.

Karla joined her and placed her arm around the woman's shoulders. Mary Ellen patted her hand. "Thank you, dearie. It's a sad, sad story. Horrible, really. Daryl was locked in here with Jenny's body and his brother Andrew was locked outside, two, maybe three days. No one was certain. Daryl couldn't open the door." She pointed to the door. "The bolt was too hard and too high, bless his little heart."

"How did Andrew get out?"

She shrugged. "That remains a mystery. He probably snuck out somehow when Jenny went to take her bath. He loved being outdoors. Daryl didn't. A papa's boy through and through." She sighed. "Daryl always preferred to be indoors and play at pretending he was his dad. No wonder he became so successful."

"So Jenny was here all alone with the boys?"

"Yep."

"Why didn't Jenny go to San Francisco with Gabriel?"

Mary Ellen shook her head. "They'd decided to take some time apart."

"Oh," she paused. "Did their aunt...kill herself?"

Mary Ellen spun angrily toward Karla and, with remarkable speed, reached the bathroom and flung the door open. "She most certainly did not! She'd been taking a bath and was getting out when she slipped and slammed her head against the side of the tub. They found her naked body holding the towel she'd reached for. Sweet Daryl had nestled himself into her cold arms."

She turned and walked toward the back of the cabin. "And little Andrew was sitting out there, shivering and staring through the window, pleading for his brother to open the door, watching him happy and safe in his aunt's arms." She turned to Karla with a piercing stare and a stern tone. "Jennifer was the liveliest woman I ever knew. No, young lady, Jenny loved everything, and most of all she loved living." She paused when her voice cracked. "Like her sister Martha, she was full of life." Mary Ellen tried in vain to hold back the tears welling up in her eyes.

The kettle whistled and Karla headed to the stove to turn off the burner.

# 14

# THE TEAM

"**S**arah." James shook her shoulder. "We're here."

Sarah blinked and glanced around. "I did it again, didn't I?"

"Yes, indeed."

"How long did I detach?"

"Not too long. Make any meaningful progress?"

"Yes. But I need to figure out how to relate it to you."

"Conrad called back. Said he's on his way. Said he can't have you *gallivanting*—his word—around the countryside with *a handsome old man*—my words." He chuckled, amused at his own joke, but Sarah remained serious.

"What do you mean, he's on his way?"

"He's taking a flight to Eureka and driving here. He'll be here tomorrow mid day."

"When did he call?"

"He returned my call when you were otherwise engaged."

"Boy, I didn't even hear the phone."

"Nope."

"A flight to Eureka—"

"Well, technically it lands in Arcata, a few miles north of Eureka."

"But those flights are so expensive."

"What can I tell you? That's what he said. He didn't sound open to suggestions to the contrary."

"I can imagine."

"He mentioned you had seen me in a dream. That I bumped into the woman you're supposed to help."

"Yes, I did. On a street called Mc—"

Martha screamed.

"Oh, boy! I heard that one," James said. No mention of names, not even street names."

"I doubt that's the real name of the street, anyway."

"But if I appeared in the narrative, it may indicate she wants us together."

"That's my thinking."

He smiled and squeezed her arm. "Ready to chat with the team?"

Sarah shrugged. "Let's give it a go."

They left the car and walked into the sheriff's station. Sarah followed James through the main office and into a meeting room.

A group of men and women, some in uniform, some in shirts and jeans, and some in suits, sat around a large, oval table. James wasted no time. "Folks, it's my pleasure to introduce you to Sarah Thompson. As I mentioned she is ten times more gifted than I am and she has some interesting facts to share with you."

"Good afternoon," Sarah said as she sat on the chair that James had pulled out for her.

Each of them introduced themselves in turn. The team included local officers—some on duty and some off—from the county's sheriff's department, an FBI agent and a profiler, an attorney, and James.

"I'll brief you on what I've learned in a minute," said James. "But first I must warn you that the being, or ghost, as you like to call them, that's communicating with Sarah, is not sharing freely. This particular being is extremely private, and protests very loudly when information is provided that he or she doesn't permit."

"How does the protest manifest itself?" asked the attorney.

"My brief experience with it was by a loud shriek. Sarah can hear it. On two occasions, I heard it as well. Whether you will or not, I'm not sure."

"So," Sarah interjected, "if I stop myself as I'm informing you of what I've learned, please appreciate that I'm attempting to respect the wishes of the person who is communicating with me. Should I fail to do that, the person will provide no more information."

"How does it communicate with you?" queried the Chief.

"It's narrating a story in the form of a novel."

"A story?" he questioned.

"Like a book?" the profiler wondered.

"In bits and pieces, disjointed chapters, if you will. All with fake names and locations. And even though these locations and names are fabricated, I'm not allowed to share those with you. So no names or places at all."

"In addition," James interrupted, "this spirit is urging Sarah to help a woman. This woman could be the next victim."

Every man in the room stirred and glanced at each other with obvious discomfort.

"The woman I'm expected to help is not a... working—" she hesitated.

"You mean a prostitute," an officer said.

"She's a..." Sarah paused to sense if Martha would allow her to describe Karla. Feeling no resistance she went on, "...a reporter for an art magazine. According to the story I'm getting, she comes from a family with significant wealth, is well-educated, beautiful, and successful." Sarah inhaled deeply, relieved that she'd been able to describe that much.

"Now," James said, "I'll tell you what I've learned so far that coincides with our findings."

As James spoke, Sarah took out the book and opened it, hoping it would continue the story and give her more information. Instead, it simply offered a poem.

She read the poem in case it offered a clue.

## SHE SAID

She said, "You're clever."
I said, "Oh?"
"You know things
You don't know you know."

Slowly
I put down
My empty glass of wine,
Slowly
I did raise my gaze,
Until her eyes met mine.
"Can't you see?" said she.
"No, I can't," said me.

"Things are not just things for you,
For you they're special things."
I tried to look intelligent,
Pretend I understood,
I tried to look like I could find
In all things
Something good.

I wanted to believe the words
This maiden spoke to me.
But deep inside
I think I knew
It really couldn't be.

"You're really very..."
The waiter came
To bring the check
So I never knew the rest.
But she almost persuaded me
I really was the best.

201

"Sarah?" James gently placed his hand on hers.

She looked up from the book. "I'm sorry—I opened the book in the hope that it would offer more information."

"You have the actual book with you?" the chief asked.

"Yes."

"Why don't you simply look at the last chapter and read the ending?" asked the FBI man with a hint of sarcasm.

"The story isn't in the book," she answered patiently. "This is a book of poems."

Skepticism permeated the room as the group sniggered, grunted, or sighed.

"The entity or ghost is attached to the book," explained James. "It uses it to communicate with Sarah."

They shook their heads.

"Sounds odd, I realize," James added, "but in the worlds we psychics travel in, it's not uncommon. Sarah, did you find out anything new?"

Sarah shook her head with obvious disappointment. "No."

"May I look at the book?" The FBI agent reached out to take it.

"No!" James held his hand. "Please Steven, don't touch it."

Steven withdrew his hand. "Why the hell not?"

"The book," James shrugged, "doesn't wish to be shared."

*Sarah, leave. Leave now!*

Sarah stood up. "I'm sorry gentlemen, but I must go."

James looked into Sarah's eyes. She nodded.

James stood up. "It appears that our ghost is not comfortable with Sarah being here."

The FBI agent said, "I'm sorry if I—"

"Steven," James interjected, "trust me, it's not your doing. These types of interactions have a flavor of their own, and in this case the spirit prefers to deal only with Sarah."

The chief rose to protest, "But—"

"Sheriff, you have to trust me," James interrupted. "I'll act as liaison between Sarah and the team and keep you posted on any new developments. The group has enough to do in following up on the details Sarah has already provided, which I've shared with you."

Without waiting for a response, James took Sarah's elbow and escorted her out of the room, across the office, and out to the parking lot. When they reached his car, he opened the passenger side door for Sarah, helped her in, and shut her door. He got into the driver's seat, and locked the car.

"Good thing we're locked in. No entities allowed!" Sarah chuckled.

"Why in the world did I do that?" He laughed, as he placed his hands on the steering wheel. "I have this irrepressible urge to protect you."

"Well, I thank you for that, and the quick exit. Did you hear the voice?"

"No, not a thing. I knew by the look in your eyes that I needed to whisk you away. What did it say?"

"To get out of there. I assume it didn't approve of me being near the team. Too much risk of exposure."

James started the car and exited the parking lot. "What if we take a walk down by the lake and hopefully you can tell me more. You've detached a couple of times and I'm sure there's more to share."

"I'd like that. I could use some fresh air."

"Have you figured out how to give me more details?"

"No, there's no way for me to be sure what's allowed and what's not. I'll have to go for it. Shall we give it a try?

"Sure."

"The person I'm supposed to protect is involved with a set of..." she paused expecting a screech, but when nothing happened she finished, "...twins."

"Males?"

"Yes. Identical."

"Connected to the murders?"

"Maybe."

"That's quite vague."

"I'm unsure. Let's say probably."

"At least there's been no opposition to this bit of information."

203

"As for the rest, I'm afraid that the locations will be hard to describe. Plus I can't use the names, fake or not. I can try to describe the look of things, but—"

"It won't help anyway if you're being steered falsely."

"But you might recognize them if there are similar locations around here that you're familiar with."

"It could be, but," he shrugged, unconvinced, "it's a bit far-fetched."

"Yeah, you're right. But it's all I've got."

They drove on in silence.

# PURSUIT

Karla left her motel room, shut the door, and climbed into her car. She exited the parking area and headed toward Highway 20 to follow the road that circled the lake. The fog had lifted, allowing the sun to shine through the trees and reflect off the tranquil waters of the lake.

Karla turned onto a small side road that appeared to snake down to the water. She arrived at a driveway that resembled the entrance to a southern plantation-style home. Two brick posts anchored ornate iron gates with an escutcheon in the center that bore the letters *RM*.

She parked the car and approached the gates. She noticed a security system that seemed to control the gates' mechanism. It didn't appear that the gates were designed to prevent entry, but merely suggested a borderline.

She slid through the side opening to the driveway, cautiously walked to the front door, and rang the doorbell. No answer. She stepped back and studied the house. Tucked into tall trees, the building had a splendid view of the serene lake, and stood nestled against the hill that slanted down from the main road. All the windows were closed with the curtains drawn.

"Andrew," she called out. "Andrew! It's me, Karla."

She walked around toward the back of the house. "Andrew, if you're here, please say so." She shouted, "I saw you driving the Jeep last night—I'm sure you're around here."

From the back of the house she spotted an old boat tied to a small pier down the hill. "Andrew!" She yelled.

Her voice echoed through the forest. Only the birds answered. She examined the house one more time, returned to her car, and drove back into town.

# 15

## THE DISCLOSURE

"James," Sarah reached for his arm as they strolled along the lakeshore. "I can describe the house where the first woman—the older woman—died. It's a plantation-style home." She furrowed her brow. "Although, come to think if it, the house I just saw, looked way bigger than the first one."

"Is that where you were?"

She nodded. "How long this time?"

"You were silent a minute or two. Not long."

"And I continued walking with you?"

"Without hesitation. The fact that you're detaching so often tells me that you're getting closer and closer to the woman you're supposed to help."

She looked around the lake in search of the house, but to no avail.

"From here, I can't find anything resembling what was shown to me." She turned on her heels and took off. "C'mon, we need to drive around this lake and explore some of the small roads that lead down to it. Let's go."

James chased after her. "Listen, Sarah. I'm all for doing the gumshoe bit, but it's nearly dusk, in case you hadn't noticed. Not a good idea to go searching for this house in the dark. Clear Lake is very big and you've only seen a small—"

"How big?"

"It's the biggest lake in California."

"Bigger than Lake Tahoe?"

"Tahoe is bigger, of course, but technically, part of it is in Nevada. Clear Lake is huge and has many communities, coves, points, and—"

"That's going to make the search very difficult. How in the name of God are we supposed to find it?"

"I'm sure you'll be guided when it's time, but we certainly can't find it when it's dark."

"True. I hadn't noticed it's almost sunset for us. It was daytime in the vision I had."

"Hmm. That's interesting. If it's daytime for the story and nearly night for us, you may be catching up. At least we may be within twenty-four hours of her, given what you've told me."

"If that's the case, it's even more urgent that we find her."

"I'll tell you what, let's get a quick bite and afterwards I'll take you back to your cabin. Maybe when you're alone tonight more information will come to you."

Sarah took a deep breath. "I am hungry, now that you mention it. Bet you are, too."

"You win that bet." When they reached the car, he stopped. "She's becoming more comfortable with me. I don't sense that strong resistance any longer."

Sarah raised her eyebrows. "She?"

He tilted his head and his brows arched as well. "How about that? It's a woman. She's allowed me that."

"Can you feel her presence?"

"No. And I can't hear or see her, either. C'mon, let's hunt down some food and get you back to your cabin. I'll connect with the chief and give him the latest developments. Maybe they'll find the key given we're now in search of a set of twins."

Sarah grabbed his arm. "I'm not sure it's the twins."

"Maybe not, but we can take a look. At least it's a possibility."

She tightened her grip on his arm. "No, no! It's not certain."

He placed his hand over hers. "I'll make sure to tell them it could be a red herring, but it's worth looking into it."

"I'm very uneasy about that."

"You or she?"

Sarah paused. "Both of us."

James gave her a conciliatory nod. "I'll caution them, all right?"

She released his arm. "I'll drive while you're on the phone."

"No need. I've got blue tooth in the car."

She laughed. "You don't trust me. You're worried I'll detach and lose myself in the story. Can't say I blame you."

"I trust you, but I *don't* trust your entity, at least not yet."


# ALLUSION

Karla opened the door to the Pines Diner and stepped in.

Elisa and the elderly couple were in the exact same positions they'd occupied the night before. Several other tables and booths were occupied with patrons eating and chatting. The television played a cooking show.

Elisa greeted her with a grin. "Good afternoon, sweetie. You know the drill, sit anywhere you like."

"Hello, Elisa."

"Hungry?"

"A tuna salad and some iced tea please."

"Tuna and tea coming right up."

Karla picked a table and sat back as Elisa disappeared behind the counter. Moments later she reappeared with the iced tea, and stood by Karla's table, waiting.

"Yes?" Karla asked.

"Thought maybe you'd like to ask me some questions for that story you're writing." She winked. "Always dreamed of seeing my name in the paper. Ned said I might make it into the paper if I opened up to you." She grinned.

"Sure thing. Please join me."

Elisa squeezed into a chair across from Karla.

"What can you tell me about the McKenzies?" Karla asked.

"They're good people. Real hard working, church going, and all that, except that boy Andrew. He was always different."

A bell rang by the kitchen counter. "That's your salad. Give me a moment." She sashayed all the way to the kitchen counter and picked up the salad. On her way back she grabbed a basket with crackers and a holder with four plastic bottles.

"Here you go, hon." She resumed her seat across from Karla. "These are our salad dressings, made right here and with no preservatives."

"Thanks. But if it's not too much trouble, could I have some lemon wedges?"

"Sure, no bother. In a sec." She turned toward the kitchen, and called out, "Jimmy, cut me some lemon wedges she can squeeze." She returned her gaze to Karla. "Watch, he'll plop the dish on the counter in no time."

Moments later, Jimmy placed a little bowl with lemon wedges on the kitchen counter.

"Didn't I tell you? He's quick. Be right back." Elisa pushed her chair back, and strutted toward the kitchen counter, grabbed the bowl, and zigzagged back to the table. She set the lemon wedges down, and plopped onto a different chair next to Karla.

"Anyways, them McKenzies kept pretty much to themselves, on account of having so much money." She leaned back, making herself at home.

Karla squeezed the lemon wedges over her salad. "Did they have any special friends in the town?"

"Sure. Lots. We all used to go over to the mansion all the time, the one by the lake."

Karla nodded.

"They invited us common folks for Easter, Thanksgiving, and Christmas parties. They were some-thing else, I'll tell you."

"Didn't you say they kept to themselves?"

"That, too."

"I'm afraid I don't get your meaning."

"Well, it was like this. You knew who they were and where they lived, and of course what they did, and how rich they were, and all that stuff, but that was all you knew. Get it?"

"I guess so. What about the two boys, didn't they go to school here?"

"You mean Robert Junior and Gabriel?"

Karla chewed and swallowed before answering. "No, I meant Martha's children."

"Oh, I get it." She leaned close. "Well, that's a story. After Jennifer died things went bad. No more parties at the mansion and the kids were kept far away from us townsfolk. Them boys were what they call home-schooled. They had a bunch of tutoring. Yeah, that's what they called it."

"Why do you suppose things changed?"

"Well, Jenny's death. Awful business that was. Martha was real shook up. The boys were little but it's clear that they were—well, *disturbed*, I'd say."

"Yes, I can only imagine. What did you mean when you said that Andrew was different?"

"Them boys were like mirrors of each other. You couldn't tell them apart when they were little. They dressed them the same, cut their hair the same, it was something to behold. Yes sir, the spittin' image of each other. But after the accident, and as they grew up, Andrew, he—well he let his hair grow and went all hippie-like, he was moody, and took to roaming the woods. Mostly at night."

"When he was that little?"

"God, yes. Many a time they formed search parties 'cause he'd gone missing out there." She leaned closer to Karla. "Not once did he get found."

"Really?"

Pleased with herself at having aroused Karla's attention, Elisa leaned back and crossed her arms. "He came back on his own every time."

"So, he wasn't actually lost."

"Not as far as *he* was concerned. I tell you that boy was different. He sort of knew how to talk to the wild. Like one of them beasts out there instead of a boy."

"Really?"

Elisa beamed with satisfaction. "A wild one he was."

"And Daryl?"

"A papa's boy all the way," she said dismissively. So prim, so proper, and always glued to his daddy."

Karla finished her salad and sipped her iced tea while she mulled over this new information.

Elisa, unable to withstand Karla's silence, finally spoke up. "They all went away for a long while—at least Martha and the boys." She tilted her head back as she searched her memory banks. "I suppose Mary Ellen went, too. She has loads of foreign stuff in that cabin of hers."

"Where did they go?"

"Some other country is what I was told. France, I think. Where Gabriel lived."

"They went to stay with him?"

Elisa shrugged. "Dunno. They could've—after all, they were family."

"And Robert McKenzie, their father? What happened with him?"

"He stayed behind. He came here often, and when he wasn't here, I imagine he'd go to their place in the city or over to Napa. He kept an eye on the business. Good thing he did, too. Folks around here needed the work from his tree farms and wineries. Still do."

"Did the boys ever come back?"

"Yeah, early in their teens. They looked different from one another by then, mind ya'. Andrew with the long hair, gypsy-like all the way, and Daryl all proper and fancy, a carbon copy of his daddy. One day we got wind that Andrew had been shipped off to some fancy school. Later Daryl went off to school, too, or something like that."

"Does either of them come here anymore?"

"We saw them here and there over the years, mostly Andrew, but Daryl too, sometimes." She leaned forward. "Some folks say they've seen him recently. I haven't."

"Him?"

"Andrew."

"Tell me more about him. What did he do when he was younger?"

"Not much more to say, really. He painted strange things on walls and pavements and scared his poor mama to death by disappearing into the woods all the time. Bet he didn't amount to much."

Karla finished her iced tea and reached for her purse.

"Oh, that's okay. This one's on the house," Elisa said with a wink.

"Thank you, but it's not necessary."

"Sure it is, honey. Shall I tell you more?"

"Thank you Elisa, you're most generous. I'd like that, but I need to get to the registrar's office and check something out."

Elisa leaned over and whispered conspiratorially to Karla. "Bet you Andrew is the one who killed all those women."

Karla felt her mouth go dry. "What women?"

Elisa made a face to shush Karla and glanced around to make sure no one had heard her. She motioned for Karla to lean closer. "Just my opinion, mind you, but there were these women found in the lake over in Rosewood—"

"Rosewood?"

"A town by the lake, several miles from here. Anyway, these women, the kind that men pick up in bars, well, they kept disappearing left and right. Poor souls."

"When?"

"This is some years back, mind you." Elisa got even closer to Karla, practically tilting her over. "Anyways, two of these old good-for-nothing women turned up dead and washed ashore on the lake." She shook her head in disgust. "The sheriffs made a big thing of it. They came through the town asking questions, stirring everything up. They couldn't find a thing." She leaned back in the chair for a dramatic pause, tilted forward, then whispered, "And, what do those fools say now? Martha McKenzie drowns herself? Please." She leaned back and grinned, satisfied that she had presented conclusive evidence of something incontrovertible.

Karla could only stare at her.

Disappointed, Elisa frowned. "Don't you get it?" Karla shook her head. "Martha's been coming to Clear Lake with her family to swim since she was a little girl. Her folk's vacation home down in the eastern south lake was a beauty, right by the water. That girl knew how to swim before she learned to walk. It's as plain as day."

"So?"

Elisa rolled her eyes, leaned forward, and drew Karla toward her. "Martha figured out who had killed all them women. So, *he* had to kill her, too." Satisfied, she sat back, folded her arms, and smirked. "Newspapers said *feared drowned*. But, I know better. No way in hell Martha could drown. No way."

"You can't mean to say that Andrew killed his own mother?"

"I sure do."

Karla bolted up, pushing her chair back. "Thank you, Elisa." Without looking back she hastened out of the diner, desperate for fresh air.

# 16

# THE EXPOSURE

"The gossip is that that one of the twins killed his own mother," Sarah whispered.

James half smiled at her from across the booth in the roadside coffee shop where they had stopped for a quick meal. "There you are," he said with mock recognition. "Welcome back."

Sarah realized she held a hamburger in one hand and a French-fry in the other. She shook her head and rolled her eyes, suddenly aware of how silly she looked. "How long was I suspended like this?" She bit into the fry.

"A minute or so. You got out of the car and came in here perfectly fine, although I knew your mind was clearly elsewhere. It's truly amazing."

"Did I order my food?"

"No, I did. You don't speak, but you look like you're here in the moment. You're completely aware of your surroundings while your mind is occupied elsewhere."

"Oh, boy. That's got to be freaky."

"I find it remarkable. It's a bit like when one is driving and our mind is deciphering a problem or some such thing. We function perfectly behind the wheel, but we may overshoot our destination. That certainly has happened to me."

"James, any of the spirits around here recognize where I went, or witness it?"

"No, it doesn't work that way, Sarah. This woman that's guiding you is communicating with you and you alone. What's this news you just gave me?"

"What do you mean?"

"When you returned to me, you said something about killing the mother."

Sarah reflected for a moment. "Oh," she said at last, "the woman I'm supposed to help is seeking one of the twins. He's disappeared. She continues to dig up information, and obviously I'm being shown what she's learning. She was told that one of the twins killed his mother."

"I take it the mother you're referring to is your entity?"

Sarah nodded.

"The same older woman you saw falling down the stairs?"

"Yes."

"Did this new tidbit come from a reliable witness?"

Sarah grimaced. "Far from it, a gossipy waitress. Unreliable, but disturbing nonetheless."

"I'd say. The one blamed for killing his mother is the twin she's looking for?"

"Yes."

"But you're uncomfortable with that."

"I am."

James simply shook his head and went back to his burger.

They ate in silence for a while.

"Let's try to dissect the situation you're in," James said at last. "Why do you suppose she offers up untraceable locations, forbids you to say the names, encircles you with secrecy, and yet spoon-feeds you information?"

Sarah swallowed a bite and leaned back. "She's unwilling to divulge her own secret."

"That's one reason. But, she could guide you directly to this woman you're supposed to help, and give you the real location."

Sarah shrugged. "Could it be she doesn't know?"

217

James arched an eyebrow. "Not likely."

"Why not?"

"Well, let's examine the situation. The woman is in the town where the entity resided, where her twin sons were raised, and where her family's business is."

Sarah finished her burger and fries as she pondered James' assertions. "Maybe that's the reason why. She's fearful of bringing shame to the family."

"So, she needs you to help this woman, but doesn't wish others to discover who's behind these killings."

"Particularly if it's indeed one of her sons."

"Why the delay tactics? What do you make of that?"

"To exasperate me."

James laughed. "I seriously doubt she wants that. It's probably the opposite."

"Meaning what?"

"This entity is using an enormous amount of energy transferring information directly to you to the exclusion of any other entities or persons."

"Including Conrad."

James nodded. "That's not an easy task. Spirits are pure energy, and for her to convey the story as it's developing requires focused exertion."

"You're saying she stalls because she's tired?"

James laughed. "No, spirits don't exactly get tired, but they do get drained. I suspect that's the reason for the delays in communicating with you. She needs to gather enough energy to enable the transference. Think about it, she's present with you and with the woman she wishes you to help. That's quite remarkable. Even for a spirit."

"I never thought of that, but it makes sense."

"I would imagine that she's gathering and passing on information, in equal measure."

"Plus, if she's unwilling to accept that one of her sons could've killed her—"

JACKAL IN THE MIRROR

"She's well aware of who killed her. She's accepted that. But she may be unable to accept that he's a serial killer. It could be that she's not sure. She's waiting, and hoping that he's not."

"That makes perfect sense, James. If that's the case, I feel sorry for the poor woman."

"Well, we'll find out soon enough who the perpetrator really is."

"What do you mean?"

"With the clues you've given me, the investigative team will soon locate a family that answers the description you've given us."

A loud scream deafened Sarah. She slapped her hands over her ears as tears of pain trickled down her cheeks.

James rushed to her side. "What can I do?"

Sarah shook her head. "I'm all right, James. Thanks. She's angry. Her scream was so loud it battered my ears."

"I didn't hear this one. I brought this on. I've gone too far. I need to distance myself from her. C'mon, let's get you back to your cabin."

# REVELATION

Votive candles illuminated the tiny attic. Through the small window, the lights of the Eiffel Tower, barely visible above the rooftops of Paris, offered a dim counterpart to the flickering glow of the candles. The bed occupied almost the entire room. A small table to one side held an open bottle of wine and two half empty glasses.

He rested on top of her, his hands cradling her head, his mouth caressing her lips as he spoke.

> *"My love,*
> *I'm happy when my skin*
> *Is full of your bouquet.*
> *I suffer when I know*
> *That you are far away.*

*Each drop within mine eyes*
*Holds the flavor of your life,*
*So, when you're gone,*
*My eyes grow sad,*
*For there's nothing*
*I can see."*

"Gabriel," she whispered, "your words…" Tears overflowed her eyes. "Your poems are—"

"For you and about you." He kissed her tears away. "Don't cry, my love."

"I'm not crying out of sadness. The passion your words create within me needs an outlet. My tears are simply that. Something has to give."

He sighed. "I'm glad you like them."

"Like them!" She pushed him off her and straddled him, the candles illuminating her sensuous nude body. "You're fishing for compliments. Well, you're going to get them." She took him inside her and began a slow and deliberate undulation of her hips.

He groaned with mounting pleasure.

Her breath quickened. "Is this compliment enough for you?"

"No," he gasped, "I need more."

She tightened her thighs and increased the pulsation.

"Oh." He shut his eyes.

"Is that all you can say?"

"No." He seized her hips, tugged her to him, tossed her on her back, and plunged in.

"Oh!" she squealed.

"Is that all you can say?"

She pulled him to her.

The boy hadn't meant to watch. The door was ajar. He simply peeked in and saw.

"Mother..." he whispered.

"Dear God." Sarah found herself behind the wheel of her car, driving through the night, surrounded by trees. "Who saw you? Daryl or Andrew?"

She looked all around, but in the darkness nothing looked familiar. "Where in God's name am I?"

She leaned back and sucked in several deep breaths in an attempt to remain calm.

"Martha, what on earth am I doing on this road?" Her eyes flicked to the dashboard, then back through the windshield to follow the headlights that illuminated the roadside. "You got me out of bed at four in the morning to bring me here? You realize that no one has a clue where I am? Hell, I don't even have a clue where I am. I complied with your wishes, now you have to help *me*. Talk!"

Silence.

"Please, Martha. I need to call Conrad and tell him where I am. He's on his way to meet me this morning." She paused. "You needn't worry about him. He won't divulge your secrets."

Silence.

"Are we going to Rosewood?"

Silence.

She veered onto the shoulder of the road and slammed on the brakes. "If you don't answer, I'll turn around and go back."

*Karla needs you.*

"I get that. But where am I going?"

*Toward her.*

# Entangled

Karla stepped into the registrar and newspaper office and glanced around. File cabinets, papers, files, and hundreds of office knick-knacks crowded the small office. Beyond the front counter at the back of the office, parked at a beat-up desk, a very large and overweight man devoured a hamburger, while he hummed off-key, and sluggishly filed food-stained cards into a little box. His bulging hips and legs hung over his chair, the sagging skin on his arms flopped about with every move he made. His shoulder-length hair showed signs of long-time neglect, and his beard was littered with the bits of foods that had escaped his mouth.

"Good afternoon," Karla said.

He glanced up. "Good … you, too," he managed to mumble between bites.

"I'd like to read the news reports that were published around the time when Jennifer McKenzie died. Do you have something about that?"

He pointed his hamburger to one side of the office. "Big books, right there on the shelves. Look for one that's labeled 1977." He signaled to his left. "Table and chair over there." He returned to his burger.

"Thank you." Karla headed toward the row of shelves, dropping her purse on top of the cluttered table on the way. She scanned the large tomes, found the one she needed, and brought it to the table. She pushed some of the dust-covered files, folders, and binders aside, took a seat, opened the tome, and flipped through newspaper clippings one after another.

She stopped at one that read, *April 15, 1977 – Jennifer Trenton McKenzie Dies. McKenzie Boys Left With Body for Three Days.*

She took out a notebook and pen from her purse and read the news articles describing the accidental death and the events that followed. She resumed flipping the pages until she finished the tome, closed it, and placed it on top of the pile on the table.

She rose and approached the cluttered counter in front of the large man who now avidly devoured a cinnamon roll. "Excuse me, sir, can you tell me where to look for any articles written on the deaths of the women found in Rosewood?"

The man continued to eat, hum and file, ignoring Karla's question.

Karla dug in her purse, pulled out a fifty-dollar bill, and stepped toward him. She held out the money in front of him. "Excuse me, but I'd like to find the articles on—"

"I got you."

Karla stood by him, while he ate, hummed, and filed. "Do you—"

"I'm thinking. Leave the money here and go behind the counter."

"Okay." Karla did as he asked.

He continued to eat, hum, and file.

Karla leaned on the counter, resigned to wait.

He looked up at her and grinned sarcastically. "They were bought. Exactly sixty-eight days and four hours ago."

"Bought? How could someone buy articles from this office?"

He took a big bite of his pastry and held up the fifty-dollar bill. "With money."

"You're expected to keep the original articles."

"Not if someone needs them bad enough."

"Would the newspaper office in Rosewood have
them?"

"They don't got one. This is it."

"How can you be so flippant about selling them?"

"Hold it, lady. What's it to you anyway? You a relative of one of them hookers or something?"

"No. I'm a reporter and I'm looking for—"

"Looks like you'll have to go looking somewhere
else." Gradually, he rose to his feet until he towered over
Karla. "Don't care for reporters. Get your stuff and leave."

"I'm not done yet."

He came around the counter. "Yes, you are. Leave
now—or shall I escort you out?"

"Wait a minute. You can't—"

He moved closer. "I can, and I will."

Karla backed into the table. The pile of books, folders, and binders tumbled to the floor. She gathered her
belongings and turned to face him. "Who bought them?"

"Don't care to remember." He grabbed Karla's arm,
shoved her out the door, and shut it in her face.

"Enjoy cleaning up that mess!" she shouted. She
spun away and charged across the street, mumbling.

As she regained her composure, her gait slowed.
She took in a deep breath and noticed the displays that
filled the windows of the various curiosity shops. She
lingered for a while and became enthralled with the window of a quaint store that sold miniatures.

A hand gripped her shoulder. Startled, she turned. "Andrew?"

Daryl laughed. "I thought by now you could tell the difference."

Karla forced a smile. "I didn't expect to find *you* here."

"You're trembling. Anything wrong?"

"You startled me."

"Sorry, I'll make it up to you." He grasped her arm gently and guided her toward a small wooden bench in front of the miniatures store. He eased her down, sat beside her, and took her hand in his. "I didn't mean to scare you."

"I'm fine. All this stuff about Andrew's got me all shook up."

"What stuff? What have these good people been telling you?"

Karla looked deep into Daryl's eyes. He appeared calm and caring. "I'm glad you're here."

He grinned, his face aglow despite the shade. "I'm glad to be here, particularly if that makes you happy."

"What are you doing here, anyway?"

"I come here all the time to check on the tree farms and the vineyards, to talk to the managers and suppliers, and all that good stuff. I was driving by when I saw you." He slid closer to her. "Don't give credit to all the stories these people dish out. This is a small town and folks here live on gossip." He threw her a comforting grin and squeezed her hand.

Karla retrieved her hand and eased away from him. "It's horrible what they say. And to top it all off, Andrew is here."

Daryl tensed, and his cordial demeanor vanished. "Are you sure?"

"Yes, I caught a glimpse of him last night."

"Where is he?"

"I couldn't catch up with him. I went to your house, but it's deserted."

Daryl glowered at her. "You've been to the cabin?"

"You call that a cabin?"

Daryl's face and body relaxed. "You've been to the house."

"Isn't that what I said?"

Daryl cast her one of his alluring smiles. "To me, the cabin is home."

"What cabin? You mean Mary Ellen's place?"

"No, of course not. That's *her* home. I meant *our* cabin."

She looked at him inquisitively. "Nobody's told me anything about another cabin."

"They'll only tell you what they want you to hear. Especially since you told them you're a reporter."

Karla looked at him in dismay. "How did you reach that conclusion?"

An almost imperceptible hesitation preceded another winning smile. "What else could you tell them to get them to talk to you? C'mon, give me a little credit."

He stood and pulled her up. "Let's go. It'll soon be dark and that means dinnertime. I'll fix you the best steak you've ever had. Promise."

He hooked her arm over his and headed down the street.

She retrieved her arm and stopped. "Where are we going?"

"To the cabin. Home."

He grabbed her hand and pulled her to him but she stiffened and pushed him away. "What are you doing?"

"Relax. You've got nothing to fear. I'm here to protect you. Trust me, you're going to love our place."

After a moment's hesitation, she yielded, and side-by-side they walked down the street.

He reached a silver Porsche, opened the passenger door, and helped Karla in. He folded himself into the driver's seat, started the car, and sped away.

After a few silent minutes, he swerved off the main road and veered onto a narrow mountain road. Deftly, he raced around one curve after another with mere inches to spare.

"Are we trying to catch somebody?" Karla asked nervously.

"In a way, I suppose so. Don't worry, I know this old road like the back of my hand. I'm really looking forward to showing you the old place."

"It'll be a lot more fun if we get there in one piece. I don't particularly enjoy the feeling of impending doom."

"You could always use the feeling for a future story."

"Assuming there *is* a future story." Karla placed her hands on the dashboard to steady herself.

The speed with which Daryl maneuvered the curves increased along with his smile. "Where's your writer's spirit of adventure?"

"It's waiting for me at the end of the road."

"Would Hemingway have passed up an opportunity to experience a new emotion? Would F. Scott Fitzgerald have let an unexpected reaction pass fleetingly by? Not a chance."

"The latter would have fled and the former would—"

Abruptly, Daryl slowed down. "You're right, he probably would have. I promise not to challenge the Hemingway inside Karla Jordan. Scout's honor."

"You couldn't possibly have been a scout."

"That obvious?"

"A real scout would never have the temerity to frighten a lady."

"And here I was convinced I'd rescued a damsel in distress."

"Really?"

He laughed and drove on at a slower pace.

"Tell me about your parents," Karla said.

He glanced at her for a moment then turned his attention back to the ever-darkening road. "I'm sure you've done your research and dug up the skinny about them."

"Some things are not in the public record. For instance, where did the two of you go when your mother took you away from here?"

He turned to her. "Paris."

"To stay with your uncle Gabriel?"

Abruptly, he pulled over and stopped the car. "The sun will be setting soon and the view from here is spectacular." He jumped out of the car, dashed to the passenger side, and opened her door. "Let's enjoy the scenery." He proffered his hand and helped her out of the car.

"So, did you stay with your uncle?"

Daryl leaned against his car and sighed. "We did."

Karla joined him. "You don't like to talk about that. Why?"

He became visibly somber. "I hated being there. I missed my father. Besides, we had no business being with that man."

"Why did your mother take the two of you away?"

"Because she wanted to, end of story. I don't care to relive that trip, if you don't mind. Let's enjoy the view. Would you like to hear a poem?

"Sure."

*"Now*
*That I'm used to smiling again,*
*Don't*
*Remind me of so long ago.*

*It isn't as easy*
*As some people think*
*To forget all the things*
*That make us hate.*

*All we can do*
*Is pick up our lives*
*And pray*
*That it is not too late.*

*Now*
*If ever you meet me again,*
*Don't*
*Ask me where I have been.*

*Summers are lucky*
*In so many ways*
*When the snow melts*
*And the scars disappear.*

*When*
*My nights turn to days*
*And I hope*
*New love will banish my fear.*

*Now*
*That you've died in my mind,*
*It almost feels*
*That you never were here.*

*My heart has survived*
*More than I thought it would.*

*Now*
*It simply looks*
*For a love it can share."*

Karla studied Daryl. His eyes were lost in his memories and filled with unshed tears.

She reached over and touched his arm. "That's so sad."

He turned to her. "It's sad and happy. It's the end of what shouldn't have been, and the beginning of what might be."

"You wrote it?"

"No. It's from a book of poems I once had, and lost."

"You like poetry?"

He shook his head. "No, only that poem. So," he gestured toward the horizon, "what about of the view?"

She turned toward the scenery. "You're right, it's stunning."

His gaze remained fixed on her. "It is indeed."

"How long before the sun sets?"

"Long enough for us to enjoy it." He slid closer to her.

Sarah looked around to find herself parked on the side of the road, the sun glistening off the lake below. She whispered, "Martha, is Daryl referring to your book of poems? Is he the one who saw you with Gabriel?"

She emerged from the car, stretched, and stepped to the edge of the road overlooking the lake. Mesmerized by the serene beauty of her surroundings, she gazed into the distance.

"Okay, Martha, enough. I'm standing here, in the middle of nowhere, completely baffled, and with no cell reception, thanks to you. I certainly deserve your help. You've had enough time to recharge."

*Left bank.*

Sarah turned left and squinted. In the distance, she managed to spot a small pier with a rowboat floating nearby. Above it, surrounded by trees, she discerned the top of a dwelling.

"Oh, my God! Finally. Thanks, Martha."

She ran back to her car and sped off.

# 17

# THE TRAIL

"Where the hell is she?" Conrad paced back and forth inside Sarah's empty cabin.

"I have no idea." James stood by the door, dumbfounded. "I left her here last night after dinner. She wasn't planning on going anywhere, or at least she didn't tell me. I'm so sorry, Conrad."

"It's not your doing, James, nothing to apologize for. Darn woman. She gets like this when someone is in her head. She reacts on instinct." He looked at James standing sheepishly by the door. "Please, come in. Sorry for ranting and raving."

James stepped in and closed the door behind him. "She's been detaching—the story in her head—"

"Yeah, I'm well aware of what she does. It must've freaked you out."

"No, not really. I understand what she's going through."

"Good. What was the last vision she had?"

James sat on one of the chairs next to the small table. "While we were having dinner, she learned that the gossip in town was that one of the twins had killed his mother, but Sarah wasn't convinced. She also said she knew where the first woman had been killed—she wanted to go right then and there to look for it. But it was dusk and I talked her out of it. Or thought I had."

"Any idea where that might be?"

"Not a clue. She mentioned a house by a lake with a pier and row-boat. She said it reminded her of a plantation-type home, but on the other hand she doubted that was the one because the first house she saw was smaller. So in essence, no real clues."

"Well, at least it's a beginning. We can start there."

"The problem is that most folks who live by the big lake or any of its tributaries have a pier and at least one boat."

"Yes, but she described the rowboat as being old and rickety."

"I suppose we can drive around and try to spot it."

"At least it would give us something to do."

James got to his feet. "Let me call the sheriff's office and find out if they've made any progress in identifying the family she described."

"Can you check if they can trace Sarah's location from her cell phone, too?"

"Yes, of course. I'm sure they'll give it a go. The problem is that around the lake reception is very sporadic, and to top it all off, the entity is interfering with her signal."

"Interfering? How?"

"By using her energy to block the phone connections with ear piercing static."

"That explains why I couldn't reach her."

"Exactly. C'mon, let's try to find that lovely wife of yours." James stepped out of the room, grabbed his cell phone, and dialed the sheriff's office.

Sarah painstakingly followed the road around the lake, search-ing for a driveway that might lead toward the house on the left bank. However, the density of the trees impeded the view of the lake or any homes.

After numerous attempts that ended in dead ends, her frustration, fed by increasing exhaustion, began to mount.

"Martha, I'm having trouble finding the house, and I'm not going to trespass, so you need to guide me."

Silence.

As she returned for the umpteenth time to the main road, she spotted a gas station a few hundred feet ahead. A quick glance at the gas gauge indicated that the encounter was indeed fortuitous, since the car was nearly empty.

After filling the tank, Sarah pulled the hose from the car and headed toward the store. She reached the counter and spotted a young man crouched behind it retrieving packs of cigarettes, which he moved to the shelves behind him one by one.

"Excuse me," Sarah called out, "do you have a restroom I could use? Been on the road for a while."

"Here's the key, it's straight back on the right."

"Thanks." Sarah headed back.

A few minutes later, she came out, grabbed a bottle of water, and headed toward the counter. "I'll take this. Would you happen to know if there is a house around here that belongs to the McKenzie family?"

"Doesn't sound familiar. You're sure they live here in Clearlake Oaks?"

"Not sure at all. But the house has a small pier and an old rickety rowboat."

The young man laughed. "Lots of folks have houses like that on the smaller inlets. Right around here you'll find the big yachts. Just head north and veer off towards Alderwood. It's more likely you'll find small piers and old rowboats around there."

"Thanks." She paid for her water. "You think I could use a phone? My cell is dead and I need to let my husband know where I'm headed. I'll pay you for the call."

"Sure thing." He reached for the phone under the counter and plopped it on top. Sarah picked up the receiver, but loud static kept her from putting it to her ear.

"That's bad," the young man said, taking the receiver from her. "The lines go dead here and there, but I've never heard something that loud."

"Thanks, anyway." She left the store, got in her car, and pulled out onto the road.

"Martha you better tell me if I'm heading in the right direction."

# RELATE

Daryl and Karla drove in silence.

"Why so quiet?" Daryl asked.

"Nothing special. Admiring the fading scenery as the sun disappears and thinking."

"About Andrew, no doubt."

Karla continued to peer out the window.

"You're a fascinating woman."

Karla turned toward him. "Thanks."

"So, what attracted you to Andrew?"

Karla stretched in her seat and grinned. "You mean what's a nice girl like me doing with a mystery man like Andrew?"

"That's one way to put it."

"What could've made you hate him so much?"

"I don't hate Andrew. I told you that already."

Karla sighed and turned toward the window.

"We're different, that's all. Very different."

"You can say that again. Like night and day."

"What do you find attractive about him?"

She rested her head against the window. "Well...I love his unusual combination of strength and fragility."

Daryl shifted gears and gunned the engine. "Fragility?" he asked.

"Why does that surprise you?"

"Unless he's become someone entirely different since I last saw him, my brother could never, and I emphasize *never,* be described as fragile."

"Well, he is."

The car tore along the winding road with increasing speed. Karla grabbed onto the dashboard. "Please stop this."

Daryl turned to her with an impish look. "You're beautiful when you're frightened."

"That's a compliment I can do without."

He slowed slightly and she turned away from him. "Relax. I delight in beautiful women, and I enjoy telling them so."

"Now, you have, so you can stop showing off."

"As you command."

"Where's this cabin anyway?"

"It's in Rosewood, a—"

"Rosewood?"

"What's wrong?"

"That's where they found the bodies of all those women that were killed."

Daryl pulled over and stopped. He turned toward Karla and reached for her hand. "Listen to me. Don't believe all those stories they told you back there. Rosewood is nothing more than a sleepy old town. Relax. Anyhow, I'm here, and nothing is going to happen to you."

"To me?"

"Isn't that why you're scared?"

"I'm not scared. It surprised me to hear that we're actually going there, that's all."

"Good. I'm glad you're not frightened." He engaged the gear and accelerated back onto the road. "All is well?"

"All is well."

As the car careened along, the shadows of the night descended like a black curtain. An occasional light emanated from the smattering of homes along the mountain road.

"You've entered Rosewood," Daryl announced.

"What? No welcome sign?"

"No, they took it down."

"Why?"

"To avoid notoriety."

"Can't say I blame them."

A few minutes later the car approached an L-shaped building on the side of the road. The front was lit by a couple of old-fashioned lampposts and a sign that read "General Store."

Daryl parked in front of the store, got out, and walked around the car. He opened her door and offered her a hand getting out. "You'll like this place. It hasn't changed much since the early '40s."

"Really?"

"Yep, been here forever. My dad loved it. He used to bring me here to get sweets and other things. It was our secret."

"Sounds like you were close to your dad."

"I was," he answered with pride. "He was a great man and I learned much from him. C'mon." Daryl dashed in looking like an excited kid on a visit to the neighborhood store.

The moment Karla entered she felt immediately transported back in time. The store was stocked to the rafters with groceries, household products, and items such as shoes, shirts and jackets. To one side, the typical mid-century counter offered a myriad of sweets, sodas and ice creams. On the far end, behind a smaller counter, medicines and herbal remedies made their home.

A balding middle-aged man wearing an apron tied around his rotund belly emerged from the back. He caught sight of Daryl and beamed. "Daryl, my boy, so nice to see you." He strode over to him, picked him up in a bear hug, and laughed. "You're definitely too big for me nowadays." He set him back down and bent over to catch his breath.

Daryl patted him on the back and laughed. "I've been too heavy for you for many years, but I love it."

The man straightened, holding on to Daryl to steady himself. "Nice of you to say, dear boy, considering I'm about to croak with the effort." He glanced at Karla.

"Oscar, this is Ms. Karla Jordan. She's a reporter from the big city. Well, she's actually much more than that." He winked at her.

Karla smiled and extended her hand. Oscar held it in both of his and shook it vigorously. "Nice to meet you, Ms. Jordan."

"Please, call me Karla."

"So be it. You writing about my boy here, Karla?"

"No, actually about his brother, Andrew. Has he been here lately?"

Oscar glanced at Daryl, who shrugged. He then turned back to Karla. "Not lately. In fact, I haven't seen him in quite a while."

"When was the last time?"

"A very long time. C'mon, join me at the counter and I'll fix you a nice milkshake while we chat and catch up. We—"

"No time for that, I'm afraid," Daryl interrupted. "We're off to the cabin and I'm cooking this lovely lady some nice steaks, so don't spoil her appetite. Got any good ones hidden in your stash down in the basement?"

"Sure do. Come, you can pick them yourself."

"No, I'll hang around here and get some veggies and such. Take Karla with you. She's never been in a place like this." Karla frowned at Daryl. "Well, you haven't." He patted her on the shoulder.

"How would you know?"

"By the way you looked when you stepped in," he said with another wink, "a sure sign." He turned and walked away.

"Miss Karla, you're in for a nice trip down memory lane. Follow me." Oscar headed toward a door at the back of the store. "This good-old store has been in my family since Robert McKenzie senior and his bride Anastasia first set foot in this part of the world. Well, almost."

Karla followed Oscar. He swung the door open and invited her to go in first.

"This here is the office. The furniture is from back in the late thirties, early forties. I'm a bit messy, but my son keeps me on the straight and narrow. He runs the place these days and tries to show me how to organize things. When left alone, I create clutter. He's away with his brood for a holiday so, as you can see, I've made a mess of things here. He'll have a cow when he comes back."

Karla laughed. "I'm sure it's not that bad."

"Oh, but it is. I'm just for show, like the rest of the antiques. So if I need to find something when a customer calls and I have no clue where it is, I flutter about and let them find it themselves." He opened a door to one side of the office and switched the light on, illuminating a narrow staircase. "Watch your step going down those stairs. They're a bit narrow."

Karla took one step at a time and descended into the basement.

"This basement was Anastasia's idea, so my grandpa said. A natural cooling system she told him, and she was right. We do have freezers upstairs, but the meat ages better down here."

"She had a hand in the store?"

"I'd say. She's the one talked good old Rob senior into the whole thing. He partnered with my grandpa and their wives stocked it. I'm sure you noticed some of the original products scattered about upstairs. Not for sale, mind you, but they give the place a nice nostalgic aura."

"Your family was in the same business as the McKenzies?"

"Heavens, no, not at all."

"But—"

"Rob senior started in the mines when he was in his teens."

"I heard that's how he got started, but these parts aren't exactly famous for mines."

"Back in those days they yielded quicksilver, gold, and borax. My grandpa gave Rob a bit of a shove when he first came here from Canada so the townsfolk around here would take a liking to him. He got into mining and hit it big, got out, bought some land, and started farming walnut, pear, and other fruit trees." He smiled. "Come to think of it, we did connect in business."

"Oh?"

"My grandpa sold Rob's produce. We still do, in fact."

"Even their wines?"

"For sure."

"How did Rob get into wine making?"

"Rob senior started it all right here with a few vineyards, but Rob junior, that's Daryl's dad, he's the one got that industry going big. When Daryl took over, he bought wineries here and all over the world. That boy has a real knack for business, like his daddy." Oscar laughed. "All the McKenzies do, really." He opened a sealed locker and exposed several shelves of prime beef, each with the date their dry aging had started. "Pick what you like."

"Please, Oscar, you do it. I wouldn't dare. You're familiar with Daryl's taste better than me. I only met him recently."

He stared at her in surprise. "Oh?"

"I'm in search of Andrew, so I went to Daryl."

"Why is that?"

"Are you asking me why I'm looking for Andrew, or why would I go to Daryl?"

"Both, if you care to answer."

"Okay. Well, Andrew disappeared out of the blue several days ago, and later his studio was ransacked—"

"Studio?"

"He's an artist."

"That doesn't surprise me. Any good?"

"Very good."

"So you're one of them investigative reporters?"

Karla laughed. "No, nothing like that. I write for art magazines."

"You're an artist, too?"

"No, I love art and can write about it. That's the simplest way to describe what I do."

"You're a critic?"

"No, more of an observer."

He grabbed a piece of butcher paper, and selected a slab of meat, from which he sawed off a couple of steaks. "How about these?" he asked when he'd placed them on the paper.

Karla eyed them. "They look great."

Oscar wrapped the steaks. "So why did you go to Daryl?"

"You ask because they don't see eye to eye?"

"You could say that. Those boys split up years ago. It's a shame. Broke their mother's heart." He shut the locker and turned toward the stairs. "Ready to go back?"

"You're sure you haven't seen Andrew lately?"

"I'm sure. Andrew is not one to go unnoticed. He used to come back often to visit his mother, but—"

"Hey, you two down there," Daryl yelled from the open door above the stairs, "are you getting steaks or herding the cattle?"

"Hold your horses, boy. We're coming." Oscar gestured for Karla to go up first.

She climbed the stairs, and when she reached the last step, Daryl took her arm and escorted her out of the office. "What were you two yapping about down there?"

"Andrew," Karla said matter-of-factly.

Daryl scowled. "Oh, of course, always Andrew."

Karla stopped and turned to him. "What do you mean by that?"

"Simply that you're always thinking and talking about him."

"Yes. That's why I'm here," she said with a stern look.

Oscar winked at Karla. "Pay no attention to him. The twins have always been at each other's necks, even when they're not in the same vicinity."

They followed Oscar to the front counter where Daryl had set a basket filled with groceries. Next to it sat twenty votive candles neatly lined up in rows of five.

"So, that's the clue? I need to find a store by a roadside?" Sarah shook her head in frustration. "Listen, Martha. First you send me on a wild goose chase to the left bank of the lake knowing full well that I would never find the house. Now you guide me toward a store that could be anywhere. I've been driving for hours and I'm tired, hungry, thirsty, and irritated."

Silence.

"Let's try another approach and find out if you can be a bit clearer. You are implying that Daryl is the one that's threatening Karla. That's why he purchased all those votive candles. Or is he buying candles in case of a loss of electricity? Which is it?"

Silence.

She pulled over and stopped. Bursting from the car she paced angrily. "You are so exasperating!"

She shook her head and leaned on the passenger door. "Look at that," she pointed toward the horizon. "It's almost sunset and—Oh! Almost sunset! I'm getting close, aren't I? They're just a few hours ahead of me!"

She got back in the car, revved it up, and took off. "Let's find that general store. With a little luck, maybe you'll let me use their phone."

She pictured Conrad desperately searching for her, until her gaze settled solely on the road ahead.

# TRUTH

"Daryl," Martha exclaimed, "what on earth are you doing?"

He had decorated the entire living area of the cabin with votive candles. The incandescence of the room illuminated his satisfied grin as he sat cross-legged in the middle of the floor facing the fireplace.

He turned to her. "Hello Mother, I'm glad you're here."

"Why are *you* here, Daryl?"

His smile transformed into an angry grimace. "I'm not Daryl, you asinine woman." He turned back facing the fire.

Martha approached him warily. She stepped over the votive candles, and sat in the armchair next to him. "Darling, you can't fool me. Not anymore. You're seventeen, and far too old for pretend games like that."

"As you wish," he growled. "Believe what you will."

"Why have you come here? And why do all of this?" She indicated the votive candles.

He grinned. "You're happy here. You're full of love when you're here."

"Yes, I *am* happy here, but I'm also happy at home. Do you realize the fright you gave us running away like that?"

He shook his head. "I knew you'd come here."

"How come?"

"The old cabin betrayed you."

"What do you mean by that?" She reached for him, but he signaled her not to touch him.

"You created us in that old cabin. But it got its revenge—and killed Aunt Jenny."

"Dear Lord, how did you get that idea?"

He looked at her with contempt. "I'm not stupid, Mother."

"What's wrong? What's upset you? Why did run off like that?"

He narrowed his eyes and stared at her, the muscles around his mouth tight with anger. "You know why."

"No, I don't."

"Are you going to pretend that those three books with all the poems that *he* so graciously gave us are not about his love for you? You've convinced yourself that we're too naive to understand the truth."

Martha blanched and felt her heart quicken. "What truth? Your uncle Gabriel is a generous man. You've said so yourself. He wished for you and your brother to have—"

"A part of him?"

"Well, yes, since you put it like that."

"Do we have to read about his obsession with you? Isn't it enough that he's our real father?"

Martha leapt to her feet. "You're wrong. What are you're saying?"

He jumped up and moved closer to her. "Don't lie Mother. I saw you in Paris, in his arms, in his bed."

Martha gasped. "No, how? You don't understand. I—"

"Oh, I do understand. You're a whore." He turned away and resumed his place on the floor. "Sit down, whore."

"Daryl!"

"Don't call me that! I'm *not* Daryl, I'm Andrew." He took the book from his jacket pocket.

"Sit down, Mother, and I, *Andrew*, will read you a poem that I'm certain will make you smile."

Stunned, Martha obeyed.

"The title is 'Star.' Do you remember it, Mother Whore?"

Martha remained motionless.

"Here it goes. I'll try to do it justice.

*"It looked as though*
*I had it in my hand...*
*A star.*

*I must have blinked*
*I guess,*
*Because now it's gone."*

He tilted his head and looked up at her. "He wrote this because you left him. Right?"

Martha was speechless, her eyes welling with tears. Daryl went on.

> *"Or maybe I saw*
> *A ray of stardust*
> *While I wished for a star*
> *I couldn't have.*

"At least *he* knew he was wrong. Did you?" He glared angrily up at her.

She remained silent, staring at her son.

> *"Perhaps*
> *I squeezed too tight*
> *And now the star*
> *Is dead.*
>
> *Perhaps*
> *I ran too fast*
> *To show you my new prize,*

"Is this about me?" He stared at the book in his hands. "Or is this his prize, these *filthy* pages filled with his poems?

> *"Or maybe stars are fragile*
> *And it broke.*
>
> *I don't know where the answer lies,*
> *Or what happened to my star.*
>
> *Maybe it just got lonely*

*And hid behind the moon*
*To shed its tears.*

*Maybe*
*I never really had*
*A star*
*At all.*

"Did you leave him for good?"

Martha noticed the flickering flames reflected in his hateful stare and remained silent.

"No matter." He grinned through clenched teeth. "It's time." Slowly, he rose to his feet and approached his mother. Taking her hands, he raised her from the arm-chair, turned her around to face the fire, and stepped behind her.

He clamped his arms around her, rested his chin on her shoulder, and threw the book of poems into the flames. "That was *your* book, not mine," he whispered malevolently. "*Mine* disappeared long ago. His memory is now as dead as he should be. Nothing left of him. The poems—gone. His love—gone. Aunt Jenny will be happy." He kissed her neck. "I'll take care of you, Mother, especially now that you're aware that I own the truth."

Sarah gasped. "Dear God in heaven. No wonder you've been cautious. No one realized except Daryl, or was it Andrew? Which one is he, Martha? Who saw you in Paris?"

Silence.

"What a glimpse you've given me into your tortured reality. C'mon, please tell me, who is he, Daryl or Andrew?"

She followed the road, increasing her speed. "Maybe you're not even completely certain which one he is." She shook her head. "It's clear that you discovered what he is, but maybe you weren't sure, or refused to accept that one of your sons is a monster. Is that why you conceal his identity from me?"

Silence.

"Well, if that's what you prefer, I'll hush up as well." She banged on the steering wheel and stared ahead, into the encroaching darkness.

# 18

## THE CABIN

The headlights on Daryl's car illuminated the facade of a two-story house partly concealed by trees. Surrounded by wilderness, it sat mere feet from the lake where a small pier anchored the old familiar rowboat.

The car pulled up to the end of the driveway and Daryl climbed out. "Stay in the car. It's very dark out here. Let me open the place up, start the generator, and turn on some lights."

"No deal. I'm coming with you. I don't want to miss anything."

Daryl laughed. "Miss what?"

"What if Andrew is in there?"

"Oh, right. Let's not forget *Andrew.*" The smile ebbed from Daryl's face. "Wait till I get the generator going. Once the lights are on, we'll go in."

He disappeared behind the house and moments later the hum of the generator's motor broke the silence of the forest.

Daryl walked back to the front door, opened it, and stepped into the darkened house.

The moment the lights came on Karla ran into the cabin. A large room glowed in the light of several table lamps. It was elegantly decorated with antique furniture dating to the early twentieth century. Though it was well kept, a discarded sweater on a chair and an empty cup on the coffee table made it look as if someone were living in it. The sizeable living room had built-in wall-to-wall bookshelves crammed with books, while family photographs and mementos covered most of the walls and available shelf space. Only a narrow door faced the windows that overlooked the front of the house, and a large stone fireplace separated the bookshelves. A furry white rug resembling a polar bear skin lay before the fireplace, and a couple of side chairs, and two sofas adorned the rest of the room.

"Looks like we've found him," Karla said.

Daryl stopped. "What makes you say that?"

"Someone's been living here. Look at this place—it's spotless. And it's not a cabin, it's a beautiful house."

Daryl snagged the cup, walked over to the dining room, and flicked on the light. A small kitchen with all the modern conveniences appeared beyond it. The stairs to the upper floor divided the dining room from the living room, but only a wooden counter with tall bar stools served to separate the kitchen from the dining room.

"Let's unload the groceries," Daryl said. "I'm famished." He headed toward the front door where Karla remained standing. He shook his head and laughed.

She stopped him. "What's so funny?"

"Your deductive powers."

"Oh? Why?"

"Mrs. Oliver has been keeping the place up for years. She comes in twice a month. She was probably here yesterday. C'mon, let's get the bags. I don't want you to miss out on helping me carry all the stuff." He grabbed Karla's arm and dragged her out of the cabin.

They reached the car, and Daryl dug out one of the bags of groceries and handed it to her.

Karla took the small bag. "Twice a month? If you ask me, that's a waste of money."

He handed her another bag of groceries, carried one himself, snagged his suitcase, and locked the car. "When you love a place you don't care about the money, especially if you have it. C'mon." He steered her toward the cabin.

Inside, Daryl put his luggage down, closed the door, and nudged Karla toward the kitchen. He relieved her of the bags and placed them on the counter in the center of the kitchen under a copper hanger crowded with cooking pots, pans, spoons and ladles.

"The main house is deserted and this *cabin* as you call it—is kept up? I don't get it."

Daryl stepped into the living room, picked up his suitcase and disappeared down a hallway off the main room. "The big house," he called out over his shoulder, "was never as warm a place as this. We all loved coming here. Particularly, Mother." A light came on in the hallway.

Moments later he came back into the kitchen. He unpacked the groceries, placing them expertly on shelves or in the refrigerator. Karla leaned on the counter watching him.

"We? Who is 'we'? Does Andrew—"

"Look,' he said, clearly exasperated, "there's no mystery here, so drop the investigation."

"Don't get so uptight. I was only wondering who—"

"You wonder too much."

In silence, he finished storing the groceries, grabbed the small paper bag filled with votive candles and strode into the living room. He placed the candles in the top drawer of a cabinet by the front door just as the lights went out engulfing the cabin in total darkness.

"Shit!" he exclaimed

"What happened?"

"The damn generator. I've been meaning to give it an overhaul, but I haven't had time." He retrieved a pack of matches from the drawer, lit a couple of votive candles, and gave them to Karla. He returned to the opened drawer and grabbed a flashlight. "Here, use this."

"What's with the generator?"

"What do you mean?"

"Why do you even have one? With all your money you could have—"

"Yes, could have, but didn't. Can you cook?"

"Yes, I can cook, but weren't you going to make *me* the best steaks ever?"

"I am, but you can help with the salad. I'll fix the generator and light a nice, cozy fire." He marched off without waiting for a response.

Karla shook her head. She took the vegetables from the counter and placed them in the sink. She searched for a strainer amongst the items hanging over the table, then continued her search through various cupboards by flashlight. She spotted a strainer that satisfied her needs and headed toward the sink. The lights came on and she blew out the candles.

Daryl came back, dusting himself off. He shut the door and headed for the fireplace. "Hope it'll last for a while. I'll get a fire going. If it shuts down again, at least we'll have some light." The fireplace was prepared, with crumpled newspapers and logs set in place waiting to be lit. Daryl stroked a long match and held it to the newspapers. They ignited, and in moments the logs were burning. As he poked the logs, he heard Karla scream in the kitchen.

He dropped the poker and sprinted to her side.

Karla stood before the sink, her face, hair, and clothes, dripping wet. "The cap on the faucet wasn't on right."

Daryl laughed.

"Don't stand there! Give me a towel!"

Daryl grabbed a small kitchen towel, and handed it to her. "I assumed you knew how to handle yourself in a kitchen."

Karla raised her head from the towel. "Don't push your luck."

"C'mon, you got to admit it's pretty funny," he said, trying to contain his laughter.

Karla frowned. "

"Really?"

"For crying out loud!"

"C'mon. I'll show you to Mother's room so you can dry off."

He escorted her through the dining room and up the stairs.

They entered Martha's elegant bedroom. Daryl opened a closet filled with clothes. "Mother was smaller than you, but one of her nightgowns might fit while we dry your clothes. The bathroom is that little door by Mother's boudoir. While you make yourself presentable, I'll get some wine from the cellar. Then I'll fix you a martini to help warm you up."

"I'll be right out. Thanks."

"Drop your clothes outside the door and I'll put them in the dryer." He left her, closing the door behind him.

Taking a robe from the closet, she dropped her clothes outside and made her way to a bathroom every bit as refined as the bedroom. She grabbed a towel and dried herself.

# 19

# THE REVEAL

Sarah left her car in the parking lot outside a familiar building. The sign read General Store. At the door, she reached for the knob just as Oscar was flipping the "Open" sign over.

He noticed her and opened the door. "We're closing, ma'am, sorry."

"Please," she gasped. "Oscar?"

He smiled and nodded. "This is a first. You know me but I don't believe I've had the pleasure."

She extended her hand. "We've never met. I'm Sarah Thompson." They shook hands. "It's really you and your name is indeed Oscar."

He chortled, amused by her comment. "Nice to meet you Sarah. And yes it is I and my name is indeed Oscar. What's all this about?"

"I'm more than happy to tell you, but first may I use your restroom? Been driving all afternoon—"

"Yes, of course. Come right in."

She stepped into the store.

"It's at the back of the store to the left of the office."

Sarah couldn't help but smile. "It's exactly like she showed me."

"What is? Who showed you?" a bewildered Oscar asked.

"Oh, don't mind me. Be right back." She headed toward the back of the store. "I'm an acquaintance of the McKenzies."

"Do you mean the McKinneys?"

"Yes, of course. Sorry, with the excitement of finding you—" she disappeared into the restroom.

Moments later she emerged to find him waiting. "Thanks so much."

"That's how come you know about me, the McKinneys?"

"Yes."

He frowned. "How—"

"May I bother you for a telephone?" she interrupted him. "I've had no reception on my cell phone and my husband must be worried sick."

"Sure thing. Better use the one in the office." Sarah followed Oscar into the cluttered room. "Sorry about the mess."

"Please, don't mention it."

Oscar pointed to an old-fashioned rotary phone. "It's old, but in good working order."

"Thank you. This town is called, uh, 'something wood', right?"

"Alderwood. Anyway, I'll leave you to it." He stepped out, leaving the door ajar.

Sarah dialed. "Hello there, handsome," she said when Conrad answered.

"Where the hell are you? Are you okay? Why haven't you called?"

"Whoa, one at a time."

"Do you realize how worried we've been? Please, answer me. Where are you?"

"I'm all right, I'm in a town called Alderwood somewhere in the middle of a mountain range, by a lake. Hard to describe. Sorry but I've had no reception on the cell phone. I'm calling you from a General Store that belongs to a guy named Oscar."

He exhaled. "Couldn't you have waited for me? Why did you leave?"

"I tried to, but Martha urged me to go. I really had no choice."

"At least you're fine. I've been going out of my mind."

"I'm sorry, darling. I tried several times to call you, but couldn't."

"Are you coming back?"

"No. I'm getting closer to Karla. She's only a couple of hours or less ahead of me. And she's in real danger. I need to get to her."

"We're coming to you. How do we find you?"

257

"We?"

"James is here."

"Great, he'll tell you how to find Alderwood. Martha's real last name, is Mc—"

The line went dead and the familiar static took over. She hung up and dialed again, but the static was so strong the connection couldn't go through. Frustrated, she hung up and walked back to the store.

"All done?" asked Oscar.

"Got cut off. Lots of static interference."

"Give it another go in a few. Hope you like chocolate."

"I love it, and I haven't had anything to eat all day. What could be better than chocolate?"

"Have a seat, my dear."

Sarah slid onto one of the stools by the counter.

Oscar set two chocolate ice cream sodas down with spoons and straws. He came around the counter and took a stool next to Sarah. "A nice pick-me-up after a long day."

Sarah sipped on her straw. "It's delicious, Oscar, thank you."

He scooped a spoonful of chocolate ice cream into his mouth. "This is the reason my figure is so stunning. I can't go without it. So, Mrs. Thompson, how—"

"Please call me Sarah."

"Fair enough, but if you don't mind me asking, Sarah, how are you acquainted with the McKinneys?"

"Through Martha."

Oscar shook his head. "Sad story."

"Indeed."

"You're on your way to visit with Daryl?"

"Yes. And Karla, whom you just met."

Oscar gazed keenly at Sarah. "How could you possibly know that?"

"Oscar, I hope I won't freak you out, but I'm going to tell you some unusual stuff that might alarm you."

"It's hard to scare me. Go ahead."

"I'm a psychic and a medium."

He laughed. "Well, if that doesn't top it all. You're going to tell me you met me in a dream, aren't you?"

"You could say that. I watched you, Daryl, and Karla right here, in this store."

"Get out of here."

"I'll prove it." She took a quick sip of her soda and a bite of the ice cream. "Yum, this is fantastic. Anyway, they came in here and you hugged Daryl like you've always done. You tried to lift him, only he's too heavy and you got out of breath, and—"

He eyed Sarah suspiciously. "C'mon. I don't buy it. You were watching from outside."

"Okay—you took Karla to your basement and told her all about Anastasia and your grandparents. You also told her about the rivalry between the twins, and you chose two steaks."

He dropped his spoon into the soda and leaned back as if needing to focus on her from a distance. After a hard swallow, he managed to find his voice. "Dear God, you're for real."

She raised her eyebrows and nodded.

He gulped the remaining soda down, wiped his mouth with his apron, shook his head, and sighed. "You saw and heard all of that without being here?"

Sarah nodded. "And here's something that's going to surprise you even more. Martha is the one—"

"Martha's dead."

"Yes, that's true. But she's worried about Karla and needs me to help her."

He slid off the stool and paced nervously up and down the length of the counter. "Let me get this straight." He approached her one step at a time to emphasize his words. "You're telling me that you, that you talk to—dead people?"

"It's more like they talk to me. If they wish to. In Martha's case, she shows me what she thinks is useful."

Oscar threw up his arms and blew out a breath. "That's something else." He climbed back onto the edge of the stool, shook his head, and stared at her. "Doesn't it frighten you?"

"The dead?"

He grimaced and nodded.

"No."

"Why did Martha…?"

"Why did she approach me?"

He shrugged.

"There are restless spirits that are looking for…let's say *closure*. So they hang around in this realm, and—"

"What realm?"

"The dimension you and I occupy. This world, the one we're all aware of."

"You mean this here moment, right now, you and me having our ice cream sodas?"

"Yes."

"And you, what, go to other realities, other dimensions?"

"I witness them."

"How come?"

"I was born with the ability to do so."

"You saw dead people when you were a kid?"

She shook her head. "No, but I knew things that I had not personally witnessed, and I could tell what was going to happen before it happened, like premonitions. It wasn't till I was much older that I finally understood the science behind it."

"Science?"

"Yes. Basically I can perceive multiple dimensions beyond these four dimensions," she said, and gestured around them. "In alternate dimensions time and space have no barriers."

"Wow. Were you born with that?"

"In some people it's hereditary, generational even. Not in my family, though. I'm pretty much it, although my Nana was very intuitive."

Eyes wide, eyebrows raised, Oscar said, "I'll be darned. Are there others like you?"

"My husband's grandmother and her twin daughters were like me, as well as one of his cousins. Now that I am more open to sharing my ability—if we can call it that—I've come to meet others who tell me that they can perceive things or sense spirits and the like. A few days ago I met a marvelous man who lives in Eureka. He lives in both realms, this one and the spirit one, all the time. For me it comes and goes."

"That's quite the story. Unusual, for sure." He laughed. "I've watched psychics on television, but—"

"You didn't believe it was real."

He shrugged. "How does it happen?"

"Apparently we all can do it when we're first born, but for some reason, as we grow up, we lose that ability. Yet for some, like me and others like me, it's part of our makeup and we can't shake it."

"So Martha is anxious about something and tells you what to do?"

Sarah rolled her head from side to side. "Sort of. She's been very, and I mean *very*, secretive and difficult to deal with. I'm amazed that she's letting me share all this with you."

"Well, that's good to hear. I loved that woman. Many of us did."

"She's comfortable with you. That's why she's letting me tell you all this. May I ask when she died?"

Oscar tilted his head in disbelief. "You don't know that?"

"No," Sarah answered matter-of-factly. "Like I said, time and space don't—"

"About six months ago," he interrupted.

"That long ago? Hm."

"Drowned, so they said."

"But all of you knew better."

"Yes."

"Well, you were right."

"Then—how did she die?

Sarah finished her ice cream soda. "An accident, a fall down the stairs…" she paused. When Martha didn't protest, Sarah told him in a few words what had happened to her.

Oscar squeezed his eyes shut and tears trickled down his cheeks.

Sarah stepped close and embraced him. "I'm sorry, Oscar. I didn't mean to shock you."

"Not shock, sadness. She loved that 'silly old cabin,' as she called it. But it's a beautiful house." He used his apron to wipe his tears. "We told her time and time again not to come on her own, but she couldn't help herself. Andrew used to come by and visit with her. Daryl too, once in a while. But mostly she came by herself. She never cared for the hoity-toity feel of the big house."

"I have to get to the cabin. She needs me to save Karla."

"From what? She's with Daryl."

"I'm not sure from what. I may need to help both her and Daryl. Martha's signals are a bit muddled on that subject."

"Karla said she was looking for Andrew. For all we know the twins are both there. She'll be well cared for by them."

Sarah sighed and forced a smile. "I'm sure you're right. But, I need to get there. Can you give me directions?"

"Yeah, I'll write them down for you. It's not far from here, but hard to find in the dark."

"May I try to place the call again?"

"Yeah, go right ahead."

Sarah returned to the office and picked up the receiver only to find the same static interference in place of a dial tone. She hung up and rejoined Oscar.

"No connection. I did manage to tell my husband, Conrad, about you and the store. He and our friend James may call you or come by. Will you please wait and tell them where to find me? They're coming from Upper Lake."

"Sure thing, Sarah. I'll stick around till they get here. Here are the directions. Drive carefully. That road can be treacherous. The house is the only structure on the left bank of the lake." He escorted her out of the store, shook hands, and watched her drive away.

# 20

# THE ARRIVAL

With renewed energy, and Oscar's instructions, Sarah hit the road with confidence. "Okay, Martha, we're about to find them."

A few miles later she spotted the fork in the road and veered right. When she caught the glow of house lights, she killed the headlights. Parking the car behind some tall bushes beside the driveway, she got out, closed the car door quietly, and walked to the cabin.

She snuck up to an open side window and peeked in. A man she took to be Daryl sat alone on the couch facing the fireplace. In the silence, Sarah could hear the fire crackling. He sipped his martini while his eyes roamed the cabin. His gaze focused on a photograph of two little boys and two women that sat on a shelf across the room. Sarah recognized a young Martha and assumed the other woman to be Jennifer.

Daryl walked toward the photograph, and picked it up. Tears welled in his eyes, and Sarah heard him whisper, "Mother."

Karla came down the stairs in a white silk nightgown and matching robe. He glanced up from the photo. "Your martini is on the bar."

"C'mon, let's get dinner. I'm starving." En route to the kitchen, she plucked up her drink.

The silhouette of her body, profiled by the light, shone through the robe. Daryl placed the photograph back on the shelf and followed her into the kitchen.

She noticed the tears glistening in his eyes. "What's the matter?" she asked.

"Nothing," he lied. "I happened to catch a glimpse of an old picture of Mother and Aunt Jenny."

Karla reached out to gently pat his arm. "C'mon, fix the faucet so I can wash veggies."

He bent down and kissed her gently on the mouth. Before she could react, he straightened up. "Thank you. You're a good woman. Andrew is a lucky guy."

He walked to the stove. "I already fixed the faucet. You're good to go. Just needed a couple of turns." He reached for a grilling pan, placed it on the stove and lit the burner.

Karla got the strainer and cautiously tried the faucet. Satisfied, she stood at the sink and washed the potatoes and rinsed the lettuce and tomatoes.

Daryl seasoned the steaks and placed them in the grilling pan. "I'll pop the potatoes in the microwave while the steaks rest. Would you like a mustard sauce on your steak?"

"Yes, that would be nice."

Sarah stepped away from the window and examined the cabin as she cautiously walked around it. Noticing the pier and rowboat on the lakeshore, she made her way down the hill toward them. Cautiously, she approached the rowboat. She held on to one of the pylons of the pier to get a better look. She recognized it, remembering with shock the role it played in the gruesome disposal of bodies.

"I'm so sorry, Martha," she murmured.

She climbed back up the hill and made her way around the cabin toward the shed that housed the generator. Cautiously, she opened the door, but could distinguish almost nothing in the darkness. She shut the door and returned to the window by the living room.

Daryl had placed the grilled steaks on a large plate and was preparing the mustard sauce. Karla opened and closed cupboards and drawers as she searched for what she needed. The dinner plates, salad, and baked potatoes were already on the table.

"If you must know, it's hard. I don't trust women," Daryl answered.

"Oh, c'mon. We're not that bad."

"No, but since I took over for my dad, I became eligible. Women pop out of the woodwork."

She stopped her search and turned to him. "That didn't occur to me. I can imagine it must be difficult to figure out if someone loves you and not your money. I understand your mistrust."

He laughed. "It does have some advantages. There are plenty of women to pick from, so companionship is not an issue. But, *love*…well, that's another story. How about you, why aren't you married?"

"I haven't found the right guy, yet." Karla resumed her search through the drawers.

"How about Andrew?"

"Maybe, if we'd had more time."

"What are you looking for? You're driving me crazy."

"Candles and candle holders, but not those churchy-looking things."

"Are you expecting a romance, or another power failure?"

"A fine dinner with perfect steaks and good wine should be eaten by candlelight. What kind of a connoisseur are you?"

"Obviously a very bad one. They're in the cabinet by the front door."

Karla walked through the dining room toward the living room. She reached the cabinet and opened the drawer. "There are hundreds of those churchy candles and holders in here!"

"Don't exaggerate. There's a couple of dozen."

Karla returned with two crystal candleholders and two tall white candles. "Why so many?" she asked. "You some kind of religious fanatic?"

"The lights go out a lot."

"I can understand regular candles, but all those creepy votive—"

"Drop it. Let's eat."


A sudden noise startled Sarah. She pulled away from the window and glanced around. She tiptoed toward the right side of the cabin in search of the source.

A muffled sporadic thumping came from beneath a small window along the bottom of the cabin. She crouched down and peeked through the window. Total darkness prevented her from seeing anything within, but she confirmed that this was the source of the dim thumping.

Sarah stood and looked for a way to enter what she assumed to be a basement. She cautiously inspected the cabin in search of an exterior door.

Finally, she found one on the opposite side of the house. A padlock that hung from a rusty old latch held it securely shut. Sarah pulled on the padlock and noticed that the screws on the latch were loose. She pulled again, but they held firm.

She slipped away to her car, silently opened the door, got her cell phone from her purse and turned it on, then popped the trunk. She found the crowbar, opened her suitcase and removed a sweater, cautiously closed the trunk, and snuck back to the side door.

She jimmied the crowbar between the fastener and the door, placed her sweater over it to avoid noise, and pulled.

When the screws gave way, she fell backward over an empty pail, causing a clatter that echoed through the forest. Scrambling to her feet, she retrieved the crowbar as the front door to the cabin swung open.

A beam of light shot from the front of the cabin into the surrounding darkness.

Sarah rushed down the hill and managed to hide behind some tall bushes. From her hiding place, she watched Daryl walk about the cabin, searching for the noise. He shone a flashlight along the sides of the house, then out toward the forest. He said something to Karla as he stepped close to the door. Shutting off the flashlight, he returned to the interior, closing the front door.

Sarah's breath came faster and she could feel her heart pounding in her chest. She stashed the crowbar, her sweater and the lock, and emerged from behind the bushes. She scurried back to the door and opened it. She could barely discern the cement steps that led down to the dark basement.

Cautiously, she stepped over the threshold and closed the basement door behind her. Darkness engulfed her. A musty odor permeated the air. She pulled her cell phone from the back pocket of her jeans, launched the flashlight app, and shone the light on the steps as she made her way down.

# 21

# THE SPLIT

Sarah reached the bottom of the stairs and shone the flashlight around the basement in search of the source of the noise she'd heard.

*There it was again.* Thump, thump.

She made her way through the narrow aisles between a series of large, dusty shelves that turned out to be a well-stocked wine cellar. The thumping came from behind one of the shelves. Sarah crept toward the noise. In the farthest corner she spotted a man, bound to a post and gagged, with a big gash on his head, feebly kicking a nearby cask.

She kneeled down, put the light on his face, and examined him. The man had been severely beaten, and a trickle of dry blood formed a brownish line on one side of his face.

"Andrew?" she whispered.

He tried to nod, but the pain stopped him and he simply closed his eyes.

Gingerly, she removed the gag.

The man whispered, "Who are—"

"I'm Sarah, a friend of your mother's."

He opened his eyes and managed to mumble, "The rope…"

"Yes, I'll take it off. But I'm afraid I have to ask you a question first. Did you see your mother in the attic in Paris?"

"What? What attic?"

"Your uncle Gabriel's."

Andrew rolled his head from side to side. "I don't remember an attic. Please."

Sarah hesitated. "Martha, you'd better warn me."

"Martha? Who are you talking to?"

"Hold on. I'll untie you." She scooted behind the post to untie the rope that bound his chest. After a few tries the knot loosened and the rope gave way.

Andrew inhaled deeply.

His hands were tightly bound behind him and secured to the post. Sarah tried to untie him, but the knot held. She struggled to loosen it, pulling and yanking, until it finally released.

Andrew dragged his hands forward and weakly rubbed his wrists. "Thank you," he mumbled between breaths.

Sarah scurried toward his feet and grabbed the rope, pulling on the knot to untie it. Andrew bent forward to attempt to help, but the pain in his head forced him back to a sitting position with a soulful moan.

Sarah looked up at him. "You have a big gash up there. No sudden movements. Try to catch your breath. I'll work on this rope."

He closed his eyes and leaned back.

Laughter seeped through the floorboards above and they both looked up.

"Is that Karla?" Andrew asked, his eyes more alert.

"Yes. She and your brother are having dinner."

The knot gave way and she quickly released his feet. "C'mon, let's get you out of here. My car isn't far."

"No. I can't go. He's going to kill her."

"That's why I'm here. To help her, and you."

He stared at her. "How—"

"Long story. I'll tell you later. C'mon, we have to get you out of here."

"No, please. I can't go." He took several deep breaths. "Listen, there's a sink back in that corner," he gestured to his left, "and some rags in the cupboard right next to it. Maybe some duct tape. Help me get my head bandaged so that I can move. Please."

"We should leave—"

"No," he said forcefully, "I *can't* leave her."

"Okay." She pointed her phone in the direction he'd indicated and headed toward the sink. She grabbed the towels and rags, wet a few, and returned to him. Kneeling down at his side, she shone the flashlight on his wound. "It looks bad, Andrew."

"I guessed as much. Don't worry I'll be fine. I heal well. Here, let me hold your phone while you work on it."

Sarah did as he said, and got to work gently cleaning the wound, careful not to reopen it. "The blood around the cut has coagulated. I'm not going to mess with that."

"Sounds good."

She cleaned the blood that had oozed from the gash onto his forehead and face, making sure there were no other open cuts. "How long have you been here?"

"Days," he shrugged, "I've lost track of time. I've been unconscious for part of it, and when I wasn't, he hit me to knock me out."

"Why?"

He looked directly at her, his exhausted eyes filled with hate. "He wants me to watch him kill Karla."

Sarah stopped and sat on her heels. "My God! Why?"

"To punish me."

"For what?"

"For killing Mother."

Sarah gasped and recoiled. "Did you—"

"Of course not. But he's convinced I did. Please, hurry. We don't have much time."

Sarah finished wiping the blood, then tore some of the rags into strips. She folded one several times over the wound to form a bandage, and wrapped his head with the other rags tightening them as much as he could tolerate. She secured the bandages with the duct tape. "That should hold."

JACKAL IN THE MIRROR

"Thank you. Can you help me up?" He put the phone on the floor facing up. It illuminated the room in elongated waves of light and cast long shadows in all directions.

"Lean back against the post and I'll try to prop you up." She rose to her feet, placed his arms around her shoulders, and pushed up, propping Andrew against the post.

He groaned softly and squeezed his eyes shut as he raised himself up.

Sarah leaned against him pressing against the post. "Okay?"

He exhaled. "Yes."

Slowly, she stepped back, her arms pinned against his shoulders, holding him steady.

He raised one knee at a time in an attempt to return circulation to his legs. "I'm pretty sure I can stand on my own."

Carefully, Sarah let go of him.

He remained upright, leaning against the post. After a few moments he took a step forward, and another, and another. "I can do this. Thanks, whoever you are. A guardian angel, perhaps."

Sarah picked up the phone. "C'mon let's get you outside."

"No. There's a way we can look into the living room. The stairs are right over there." He took the phone from Sarah. "Is this thing off?" He walked gingerly toward the back of the cellar.

Sarah followed, ready to support him if necessary. "Yes, I turned the ringer off when I got here. There's interference with reception, so no chance of anyone calling. Wait." They'd reached the bottom of the stairs. "Are you strong enough to climb?"

"Aluminum banisters on each side. I can manage."

"Won't they hear us?"

"Look, cement steps, wide enough for the two of us. If we're quiet they shouldn't hear us. Been peeking into the house for years. Mother never heard me."

Sarah stopped. "Peeking in? You spied on your mother?"

"No. Yes. I needed to make sure she was all right. She didn't like me to hang around here when she came. Last time she was here, I wasn't…and she died. By the time I got here, it was too late. C'mon."

Sarah followed.

Andrew reached the top of the stairs and gestured for Sarah to climb up next to him.

"Why a deadbolt on this door?" Sarah whispered.

He turned off the phone, and handed it back to Sarah who slipped it into her back pocket. "Dad didn't want us to come down here alone."

"So it's locked from the inside?"

"Not anymore. Back then Dad had the key, but it's been lost for years."

A couple of wooden planks in the door were separated enough to allow them to peek through into most of the main floor. They could see Daryl and Karla on the sofa, facing the fireplace, sipping brandy.

Karla had changed back into her clothes and lounged comfortably with her legs curled up under her. She glanced at her watch. "It's getting late. Maybe we should head back."

Daryl eyed her for a moment before he spoke. "You are so beautiful," he said seductively.

"I wish you wouldn't say that. Or stare at me like that."

"Why? Because of Andrew?"

"Partly. And partly because of me."

Daryl took Karla's snifter and placed it on the side table next to his. He pulled her to him and kissed her.

She struggled to push him away, but he refused to release her. Finally, she pulled free and stood up. "I'm—"

He rose and gazed into her eyes. "Not that kind of girl?" He snickered. "The polite thing would be for me to say that I'm not that kind of guy, but that would be lie."

She attempted to speak, but he leaned in again and kissed her. She shoved him away. "Please, don't."

"Why not?"

She walked away to establish a distance between them. "It's unacceptable. I am Andrew's. As much as you're like him physically—your voice, your eyes, your smile—you're not him. I can't—no, I don't *want* to be with you."

Daryl spun away, snatched his snifter, gulped the brandy down, and turned to face her.

To escape his glare, Karla turned away, and faced the bookshelf. One of the titles caught her eye. She opened it, and leafed through it, stopping to read one of the pages intently.

Daryl took a tentative step in her direction. "What's that you've got there?"

Karla remained silent.

"What are you reading?" Daryl demanded.

She continued to read then turned toward him. "It's the poem you recited to me."

Daryl leaped forward and snatched the book from her hands. He glared down, grimacing. "What the hell is this piece of shit doing here?"

"What do you mean? Those poems are beautiful."

He stared at the book with a look of disgust and contempt. "It must've been Mother. She had another book."

"Daryl, what—"

He signaled for her to stop talking and hurled the book into the fireplace.

She stepped forward to rescue the book, but Daryl barred her way.

"What are you doing? What's wrong?" She saw that his eyes were bathed in tears.

"I need some fresh air. Be right back." He raced out of the cabin, slamming the door.

Karla remained motionless, trying to comprehend Daryl's actions. Moments later, the lights went out, plunging the house into darkness, leaving the flames from the fireplace as the only source of light. "Daryl!"

Karla went to the dining room table where they'd left the two candles and brought them to the fireplace. Once lit, she placed them on the small table by the sofa, and stood there, waiting.

Behind the wooden planks, Andrew reached for the lock.

Sarah stopped him, whispering, "You'll scare her to death. Wait till the lights come on."

"But Daryl—"

The front door opened and a disheveled Daryl burst in, slammed the door shut behind him, and darted to the fireplace. Eyes wide and fixed, he stared into the flames that continued to consume the book of poems. "Good," he muttered. "That damned book is gone."

He spun around and made his way to the cabinet by the door. He pulled out the bag with the votive candles. He placed them on the floor between the couch and the fireplace.

"What's the matter? What are you doing?"

He looked up at her, but appeared not to recognize her.

"What's happened to you?" Karla asked with increasing alarm.

He returned to his task calmly, methodically arranging the candles in a wide circle.

"Why are the lights out? Did you turn off the generator?"

He retrieved the lighter from the mantelpiece above the fireplace and proceeded to light the candles, one by one. "This is all the light we'll need."

"What on earth are you doing?" she insisted.

He stared into her eyes, but did not respond.

"Daryl, if you're trying to call up a spirit to help you fix the generator—"

"Daryl?" he yelled. "What's wrong with you?" He advanced toward her, his eyes filled with fury. "I'm not Daryl." A sinister scowl crept onto his lips. "You know exactly who I am. I'm Andrew." He took another step in her direction.

"What?" She backed up. "Are you crazy?" Steadily, he approached her. "Daryl! Stop it!"

He stopped, looking bewildered. His eyes rolled up into his head for a moment and then he straightened up with a terrified look.

"Leave now while you still can," he pleaded in a childlike voice.

Karla froze, unable to comprehend what she was witnessing.

His voice became normal and eerily calm. "I'm sorry. Please forgive me."

"For what, kissing me, or burning a book of poems?"

He gripped her shoulders and held her at arm's length. "No, that's not it. Don't you understand? I've used you. I used you to trap Andrew."

"Trap Andrew? What are you talking about?"

"I knew he'd be in pain, especially if you were here, in this cabin, with me." Daryl leaned toward her, his face contorting with pain. "I must tell you something you're not going to like. What they told you is true. All of it. Andrew is a murderer."

Karla broke away from his grasp. Daryl continued.

"He killed Mother, right here, in this house." He looked up toward the second floor. "He threw her down those stairs."

"You're out of sorts." She spotted her brandy on the table and brought it to Daryl. "Take a sip of this. It'll calm you down."

Daryl gripped the snifter with such force that he crushed it, spilling the brandy and cutting his hand. "Shit."

"Oh, my God. I'll get you a towel." Karla ran to the kitchen, turned the water on in the sink, and wet a towel. When she returned, Daryl had removed his shirt and was using it to wrap his hand.

Karla tossed the shirt on the floor, cleaned the cut, and tightened the towel around his hand. "You two really are almost identical. You even have the same birthmark."

Casually, Daryl looked at his hand. "Do we?"

Karla applied pressure with the towel while she studied the look on Daryl's face. His eyes wandered about the room as if trying to determine where he was. "Why do you want to trap Andrew?" she asked in a soothing tone. "Why not turn him in to the authorities?"

Daryl shook his head. "No. I need to kill him," he said without the slightest emotion.

Horrified, Karla jerked away from him. "What? Why?"

"I can't have him arrested and put in an institution for the rest of his life. Andrew is a wild and free spirit. He can't be locked up. I can't let them do that to him." Tears flooded his eyes. "And I can't let him go on...killing." He latched on to her, sobbing like a child.

She surrendered to the embrace, patting his back to reassure him.

He looked into her eyes and kissed her. But what started as an innocent kiss soon turned into violent and desperate need.

Alarmed at his intensity, Karla pushed back.

"Daryl, please don't do that! Let me go!"

"I'm Andrew! Andrew!" His grip tightened around her arms. "Why won't you listen? Why are you playing this game?"

Karla backed up, but found herself pinned against the bookcase. "What game?"

He moved in, his face almost touching hers. "Come to me. Let me love you the way you like it."

Karla squeezed sideways along the bookcase. "What are you doing?"

He stopped and shook violently. Moments later, the helpless, trembling Daryl reemerged. "Karla, get out of here! I can't hold him back for long."

"Who? What are you talking about?"

"Andrew. He wants to kill you."

"Daryl, what are you talking about? Where's Andrew?"

His head jerked back and his eyes rolled. The shaking stopped and he grinned broadly, back in total control. He stepped back and opened his arms to her. "I'm right here."

Taking advantage of the space between them, Karla bolted for the front door, but Daryl's hand clamped onto her wrist and slammed her back against the bookcase.

"It's cold and dark out there. Miles before you'll find any help. If you leave, I'll find you first. No sense in getting cold and dirty anyway." His voice was chillingly matter-of-fact.

Karla struggled against his vice-like grip, but to no avail.

He picked her up and plopped her down in the middle of the circle of votive candles. "You're in for a special treat." He reached to open the top of her blouse, releasing her arms.

"Don't!" She pushed his hands away and stepped out of the circle of candles. "I don't understand what the hell is going on, Daryl, but I'm not going to take any more of this shit!"

His head jerked back and his countenance shifted. He looked terrified. "Yes, please go. Run! Go! Before he comes back." He clasped a nearby armchair to steady himself as he let out a shriek of pain, his face reflecting an internal turmoil that only he understood. He stared down, writhing, and when he looked up, his face looked completely different.

Terrified, Karla retreated to the opposite side of the room. She bumped into the door between the bookshelves, found a small knob, and grasped it.

Behind the door Andrew whispered, "Karla, I'm here behind this door."

Karla gasped.

Daryl froze, listening intently. "Did you hear that?" His eyes scanned the room.

Karla shook her head. "What?"

"That voice. Whispering."

"No," she lied. "I didn't hear a thing."

For a brief moment the room fell into complete silence.

Karla tightened her grip on the doorknob and waited for Daryl's next move.

He turned and glowered at her. "It must've been Daryl telling you to get away. Don't listen to him. Bye, bye, Daryl. Be a good boy and go. I'll take care of her." He released the chair and straightened up. "He won't bother us anymore. He's always trying to take love away from me. But he's gone. No more Daryl. Come to me."

He moved toward her.

She turned the knob and pulled the door slightly open. "Where did Daryl go?" she asked, attempting to seem calm.

"I told him to go outside. Forget him."

"I need to understand, so I can help you keep him there. Outside of what?"

"Outside of me," he roared. "Where he hides." He leaped across the room toward her.

She kicked a side chair in his way to slow him down, opened the cellar door, and disappeared, slamming it shut behind her.

# 22

# THE JACKAL IN THE MIRROR

A
ndrew had descended a couple of steps and was leaning on the handrail in preparation for Karla's escape. Sarah had stepped to one side as well. The moment Karla burst into the cellar, Andrew reached for her, and Sarah bolted the door.

"What—"

"Hush," Andrew whispered. "Come down here with me."

"Andrew? Is it really you?" she mumbled.

"It is."

Daryl slammed a chair against the door. Sarah wavered with the force of the hit, but held on.

"Let's go, Sarah," Andrew said.

Sarah turned on her phone, and aimed the flashlight down the steps.

"I don't like your games, Karla." Daryl yelled from the other room. "Karla? Can you hear me? There's no way out, only this door. That's it and it's dark down there." He stopped yelling.

The sudden silence halted their descent.

Sarah handed her phone to Karla and whispered, "I'll go see what's happening. Help Andrew down. He's seriously injured."

Karla nodded and continued down the steps.

Sarah returned to the door and peered through the crack between the wooden planks. What she saw unnerved her even more.

Daryl's entire demeanor shifted back and forth between meekness and rage as he carried on an incoherent conversation with himself. "What did you say?" he whispered and turned toward an empty space before him. "Don't cry to me about being alone, you pathetic coward," he growled, "Go back and hide where you're safe. You're a wretched weakling!"

He paced back and forth across the living room, shaking his head and muttering incomprehensibly to himself. Abruptly, his face turned expressionless for a second or two as he assumed an entirely different appearance. "The women? No, you're wrong. I didn't kill them," the meek personality responded.

The dominant self sneered back, "You certainly didn't. I did. You lack the strength, you lack the guts."

Sarah listened as he engaged in a dialogue between his two personalities.

"But you are *me*."

"I most certainly am not."

"Why did you kill them?"

"They were suffering. They needed peace. I gave that to them."

"You gave them nothing but death."

"Enough of this! Be a good boy and die!"

Daryl jerked back as if hit by an invisible blow. Then, he threw a punch, wavering with the effort. As the violent exchange escalated with increasing ferocity, Daryl kicked over several of the votive candles, lighting the rug on fire.

He ignored it.

Turning back to the door where Karla had disappeared, he stared at it, and drew close. He leaned his head against it and listened. Then he said, "Karla, my dear, I'm coming for you." He banged on the door.

Sarah stepped back, turned, and made her way down the steps guided by the light Karla held up to illuminate them.

"What's he doing?" Andrew asked.

"He's arguing with himself. He said he's coming," Sarah answered in a trembling voice.

Daryl banged on the door, but it didn't budge. Infuriated, he stepped back. "You've made your choice." He stormed out, leaving the unattended flames to spread.

"C'mon, you two, we need to get out of here before he comes," Sarah said, urging them toward the cellar steps that led to the outdoors.

"Who are you?" asked Karla.

"I'm Sarah, a friend of their mother. Long story. Help me with Andrew."

They each grabbed one of his arms and supported him.

"I can walk on my own," Andrew protested weakly.

"Just the same," Sarah insisted.

As they reached the steps to the outdoor exit, the door above them slammed open.

"Quickly," Andrew cried, "go to the wall cabinet, grab a hammer, or any tool. And turn off the phone." He pointed behind them.

Sarah turned off the phone, and the two sprinted to the cabinet. As the cellar darkened, Andrew disappeared behind one of the wine shelves.

"Karla!" Daryl called out as he stepped down into the cellar, leaving the door open to the night sky. An electric lantern in hand, he made his way down the steps. He reached the cellar floor and hung the lamp on a hook screwed to a post next to him.

Thanks to the glow from the lantern, Karla and Sarah were able to discern the tools. Karla grabbed a hammer and Sarah reached for a crowbar. They stepped away from the light, concealing themselves behind one of the shelves.

"Where's Andrew?" Karla whispered. Sarah shrugged.

"We love things for their beauty," Daryl called out. "We destroy them when they're suffering, so they can find peace. That's the nature of true love." He spotted the ropes that had kept Andrew captive. "Where's my brother? I had him tied up here." He glanced feverishly around the cellar. "What have you done with him?"

The women tiptoed down an aisle perpendicular to their assailant.

"Where did you hide him?" Daryl screamed into the gloom.

Karla peeked between the dusty bottles of wine and spotted her aggressor as he crept along several feet away. Without losing sight of him, she moved quietly in the opposite direction until her foot kicked an empty bottle that lay on the floor.

Daryl spun around and spotted her. "Karla, my darling girl, there you are." He charged around the shelf and faced her. He froze when he glimpsed Sarah standing behind her. "Who are you?" He stared at her and cocked his head. "I don't know you."

Sarah stepped up beside Karla. "Daryl, your mother sent me."

He shook his head. "Liar! Mother is dead!"

"That's true," Sarah, answered calmly. "She sent me, nonetheless."

Unsure what to make of this new person, he examined Sarah top to bottom. "Why?"

"To stop you from hurting Karla."

He laughed. "Liar. She never met Karla. I'm sure of that."

"But she knows you, and she knows what you've done."

He advanced toward her as a sardonic scowl came over him. "No, she doesn't."

"She confronted you. Remember?"

Daryl tilted his head to one side, staring at Sarah as if she were some strange creature that required careful examination. "How did you find out?" he asked calmly.

"She told me."

He closed his eyes and shook his head. "No, no, no. She died. She didn't talk to anyone."

Sarah stood her ground. "She talked to me. She told me how you showed up at this cabin, how she confronted you, how she reached out for you, and how you—"

*Stop! Don't say more! Please don't tell Andrew what Daryl did!* Martha's voice exploded inside Sarah's head.

Daryl stared at her. "And how I what?"

"You're perfectly well aware of what." The disdain in her voice flooded the room.

Daryl turned, marched to the woodpile, and grabbed an ax. Turning back, he advanced toward Sarah. "I don't give a shit! Whoever you are, you'll never live to tell another soul."

Andrew stepped unsteadily out from between two wine racks and shouted, "Stop!"

Daryl spun to face his brother, eyes full of rage. "I wondered where you'd gone. Using women to fight your battles again. Just like you used Mother against me. You sniveling little—"

"Listen to me. Whatever this other *you* inside does, you are still Daryl, and you're responsible for it. Only you can stop him."

"Why don't you die and let me be?" he bellowed, and then lunged at this brother, the ax clenched over his head. At the same moment, Karla stepped forward and threw the hammer as hard as she could. It hit Daryl in the back, stopping his advance. Before he could recover, Andrew leaped upon him and grasped the ax with both hands.

The two identical men struggled frantically for control of the weapon like reflections in a mirror, their birthmarks each turning purple with the pressure of their grip.

The flames from the fire above had burned the door and now licked the wooden walls down the stairs, reaching for the empty wooden crates on the floor.

Karla retrieved the hammer from the floor and lunged toward the men. Sarah held her back. "Give them a second."

"But Andrew's hurt."

"Yes, but he needs to—"

"Okay, but I'm getting close just in case," Karla said.

They both moved in. Through the struggle they heard Andrew's voice. "Daryl, if he kills me, he'll kill you, too. You'll be alone again. Please help me stop him."

Daryl stopped struggling and looked at his brother as if for the first time. Letting out a deafening scream, he pulled backward as if some unseen force had wrenched him off his brother. He struggled and groaned in a fight with his invisible foe. He buckled over as if hit in the stomach, the ax clenched in his hand. Then he flung himself against a post, slumped to the floor, his eyes shut, motionless. He appeared to be unconscious.

Andrew crawled to him. After a few seconds, Daryl opened his eyes to find his twin kneeling next to him. He moaned, "You shouldn't have left. You shut the door. You stayed outside and left me alone with Aunt Jenny. You sang with the animals. You were so happy outside. Free and happy."

"No. I wasn't happy, Daryl. I was cold and scared. I wanted more than anything in the world to be inside with you, warm and safe, but you wouldn't open the door." Tears trickled from his eyes.

"The bolt. It was too high. I couldn't reach the bolt," Daryl muttered, his face wracked with pain.

The brothers embraced.

"I should've tried harder," Daryl said. "But you scared me, yelling and threatening me from outside."

"I get it, it wasn't your fault."

Daryl's head dropped, tears streaming down his face. "Andrew, I didn't understand...all those things you said I did to you...*he* did them, not me. I didn't. I really didn't do them."

"Yes, Daryl, *he* did them. We understood."

"We?"

"Mother and I. We both understood. But she didn't have the courage to do anything about it. She hoped you'd be able to cope, clear your head, and stop pretending to be me."

"But *he* is you!"

"No, he's not me. He only lives inside of you, and you're the only one that can get rid of him. You've got to stop him. I'll do anything to help you. Please, Daryl, try."

"I can't control him. He takes over and I lose track of what happens to me. He told me about Aunt Jenny. How she was lying there in pain, crying, how she couldn't move, and then she fell asleep and wouldn't wake up. But she didn't hurt any more. She was quiet, peaceful. I loved Aunt Jenny and she loved me. He told me to cuddle with her, so I did. She liked it. I liked it."

"I understand."

"Mother didn't understand. She didn't understand that all those women hated their lives and suffered. But after he helped them, they were quiet, peaceful. He cuddled with them like I did with Aunt Jenny. Mother didn't understand. She kept asking why."

The ceiling of the cellar, engulfed in flames, snapped loudly. Several pieces of burning wood fell to the cellar floor.

Karla crawled over to the brothers, hammer clenched in her hand. "We need to leave. Now!"

Daryl swung his head to one side as if answering a call. "I can't hold him any longer. He's angry." In a flash he hit Andrew with the ax handle, knocking him unconscious.

Karla screamed and smashed the hammer into Daryl's shoulder, causing him to drop the ax.

"If you come close to him," Karla shouted, "I'll kill you."

"No you won't," Daryl answered.

"Try me," she retorted in anger.

Sarah leapt forward and snatched up the ax.

More burning embers dropped from the floor above as the intensity of the fire increased. Smoke filled the cellar, curling along the wine racks like an angry storm cloud.

Daryl howled and rolled furiously about, gripping invisible hands around his neck and fighting with himself.

"Sarah, help me with Andrew!" Karla screamed.

They grabbed Andrew's unconscious body, dragging him to the steps that led outside.

A loud crack preceded several burning planks that fell at once onto a shelf filled with wine bottles. It toppled, smashing the bottles and igniting the alcohol.

Daryl screamed. Then he laughed.

"Oh, God. Now what?" Karla stopped.

"Don't stop! Keep pulling!" Sarah yelled.

The two women began a desperate climb up the steps, dragging Andrew's limp body.

"C'mon, Andrew, wake up," Karla begged.

"Let us have some order here." Daryl rose to his feet and called out. "We can't have us both doing this all the time. One of us has to go."

From the top of the steps they caught sight of Daryl. A calm sneer crept onto his lips as he headed toward them.

The women redoubled their effort and sped up their ascent. They reached the top, and dragged Andrew out of the cellar. They managed to get him a few feet from the cellar before slumping to the ground, exhausted, struggling to catch their breath.

The contact with the cold night air reanimated Andrew. The three lay sprawled on the dirt, staring expectantly at the exit from the cellar. The only sound was the crackling of fire and the explosion of bottles. Smoke billowed from the cellar door.

Daryl emerged from the smoke. Soot mixed with tears streaked his face with hideous black lines. His hands were black with burns. He glared at them with eyes full of hatred as he took step after deliberate step in their direction. He froze unexpectedly and began walking backwards jerkily as his invisible alter ego wrenched him back into the cellar.

Andrew crawled to the door of the cellar.

"Stay out Andrew! Don't come in!" Daryl screamed from below.

But Andrew didn't heed his twin's plea and slid down the steps.

"Andrew!" Karla screamed and ran to the top of the steps.

"I'm right behind you." Sarah called out.

Surrounded by smoke, backlit by flame, Daryl rose to his feet and approached Andrew.

"Daryl, please don't hurt him." Karla pleaded.

Daryl knelt beside him. "Please, forgive me."

Andrew held firmly on to his brother's arm and sat up. The two brothers embraced.

Daryl rose, swung his brother over his shoulder, and headed toward the steps.

"Get away!" he yelled at Karla and Sarah. "Let me take him out. I need to save him."

The women retreated hesitantly, and stood by as Daryl carried his brother up from the cellar. With unexpected gentleness, he lowered him to the ground. "Take care, brother," he whispered.

Andrew reached up to grab Daryl, but he yanked himself away. He stood for a moment staring down at his twin with all the love he had failed to show before. A moment later he spun about and threw himself down into the burning cellar.

"Daryl—no!" Andrew reached for his brother, but he was gone.

Karla seized Andrew and held him back. Sarah also took hold of him, and together they gradually drew him away from the inferno.

Once they'd reached a safe distance from the burning cabin, Andrew stopped resisting the two women. The three stood silently, staring back at the blazing structure.

"Strange isn't it?" Andrew said at long last. "It ended the way it all started. He's locked inside, and I'm locked outside."

Karla looked into Andrew's eyes. "Only this time the choice was his."

Sarah heard distant sirens.

A moment later, the floor succumbed to the flames and collapsed into the cellar, sending clouds of smoke and embers out into the night air.

Clutching Karla, Andrew watched the cabin disappear in a conflagration that lit up the surrounding forest and the edge of the lake, where a weathered dock anchored an old rowboat.

Sarah watched as Andrew's face gradually relaxed, clear evidence that a heavy burden had been lifted from him, and peace had taken its place.

# 23

# THE GATHERING

The sirens drew closer. Sarah turned to find a stream of flashing red and blue emergency lights headed up the driveway. Behind the police cruisers, a big man leapt from a slow-moving car and sprinted toward them.

"Sarah!" Conrad yelled.

The intensity of the fire behind her muffled his voice and she remained motionless until he got close enough for the flames to illuminate his face. "Conrad!" she shouted and flew into his arms.

"Are you all right?" he asked without breaking the embrace.

"Yes. I'm fine. How—"

He kissed her with such force that she winced and pulled back.

"Did I hurt you?"

"Yes. But in a nice way."

A fire truck pulled up between the burning house and the lake, and several firefighters jumped out to assess the fire.

Ignoring the activity around them, Conrad cupped his wife's face and glared into her eyes. "You drive me mad with worry—"

"But I get results and that's why you love me."

Conrad laughed in spite of himself. "That I do." He kissed her again, only this time with a tender and gentle touch. "You're sure you—"

"Yes, darling, I'm all right. Look." She stepped back and turned around as he inspected her. "And so are Karla and Andrew. Although he's pretty banged up."

The battalion chief approached them. "Good evening, ma'am. Can you tell me where the fire started? We need to find its origin and identify any specific risks before we send anyone in there. Is there anything flammable?"

Sarah gave the chief a rundown of the events and possible dangers. "Thank you, ma'am." He returned to his team and relayed the information.

Moments later, the men raced off to carry out their designated tasks with the expert precision that only years of training could produce. Several firemen aimed hoses toward the blazing structure, while others focused on the back of the house.

"Those guys running to the back will be applying dry chemical agents," James told them, "to interrupt the chemical chain reaction in the cellar, in an attempt to stop the flames."

"James!" Sarah turned and hugged him.

"Dear girl," he grinned, "what will your husband say?"

"That he's eternally grateful to you." Conrad rested a hand on James' shoulder.

As the firemen trained their hoses on the cabin, much of the water, brought to its boiling point by the flames, converted instantly into vapor.

"Look up there," James said, pointing toward the top of the cabin. "The conversion to vapor dilutes the oxygen in the air above the fire and removes one of the elements the fire requires—that'll help put it out more quickly. With the constant application of water it will extinguish the flames by smothering them."

"Is there anything you don't know?" asked Sarah.

"Plenty. I have no idea what was going on before the big bang. But I'm working on it." He motioned in the direction of Karla and Andrew. "Is that—"

"Yes, that's Karla, the intended victim, and Andrew, one of the twins. The other one, Daryl, died in the flames."

JACKAL IN THE MIRROR

They watched as the paramedics placed a warming blanket over Karla, and attempted to place Andrew on a stretcher.

"I don't need to lie down!" he protested with a mixture of anger and frustration.

"Yes, you do." Karla pressed him down. "Let the paramedics help you. Please."

As they pushed the stretcher toward the ambulance, Andrew cried out. "No! Don't take me away. Not yet, please. Do your work here if you must. I can't go. *Please.*"

Karla approached one of the paramedics and whispered into his ear. The man nodded.

"Andrew?" Oscar approached him tentatively.

"Oscar," Andrew smiled. "How—"

Oscar gestured to Sarah. He patted Karla's shoulder. "Miss Karla, you found your man."

"I did."

The paramedics inserted an IV and Andrew winced. "I don't need that. Please bandage my head and let me be."

"Always the rebel." Oscar shook his head. "Let them do their job, my boy. You're pretty banged up." He turned to Karla. "Where's Daryl?"

Karla shook her head and indicated the burning cabin.

"Oh, no." His eyes welled up. "That's a shame. Hell," he said, wiping away his tears, "I'm too old for this crying business."

Andrew, tears rolling down his own cheeks, reached for Oscar's hand. "No, we're not. We never will be."

The paramedics undid the bandages on Andrew's head. "You're a lucky fella," one of them said. "Whoever bandaged you saved us lots of trouble. You'll need stitches up at the hospital, but for the time being, you'll be fine."

"Miss Sarah's doing, I'd venture." Oscar winked at Andrew.

"Who is she? Where did she come from?" Andrew asked.

Oscar leaned toward him. "I just met her. She came to the store. Followed Karla and Daryl. She's someone real special with an extraordinary talent." He turned in her direction. "Miss Sarah," he called out, "would you be so kind as to come and have a chat with this rascal?"

289

Without relinquishing Conrad's hand, Sarah approached the stretcher.

"Thank you for saving me." Andrew held out his hand. "These gentlemen tell me you did a great job with the bandages."

With her free hand Sarah took Andrew's. "You're welcome. I'm glad you're going to be okay." She looked up at Karla. "That goes for you, too."

"Sir," one of the paramedics said as he stepped up to the stretcher, "we have to go. We need to get you to the hospital."

"No, please, I need to stay with my brother. I need to—"

James touched his shoulder. "Andrew, I'm James Horton. Your brother—"

"You said James Horton?" Karla interrupted.

He nodded.

Her eyes lit up. "*The* James Horton?"

James smiled uncomfortably. "I'm not sure what—"

"The James Horton of The Hague. *That* James Horton?"

Sarah laughed. "Yes, the one and only James Horton."

Karla's gaze fixed on James. "I researched you once for a story."

"Well," James shrugged, "I hope you weren't disappointed."

"Are you kidding? It was amazing. You're a legend."

"Well, I'm not sure—"

"You were going to say something about my brother," Andrew interjected. "What about Daryl?"

James turned to face Andrew. "I can tell you that he's all right. He's at peace. He's joined your mother." He shot a quick glance at Sarah and winked.

"How could you possibly know that?" Andrew asked with a hint of contempt.

"It's a long story, and I'd be happy to tell you all about it once you're taken care of. For now, please accept that his sacrifice made your mother very happy and liberated Daryl."

Tired and confused, Andrew glanced at the people surrounding him, seeking some kind of explanation. He saw none. "How in hell could you know about his sacrifice?"

"Like I said. It's a long story. I promise to relate it all to you in due time, but we need to allow the paramedics to take you to the hospital. There's nothing left for you to do here."

Andrew stared at Oscar for a moment, then turned his eyes toward Sarah. She gave him a reassuring smile. Karla placed her hand on his shoulder and nodded.

They rolled the stretcher toward the waiting ambulance. Andrew leaned back and closed his eyes.

# 24

# THE ART

"I am so looking forward to this escapade of ours." Sarah tightened her grip on Conrad's hand as they walked down Powell toward Geary Street in San Francisco.

"I'd say. We're more than a year overdue."

"Better late than never, to quote a cliché."

Smartly attired in a navy pinstriped suit, light blue shirt, and royal blue tie, Conrad attracted considerable attention from female passersby.

"It's great to see how much I'm envied," Sarah said. "You look so handsome all dressed up."

"News flash! They're actually eying you all decked out in that sexy multi-colored dress."

"It's not multi-colored; its varying hues of iridescent blues and greens."

"Okay, Miss Hoity-Toity, whatever it is, you look stunning. You can dress like this anytime, as long as you don't run away again."

"C'mon, we've been through this. I didn't run away."

"Yeah, yeah, Martha this, Martha that. The fact is, you scared the daylights out of me. Let alone poor James. He felt responsible for you, and then he went and lost you. To top it all off, not a sign of a single spirit to offer the poor man any help. I thought he was going to lose it at one point. And that investigative team, they couldn't come to terms with the fact that he'd reached an impenetrable barrier. James simply felt incompetent."

Sarah stopped and faced her husband. "What? This is all news to me. Incompetent? James?"

"He did feel that way. It's true."

She shook her head and resumed walking. "This is all about you tooting your own horn. Just because it was your idea to dial Oscar's number doesn't make you the hero of the story."

This time Conrad stopped, grabbed her arm, and stared at her. "And why not?"

She laughed. "Granted, it was a good idea, but—"

"Good? Brilliant, that's what it was. You won't admit it."

"Fine. But James and the team had already found the family and the twins."

"Oh, really? Well, let me remind you, Miss Know-It-All, they had no idea where to look until I came along." He took Sarah's hand and continued walking.

"They would've figured it out sooner or later."

"But they didn't. *I* did."

She threw her arms around his neck. "So you did. My hero." She kissed him.

"Sarah," he protested between kisses, "we're in the middle of the street."

"In San Francisco." And she kissed him again, and again.

They resumed their walk as Conrad looked around. "No one even noticed two old fogies kissing on a crowded sidewalk."

"Told you. Hey, there it is."

Moments later they entered the gallery. The name *Andrew Strand*, etched in large black letters on a diagonal white wall, greeted them.

Sarah shook her head. "Good old Martha, she fed me 'Stuart' instead of 'Strand.' Real names, only garbled."

"She did everything she could to protect her family. What a burden she carried."

Karla spotted them when they entered the gallery, and headed their way. She wore a white pantsuit with a black blouse, and black patent leather high heels. Her hair was pulled into a tight bun adorned with a small black bow. "We're so glad you could come," she said, embracing them.

"We wouldn't miss it. I'm excited to see Andrew's paintings in real life," Sarah said.

Karla laughed. "I can't wrap my head around the fact that you've experienced—or lived or—heck, whatever it is you did." She grabbed Sarah's hand. "C'mon, let's find Wonder Boy."

They made their way through the crowded gallery toward Andrew, also dressed entirely in white with black shoes. His white jacket set off shoulder-length black hair. He looked uncomfortable surrounded by a throng of admirers. When he caught sight of Karla dragging Sarah, he smiled politely at his fans, excused himself, and came toward them.

He gave Sarah a bear hug that lifted her off her feet. "I'm so delighted that you're here."

"Me too, but I'd like to breathe," she gasped.

"Sorry!" He set her down. "I can't tell you enough how much I've been looking forward to being with both of you again." He turned to Conrad and effusively shook his hand. "Thank you for all your help."

"C'mon, Andrew, you've thanked us plenty," Conrad said.

"It's not often that one meets people willing to risk their lives to save yours."

"Well, they're here, so now we can get on with the program. The sharks are beginning to circle." Karla took Andrew's hand and attempted to pull him away.

"We need James. He's not here yet," he protested.

"He'll be here soon. Come on, it takes time to gather everyone and get them to hush up."

Andrew caught sight of James entering the gallery and lit up. "Hold on, Karla." He bolted past the Thompsons and reached him in a handful of steps. "James, thanks for coming, man."

"Of course. I wouldn't miss it for the world."

Andrew leaned toward James and whispered, "Are they here?"

Understanding exactly whom Andrew was referring to, James smiled. "Your mother is."

"Daryl?"

James shook his head. "I haven't seen him since the night of the fire."

Andrew's frown made his disappointment obvious.

Karla joined them and wrapped her arms around James. "What a treat to have you here."

"The treat is all mine. I'm looking forward to viewing Andrew's work."

They threaded their way through the crowd toward the Thompsons.

James embraced Sarah. "How's my favorite psychic?"

"Doing well, James. Quite well. And you?"

"Perfect." He turned to shake Conrad's hand. "Hi there, partner."

"Man, it's good to see you."

"Program time," Karla announced. She grabbed Andrew's hand and turned to Sarah, Conrad, and James. "Follow us, and park yourselves right in front of the stage."

They did as directed.

Karla climbed onto the riser that had been set up and tugged Andrew up to her side.

"Hello everyone," she called out. The crowd quieted down and gave her their full attention. "Thank you very much for joining us. As many of you are well aware, Andrew Strand—despite his success—has always shied away from the limelight." She turned to him and smiled. "Today, however, he's agreed not only to be here with us, but also to say a few words. Ladies and gentlemen, I give you Andrew Strand." She stepped back.

Andrew looked around at the crowd, blushed, and reluctantly stepped forward. "This is not easy for me. Like Karla said, I don't do well in crowds and I don't like to speak in public. It's even more difficult because I'm a part of the opening of this magnificent new gallery that has chosen to showcase my art exclusively. For that honor I am indebted to the gallery's owner and all-around good guy and art connoisseur, Lucien Montenegro." Andrew pointed toward Lucien and applauded. "Thanks for all your support, Lucien."

The audience joined in the applause as Lucien bowed.

"I'm not good at chatter or social talk, my art is my voice, and many of you have experienced me at my best," he said sheepishly, "which is when I don't engage in conversation."

The audience chuckled and murmured.

"But who can say no to the indomitable Karla Jourdain?"

Laughter rippled through the room.

"I certainly can't," he went on, "especially now that she has agreed to be my wife." He reached for her hand and pulled her to him. The spectators applauded. Karla blushed.

"Well," he laughed, "this is a first, Karla actually can blush. Who knew?"

"C'mon. You're embarrassing me," she chided.

He put his arm around her shoulder. "Today is far more than the opening of this gallery and this exhibit, it is also the opening of my heart." He paused to compose himself as he tightened his hold on Karla. "As you're well aware, almost a year ago, my studio was ransacked, and many of my paintings were vandalized," he sighed. "Numerous sculptures were broken or destroyed. In this room, you'll find the paintings and sculptures I had in storage, but as we open the doors to the adjacent rooms, you will observe many of the damaged pieces—reborn."

A collective gasp and murmur erupted.

"You may ask why I didn't get rid of them. The simple truth is, I couldn't. So, I recreated them, to show not only the damage they suffered, but to give them a new life full of forgiveness, despite the attempt on their existence."

The audience applauded respectfully. Andrew signaled for them to quiet down. "After that, you'll walk into a third room. That room is dedicated to my mother, Martha Trenton McKinney, a woman with an uncanny ability to love. And forgive. The work you'll observe there is a departure from my usual style, and the portraits you'll view—"

Several people reacted and a general murmur ensued.

"Yes, you heard me right, portraits. Although they're not as good as Jeremiah's." He winked at his friend.

"Loads better, I bet," Jeremiah yelled out.

The audience applauded.

Andrew laughed. "No, not true at all. The portraits are my private collection. They depict my family, my twin brother, Daryl, my mother, her sister, Jennifer, my father, Robert, and my uncle Gabriel, all of whom have sadly passed on. The portraits embody my feeble attempt to keep them close to me, to keep them alive."

Gasps came from the spectators.

"As you make your way through that particular gallery, you'll notice that I have incorporated several poems alongside these portraits. These are poems from a book my mother loved, written by my uncle, Gabriel McKinney. Thanks to this book of poems I am here with you today, opening up my soul by way of my art. I hope you enjoy them. Thank you."

The room broke into thunderous applause. Andrew looked behind him and signaled. The double doors into the second showroom of the gallery opened, and the crowd made their way in.

Karla pulled Andrew to her and kissed him. "That was beautiful."

He kissed her back. "All because of you." He turned to Sarah. "And you."

They stepped down from the small stage.

"Sarah," Andrew took her hands in his, "thank you for saving the book."

"You're welcome. I loved reading it."

An elegant couple and a young man with an uncanny resemblance to Karla walked up to them.

"Mom, Dad, Eric, these are the Thompsons, and James you've already met." They all shook hands.

"Eric has been a godsend this past year helping us with AlderCreek." Karla kissed him on the cheek. "Since my little brother took over running our father's firm, I haven't been able to spend any time with him. It's been great having him around."

"I'm glad I could help. But I can't wait to check out Andrew's creations. Catch you in a few. C'mon you two." Eric locked arms with his parents and they headed to the back of the gallery.

Andrew reached for Sarah's hand. "Let's follow them."

She held him back. "I'd like to meet Jeremiah, if you don't mind."

"You're a fan?" Andrew asked.

"No. I saw him through your mother's eyes when Karla was searching for you."

"This thing you do is so—I'll never understand it," Karla chuckled.

"Hey, Jer," Andrew called out. "I'd like to introduce you to a very good friend."

Jeremiah excused himself from the group he was with and strolled toward them. He'd tied his hair back in a ponytail and gathered his beard with a chain adorned with a beautiful hanging crystal. He wore pale blue linen pants, a psychedelic linen shirt, and sandals—formal attire by his standards.

"What's up, baby?" He kissed Karla.

"Jer," Karla said, "this is Sarah, her husband Conrad, and this is James Horton, the one from The Hague that…"

"Whoa! You don't say." He reached over and shook James' hand with unbridled enthusiasm. "I read Karla's piece. You're her hero. Thought you were all but gone, though."

James laughed. "Not quite yet, thankfully"

Sarah stretched out her hand to greet him, but Jeremiah picked her up off the floor and twirled her around. "The magical being!"

James elbowed Conrad and winked. "Now we know what to call her."

"God, she's going to be impossible," Conrad said with a laugh.

Once Jeremiah put Sarah down, he turned to Conrad and shook his hand. "Good to meet you, man. Hey, James, you get that Karla's nuts about you, right?"

"You're going to embarrass him," Karla protested.

"Well, other than your crazy-talented hubby to be, nobody gets your wheels turning like this guy. I'm jealous."

James patted Jeremiah's back. "No need for that, my friend. We've got no chance with this beautiful woman. We're lucky she even notices us."

They laughed and Karla giggled.

"Andrew, can we start in this room first?" Sarah asked. "If we're going to understand the next room, we need to look at what you created before this past year."

"Sure. Go ahead." He turned to Jeremiah. "Jer, I'd like your honest opinion of the portraits. No holds barred."

"Sure thing. Ladies and gents, catch ya later." Jeremiah walked toward the back room of the gallery.

The first room showcased sculptures of women and jackals, as well as paintings depicting many variations on the same subjects.

"You can tell that they're jackals by their size and their fiendish look," Conrad said.

"Both the women and animals possess a quiet intensity," Sarah added.

"Why jackals?" James asked Andrew.

"I became enamored with coyotes at an early age. They're known as the American jackals. Both species are opportunistic omnivores and for some reason that's been very interesting to me. As a child, I was stranded in the woods when my aunt died, and somehow I convinced myself that they were my friends. Their howl begins with a high-pitched, long drawn-out cry, and I related to that feeling. I actually cried out myself as if I were one of them. It turned out to be a great relief. I could let go of the fear and join them in the call to the wild. I also liked to mimic the coyotes' loud yelping barks. It made me laugh."

"That's the song Daryl mentioned?" Karla asked.

Andrew nodded. "It could be."

"You must've been terrified," Sarah said.

"I was."

"How long were you outdoors?" James asked.

"I was told three days."

"How did you survive?"

"I have no clear memories. Berries, I imagine. And there was the stream, so I'm sure I drank the water."

"Did you watch the coyotes?"

"I'm not sure if it was then or later. Oddly enough, after that experience, losing myself in the woods gave me a sense of safety."

"Why the shift from coyote to jackal?"

"Artistically, I liked the look of the jackals. They're better subjects for what I visualized. It worked well to connect with their darker history and biblical implications."

James looked surprised. "You mean the devil?"

Andrew laughed. "Not quite, but devilish. I endeavored to depict the duality of their ferocity and beauty."

James turned to the paintings. "You definitely achieved that, my boy."

"Did you have your brother in mind?" Sarah asked.

A sad smile appeared on his lips. "Often. When I achieved the perfect balance of good and evil in the jackals. Particularly in juxtaposition to the females in the paintings."

"Did he ever see your paintings?" asked Conrad.

"Not exactly, but he knew I liked to paint coyotes and jackals. Daryl used to make fun of me and tear up my stuff."

"Why?"

"He said they scared him. My 'friends' he called them." He paused. "Once I found one of my drawings—a jackal, fangs out—under his pillow. He said it belonged to him, that it was his drawing, his friend. At the time, I didn't understand what that meant. Wish I had."

"Ready for the next room?" Karla asked.

They entered the second gallery and Sarah gasped at the sight of the large painting of a jackal snarling at an unseen enemy while the dainty hand of a woman in the upper right hand corner of the canvas reached lovingly toward the beast. The gash on the painting had been repaired and filled with a ray of sunshine that illuminated a small pond.

"This painting hung over the makeshift bed in your studio," Sara said, "but without the ray of light and the pond."

Andrew's eyes widened. "The bed?"

"Oh," Sarah said, putting a hand over her mouth.

"Did you see us?" Karla asked.

Sarah blushed. "I did catch a glimpse of both of you in the studio. Sorry."

Andrew and Karla's eyes widened.

"No, no, I didn't watch *that* part. Don't worry. But—"

"Sarah, hush." Conrad pulled her to him.

"Don't worry. I didn't—well I did get a glimpse of the two of you in your birthday suits." She giggled.

"Sarah, please." Conrad insisted.

James burst into irrepressible laughter, and soon they all joined in.

To change the subject, Sarah turned to one of the sculptures of a jackal cradled against a reclining nude woman. "That one was in progress when I saw it. You hadn't finished it."

The sculpture had been broken in half, and Andrew had added flower petals to cover the repair and join the two figures.

"You said that the story came to you in bits and pieces," Karla said. "When you saw us, was it the last time I saw him?"

"As far as the story went, yes." She turned to Andrew. "Did Karla ever model for you?"

"No, I painted her from memory."

"What? And you didn't tell me?" Karla pinched Andrew.

He pulled away, laughing. "Oops, it was supposed to be a surprise."

"Is it here?" asked Sarah.

He winked.

"Well, let's take a look." Karla turned, but Andrew held her back. "In due time. They need to finish this room."

"All right."

They ambled around the room, examining the paintings and sculptures. Andrew had repaired the damage to each with an imaginative use of color and design. Their appeal lay in their unique mixture of anger and forgiveness.

"Andrew," James whispered, "your mother is enormously proud of you."

Andrew beamed. "Thank you, James. It still shocks me that you can actually talk to her. I'm very grateful that you can share this with me."

"How about your mother's portrait?" Sarah asked. "I don't see it here."

"It couldn't be repaired." Andrew answered. "The gash was so violent that its ragged edges made it impossible to fix. So, I painted another. You'll find it in the next room."

"C'mon." Karla yanked Andrew's hand and dragged him to the next room.

They all followed.

"Wow," Sarah said, "it's…it's splendid."

White panels set at different angles divided the large room. Each one displayed a portrait of one of Andrew's family members alongside an accompanying poem, individually encased in its unique frame and with its own distinctive font.

The panels had been arranged to allow each and every portrait with its accompanying poem to be seen from the entryway. Karla's portrait hung on the last angled wall; the only portrait not displayed on a panel hung on the back wall of the gallery. It was a stunning rendition of Martha McKinney surrounded by several poems arrayed on the wall.

To one side of Martha's portrait, a white stand held the book of poems, encased in an acrylic display case.

Karla stood frozen in the entryway. "When—how—who…?"

Andrew smiled and wrapped an arm around her. "Lucien," he turned to his guests, "the gallery curator, designed this entire presentation." He turned back to Karla. "What do you think?"

Karla looked at him, her eyes full of tears. "I love it."

"Let me show you the poem I chose for your portrait." He guided her to the back of the room.

"They're like kids in a candy store," Conrad remarked.

"I'd say," James smiled. "What a creative way to showcase Gabriel's poems."

The closest portrait to them was of Robert McKinney, with a background in mixed hues of grey. It presented a serious, detached, but elegant man in a striped dark grey suit with a yellow tie and matching pocket-handkerchief. His eyes expressed an indifference that bore no resemblance to Andrew or Daryl. The poem next to him read:

## MOOD

*Do you ever feel*
*That some nights*
*Are tailor-made for caring*
*I do*

*Tonight for instance*
*As I look out into darkest dark*
*I think of things that might*
*Be said*
*Or the joy there is in silence*

*Tonight I'm in*
*The caring*
*Mood*
*The holding onto life*
*Mood*

The next one was of Gabriel McKinney. A stunning rendering with a stylistic background depicting Paris at sunset in deep red, lavender, and crimson tones, with a touch of muted orange and yellow accents. Locks of Gabriel's shoulder-length hair caressed a burgundy velvet jacket. Gabriel's unbuttoned rose shirt and the fuchsia scarf loosely tossed over his left shoulder, offered powerful juxtapositions. His masculinity emanated from the canvas despite the colors Andrew had selected. He bore an uncanny resemblance to Andrew and Daryl, his eyes filled with love and melancholy. The poem Andrew had selected fit him perfectly.

## MY LOVE

*It's wondrous to see*
*How you fill up my life*
*With the things that my dreams said were real*

*It's grand just to feel*
*That you're there by my side*
*All your warmth and your love just for me*

*The things that you do*
*Without asking you to*
*Say that your love is one of a kind*

*The things that you say*
*On those cheer me up days*
*Make me leave all my sorrows behind*

*Bring in the rainbows*
*And turn on the stars*
*Fill the world with the colors of life*

"Does he know that Gabriel was his father?" Conrad asked in a soft voice.

"Yes. He figured it out," James answered.

"He told you?" asked Sarah.

"Martha did."

"How did Andrew react?"

"I'm not sure, but Martha is not upset, so I imagine he's okay with that."

The next portrait they came to was of Jennifer McKinney. This painting illustrated a sunrise in the redwoods filled with bright colors. Jennifer appeared as a young ethereal beauty, her eyes and smile conveying a combination of bliss and ache.

### LOVELY

*All throughout my lonesome life*
*I looked for someone who would care*
*A voice*
*A hand*
*A smile*

*To save me from despair*

*In every lonely dream*
*I wished the*
*Sun to shine*
*But every lonely day said*
*That wish would not be mine*

"Could she have learned about her sister and Gabriel?" Conrad asked.

"It's clear that Andrew believes so." Sarah reached for her husband's hand. "It's so sad."

"C'mon, darling, be proud. Andrew has truly opened his heart through all the paintings and poems. For someone who's been hiding from the public eye for years, he's sure exposed himself now."

"That took a lot of courage," James commented.

They continued forward and stopped before Daryl's portrait. Andrew had captured his brother's duality by superimposing mirror images of the man, in profile, staring at a cabin isolated in the woods, his hand gently placed over a snarling jackal.

"Wow," Sarah whispered.

"What a striking portrait… all in blues and greens," James echoed.

"What do you make of the faint touches of yellow and red?"

"Daryl's colors?" he asked.

"You could say that," Sarah answered. "His moods—happy, sad, and angry. The contrast of the ferocity of the jackal against the gentleness of his touch illustrates the intensity of his internal battle."

"Andrew's very talented," Conrad commented.

Sarah walked up to the poem and read.

### *ENOUGH*

*Enough*
*I say*
*Enough*

*Don't color me*
*The way you think I am*

*Stop*
*Making me believe*
*What is untrue*

*The image in your mind*
*Belongs*
*To you*

*What you*
*Expect of me*
*I'll*
*Never meet*

*I find it*
*Hard enough*
*To just be*
*Me*

"These poems were meant for Martha," Sarah whispered. "And yet they fit in so well with each portrait."

"I'm sure that in life Gabriel never imagined that his poems would be exhibited in such a manner. Let alone that his son would pick certain poems for each member of the family. Martha is delighted by what Andrew has created," James said.

They walked up to Karla's portrait. It was set in a nondescript futuristic background in tones found in deep space nebulae, saturated colors that contrasted with the pale tones of her skin and her loose auburn hair. A coquettish glare in her eyes conveyed an invitation to trouble.

"What do you think?" Andrew turned to Sarah.

"I'm in awe of your talent," she answered.

"We all are," Conrad added.

James nodded effusively. "Her lips, slightly parted like that, are a true enticement."

Andrew laughed. "You got it, James. That's exactly what I sought."

"Enticement? Really? To what?" Karla protested.

Lucien, the gallery director, leaned forward from behind Karla and rested his chin on her shoulder. "That's what we're all wondering." He laughed and extended his hand to Sarah.     "Hello and welcome, I'm Lucien Montenegro."

"Sarah Thompson," she said, smiling.

"Conrad, her lesser half." Conrad gestured to Sarah as he shook Lucien's hand.

"James," Lucien turned to him and kissed him on both cheeks. *"Estoy feliz de verte."*

*"Y yo también,"* James answered.

"You two know each other?" Karla asked.

"For many years," Lucien answered as he patted James's back.

"My friend, you are to be commended," James said. "Your design of this exhibit is tremendous. This room in particular is spectacular."

"All due to Andrew," Lucien said with pride.

"Well, you've created a magnificent way to show his work," Sarah said. "Did you pick the font and frames for the poems?"

"No, no. Andrew did all that."

"Excuse me a moment. I haven't had a chance to read the poem he chose for Karla's portrait." Sarah stepped past them to the poem.

### *EYES*

*Within the realm of nature*
*They say all wonders lie*
*Some are man's creation*
*And bewilder his own eye*

*But canyons made of stone so hard*
*And roses sweet and soft*
*Sunsets dying in the sky*
*Were meant to touch my heart*

*Now there's the wonder best of all*
*That I could learn to see*
*Not with eyes that tend to lie*
*By making great the thing that's small*
*But with my heart perhaps my soul*
*The answer to my feelings' call*

*There was a time not long ago*
*My eyes were nearly blind*
*Forsaking to see anything*
*My mind elected to forego*

*But one day you brought to me*
*The kindly fragrance of the rose*
*And made its soft and gentle bloom*
*A thing that I could see*

*You showed me all the majesty*
*Of mountains strong and riverbeds*
*And brought my soul to recognize*
*That stone can speak to me*

*Then all my senses*
*Frantically*
*Were forced to open up*
*And take this gift from you*

*At last they saw reality*
*Not in things that nature made*
*Not in endless dance of sea*
*Not in wind and trees that sing*

*It wasn't there that wonder stayed*

*The truth is very simple now*
*I don't know how I missed it*

*For the majesty in everything*
*The setting sun the newborn fawn*
*The birds' sweet harmony*
*The changing leaves*
*The endless seas*
*The rolling hills the gentle breeze*

*Live only in the poet's eyes*

*And being blind I needed you*
*To be my loving guide*

"Well, Sarah?" Andrew asked.

"It's perfect. Better than perfect. But I can't find a word to describe what that is."

"I do. Call it the Andrew Effect," Lucien laughed. "If you'll excuse me, I need to go sell more of this man's work. I am now taking orders on commission—everything in the front rooms has sold. Too bad you won't allow me to sell these portraits; people crave that part of you."

"These are mine, Lucien. Never for sale." Andrew's tone left no room for debate.

Lucien shrugged. *"Dommage.* It was a pleasure to meet you." He bowed toward Sarah and Conrad, and walked away.

"Let's go to Mother's portrait. I'd like your opinion." Andrew nudged Sarah forward.

Martha's painting didn't disappoint. The largest of all the portraits, it hung in an ornate gold leaf frame and portrayed a gracious, sophisticated and beautiful woman. The background was a mixture of de-saturated hues of phthalo green and cadmium yellow, and her smiling image exuded devotion and tenderness. The observer had no choice but to smile back at her.

"You captured her spirit." Sarah touched Andrew's arm. "You knew her well."

"I did." He blushed. "She allowed me the freedom I needed. Her blind spot was Daryl." His eyes filled with tears. "She couldn't accept what—"

"Andrew," James called his attention away from the painful memories. "Tell me, was Matthew able to help you with AlderCreek?"

Andrew nodded, quickly wiping his eyes. "Yes, very much so. Great referral. Thank you, James. He met with the Board of Directors and me, and of course Karla and Eric. He's doing quite well."

Sarah turned to Karla. "You're on the Board?"

"Only because otherwise Andrew wouldn't attend. Matthew runs the company, but Andrew is chairman and needs to run the darn meetings. He has to keep on top of things, but he hates it."

"I really don't hate it. It's all a ruse to keep her at my side." He winked.

Karla stepped back and looked up at him. "Well, buddy, you've shown your cards now."

They all laughed.

"What about the poems that surround Mother?" Andrew asked.

"Way to change the conversation," Sarah laughed. "We haven't spent time with them. Give us a moment."

"By all means, be my guests." Andrew said, and stepped back out of the way.

The poems closest to Martha's portrait were arranged in what appeared to be an uneven circle. Sarah recognized them as the love poems she'd read when the book first presented itself. They were all in gold-leaf frames—not as ornate as Martha's, but in a style that belonged together. Beyond this inner circle were other poems scattered about in darker gold-leaf frames.

"I bet these represent Gabriel's mood after she left Paris." Sarah said.

"Clearly it broke his heart," Conrad said.

"He really loved my mother," Andrew whispered. "She was very easy to love and she gave back so much."

"Did you—" Sarah stopped herself.

"Find out that Gabriel was my father?" he said in hushed tones. "I figured it out many years ago. The artistic side of me had to come from someone other than Robert." He smiled. "I sort of discovered it when I stayed with Gabriel in Paris. I was with him the last years of his life. No one knew I'd been there."

Sarah turned to him astonished. "Your mother didn't find out?"

He shook his head. "He insisted we keep my visit between us. He gave me some lame excuse about my art reflecting his influence and wanting to find out if she could tell."

"Did he influence you? Did she notice?"

"I'd say. Thanks to him, I discovered the softer, more tender side of people, along with the animals I'm attracted to. Mother noticed the difference, but never made the connection. The book you returned to me is actually the book he gave me. I found my notations in the back."

"Those were yours? How did it end up in the bookstore in Eureka?"

"I lost track of the book many years ago. I must've left it behind somewhere and someone found it and sold it."

"James told me a man bought it for his wife. She auctioned it off and a publisher got it."

"So how—"

"The publisher tried to get the rights and made a big public fuss about it to attract the author. After that, all of sudden all talk about the book ended. It was left in the bookstore and it patiently waited for me to find it."

"I imagine Mother did that. She must've gotten it from the publisher. Maybe she hid it in the bookstore, afraid that Daryl would destroy it, like he destroyed his."

*Thank you, Sarah. Thank you for my boy's happiness.*

Sarah jerked back as James stepped between them and put his arms around their shoulders, giving Sarah a small squeeze. "Whatever you two are whispering about has pleased Martha immensely. She's found peace. She's gone."

"Gone? What do you mean?" Andrew's shock was evident.

"I only engage with those who are attached to his earth to resolve issues. She no longer needs to be here, so she's left."

311

"Did she say anything?" Andrew asked.

"Would you like to tell him, Sarah?"

"You heard what she said?" Andrew asked her.

She nodded. "A second ago. She thanked me. But seeing your happiness is what freed her, as well as hearing that despite knowing about Gabriel you never stopped loving her."

"Look," James stared at one of the framed poems.

"It's glowing," Andrew whispered.

Transfixed by the effect, they observed the words as Andrew's mellow voice softly brought them to life.

### HELLO

*To be away from you*
*Is the same as being lost*
*With only vaguest hopes*
*Of finding home again*

*Maybe I should simply let*
*My imagination fly*
*Toward far away and long ago*
*And remember where I've been*

*Abandoned in a desert*
*Where the hot sun bakes the sand*
*Assaulted by the nature*
*That inhabits such a land*

*No water left my strength all gone*
*I head toward a horizon*
*That I know you lie beyond*
*And so my search begins*

*The fight is strong against the wind*
*The sandstorms rage all round*
*But the memory of your face*

*Makes my weakened heart rebound*

*An oasis I have found*
*That helps to ease my pain*
*The palms give shade*
*A spring fresh hope*

*I've had a breath of air at last*
*And now my life resumes*
*But in the distance I can see*
*That new storms head for me*

*The desert stretches forth once more*
*I steel my will and start anew*
*Each step becomes an agony*
*Each breath a cry for you*

*In the vastness I can see*
*The road that leads to you*
*The stars that sing for me*
*The moon that lights my route*

*I have found a place of light*
*Where flowers' sweet perfume*
*Permeates the air*
*As proof that you are there*

*Hello my love*
*You're here at last*

Andrew sighed. "Gabriel?"

"Welcoming her?" Sara whispered.

"It's a possibility," James answered.

Andrew grinned. "I believe that is the case."

Sarah reached for Andrew and squeezed his hand. "Then all is as it should be."

# V. & D. POVALL

A husband and wife writing-team that has authored and published nonfiction manuals and articles as wells as written four short screenplays, six full-length screenplays, several novels, and a science-fiction epic.

*Jackal in the Mirror* is the third title in *The Perils of a Reluctant Psychic* suspense-mystery series. The first, which introduced Sarah and her remarkable psychic powers, was *The Gift of the Twin Houses*. The second, *Secrets of Innocence*, cemented Sarah's extrasensory abilities, and her exceptional talent for unraveling mysteries.

The authors bring a variety of experiences to their work. Between them they possess a doctorate and years of practical experience in film, television, and theater.

Thanks to their rich international family backgrounds, they bring to the page a wealth of experiences and points of view. They speak several languages and have lived in different cultures.

For more information, please visit their website at www.2authors.com.

Made in the USA
San Bernardino, CA
14 September 2019